HAUNTED
HIGHWAYS

SECOND EDITION

HAUNTED HIGHWAYS

SPOOKY STORIES, STRANGE HAPPENINGS, AND SUPERNATURAL SIGHTINGS

TOM OGDEN

Globe Pequot

ESSEX, CONNECTICUT

Globe
Pequot

An imprint of Globe Pequot, the trade division of
The Rowman & Littlefield Publishing Group, Inc.
4501 Forbes Blvd., Ste. 200
Lanham, MD 20706
www.rowman.com

Distributed by NATIONAL BOOK NETWORK

British Library Cataloguing in Publication Information available

Library of Congress Cataloging-in-Publication Data available

978-1-4930-4696-6 (paperback)
978-1-4930-4697-3 (electronic)

♾™ The paper used in this publication meets the minimum requirements of
American National Standard for Information Sciences—Permanence of Paper for
Printed Library Materials, ANSI/NISO Z39.48-1992.

For family—Nancy, Albert, Jeanne, and Linda.

CONTENTS

ACKNOWLEDGMENTS

My thanks go out to Mark Willoughby, Joan Lawton, and Michael Kurland for acting as sounding boards while I was writing both the first and second editions of *Haunted Highways*. Special thanks to Shawn McMaster and Bill Hamner for sharing their ghost encounters with me and to George Seigel for giving me so many leads to research. Thank you, Gary Krebs, who originally recommended me to Globe Pequot and who has continued his enthusiasm and support these many years. Finally, thanks have to go to my very patient editor for this second edition, Greta Schmitz.

INTRODUCTION

Boo!

Are you ready for some spooky tales of ghosts, supernatural creatures, and things that go bump in the night? If so, turn down the lights, curl up under the covers, and get ready to be scared as some of the most famous highway hauntings in America unfold before your eyes.

All of the ghost stories in this collection are urban legends, many of them based on even earlier myths retold through the centuries and by different cultures. Every story has one thing in common: It occurred on or near a highway, street, trail, or other pathway.

You may be surprised to discover that not all of the spirits that you find in this book are "ghosts" at all, at least not in the usual sense. That is to say, they don't all fit the popular, narrow definition of a ghost as the returning soul or essence of a deceased human.

Rather, some of the best-known haunted tales in history, including several found in this book, involve apparitions such as animals (like the horse ridden by the Headless Horseman), noises (such as the sound of invisible car crashes), or—and this is especially relevant to the subject of *Haunted Highways*—vehicles (such as phantom cars, trains, or stagecoaches).

What makes this book possible is that ghosts haunt *places*, not *people*. That's why you'll read about hauntings that reoccur on a particular roadway. The spirits are coming back to a specific street or path to relive or deal with an event from their own lives, not to interfere with the living who encounter them. In fact, almost without exception, the people who see ghosts have no clue as to the apparitions' identities. So if you bump into a ghost out there on the street, you've interrupted *them*, not the other way around.

There were, of course, thousands of wonderful stories to choose from, so selecting which ones to retell was difficult. For the most part, I've stuck to vehicular roads rather than hiking trails or walkways.

Likewise, I've tried to concentrate on hauntings that occur on the roads themselves rather than inside the houses, hotels, cemeteries, stores, restaurants, or other venues that line the highways. I do include a few bridges, but only if ghost activity also occurs on the roads leading up to the overpass. (There are enough ghost stories about haunted bridges to merit their own book!)

So what *will* you find in *Haunted Highways*? The sixteen tales found in part one are original, fictional short stories based on long-existing ghost folklore. At the end of some of these chapters, you'll find a box containing additional details about the haunted sites that can be visited.

New to this second edition is a part two containing more than one hundred additional legends of highway ghosts, sorted by state. In this section, the old wives' tales are recounted with little or no embellishment beyond what's been passed down through generations. Information on how to find the site is contained within each story.

At the back of the book, you'll find "'BOO'k Reports," a descriptive bibliography of the works I consulted while conducting research for *Haunted Highways*.

Finally, most of the haunted places mentioned in this book are in public areas. Parks and other tourist-related locations may require a fee and are subject to limited hours of operation. Some, such as restaurants and theaters, are businesses and require you to patronize their establishments to enter. A few are private properties or residences and can be viewed only from a distance or the outside.

If you're planning a special trip to visit any of these locations, especially if it's a great distance away, please call local information lines before you travel to make sure the site or attraction will be open when you arrive. And at all times it's important that you follow any laws or regulations regarding visitation, especially if it's private property.

Above all, safety comes first. It's common knowledge that phantoms appear primarily at night, so it's tempting to visit these places after dark. This can be dangerous for any number of reasons. Be careful: You don't want to wind up haunting the site yourself!

Let's hit the road!

PART ONE: OLD LEGENDS TOLD NEW

Chapter 1

RESURRECTION MARY

Sometimes it's too much to ask a spirit to stay put, especially if she loves to dance. Take the case of Resurrection Mary, whose ghost often appears on the wooded stretch of highway between the ballroom that, in life, she used to frequent, and the cemetery in which she now rests for eternity. If you give a ride to a hitchhiker some night outside Chicago, you might just meet her.

What Depression? It was 1939. As Mary danced away the wintry night with her boyfriend and hundreds of others on the hardwood floor of the ballroom at Oh Henry Park, the economic hardships of the preceding decade seemed a distant memory.

Even the dance halls had changed. The desperate, weeklong dance marathons were gone. It was the Jazz Age, with couples throwing away their cares and worries by swinging to the big bands. From dusk almost to dawn, the music transported the crowd to a world of fantasy and illusion, far away from the drab, dull lives waiting for them back on the other side of the ballroom's doors. There were almost four hundred ballrooms and dance halls within an hour's drive of the Chicago Loop some fifteen miles away but for many people the Oh Henry was the hottest place to be on a Saturday night.

Twenty years earlier, nothing had stood on the site. In 1921, Austrian immigrant John Verderbar bought five acres of land along that part of State Highway 171, known locally as Archer Avenue. He had intended to build a summer home on the property, but his high-spirited young son Rudy convinced him to construct an outdoor dancing pavilion instead. From the time the open-air dance hall opened as Oh Henry Park, the place became a magnet for young people. (The Williamson Candy Company, which manufactured the Oh Henry candy bar, reportedly paid for the naming rights.)

The original building was destroyed in a fire nine years later. But the new hall that rose from the ashes, the one in which Mary was now dancing, was bigger and better than before. Thousands of people made their way there each and every week to dance, meet friends, and listen to the bands.

The strains of "Over Somebody Else's Shoulder" wafted from the bandstand. Mary looked up to see the petite vocalist, Harriet Hillard, singing as she flirted with the bandleader who had introduced the song, her husband, Ozzie Nelson. His group was a favorite at the Oh Henry, especially since Nelson had scored a number-one hit single with "And Then Some." It made Mary smile to see Ozzie and Harriet together, a couple who were obviously so much in love. Just like her and . . .

Where was he? Her boyfriend had offered to get them something to drink— they had been dancing nonstop for almost an hour—and he said he would be right back. But that was fifteen, no, twenty minutes ago! It wasn't like him to leave her all alone for so long.

She pressed her way across the dance floor, slowly working her way toward the bar. And then she saw him. He was *not* alone. Mary stood speechless as she saw her boyfriend pressed up against the girl he had dated before he met Mary. He had a sly, playful smile on his face and was whispering in her ear.

Stunned, Mary couldn't believe her own eyes. He had told her how difficult the breakup with the other girl had been, what an "evil" person she was, and how he never wanted to see her again. But now that Mary thought about it, her "boyfriend" did nothing *but* talk about his ex-girlfriend!

She didn't wait for an explanation. She turned on her heels and, in a daze, headed straight to the door and stumbled outside. She was blocks away from the ballroom before she even realized she had left the building—without her coat in the middle of winter.

What was she going to do? Walk home? Well, she could do it. It was only three miles back to her parents' house in Justice. And with this brisk weather, why, she had every reason to move quickly. If she was lucky, maybe someone she knew would be leaving the dance hall, see her on the side of the road, and give her a ride.

Walking down the shoulder of the street, Mary was lost in her own thoughts as the truck approached from behind her. Perhaps the driver's mind was somewhere else, too, or maybe he was nodding off at such a late hour. Otherwise, he might have seen Mary sooner. By the time his eye caught a flash of white—her dress—she had drifted onto the roadway. He slammed on the brakes . . .

Mary was buried a few days later in Resurrection Cemetery, just east of Justice. Her parents dressed her all in white, wearing her favorite dance shoes, the ones she had worn the very night she died.

At one in the morning there was little traffic on the highway in Joliet. Still, Jerry had to be careful. There were lots of people living in the area, and the road wasn't well lit outside the city. As he passed through Lockport, State Road turned into Archer Avenue, and he followed it through Sag Bridge heading toward Chicago Midway Airport.

Jerry had been on the road for about a half hour when he entered the town of Willow Springs. The legal limits of Chicago had grown to within ten miles of the sleepy town, but it might as well have been in another world. Only six thousand people lived in Willow Springs. The city hadn't grown much from its heyday in the 1940s, when so many people flocked to the doors of the fabled Oh Henry Ballroom that there had been direct bus service to from midtown Chicago.

And there it was. Jerry knew the place only from its storied past. He had never been inside. The fact that it even still existed more than seventy years after it opened its doors was a miracle. In its time, everyone had played at the Oh Henry: Count Basie, Harry James, Jimmy Dorsey, Glenn Miller, Guy Lombardo. A who's who of big bands could have been compiled from the acts that passed through the dance hall's dressing room.

Of course, the ballroom was no longer called the Oh Henry. As the swing era came to an end, other dance halls throughout the country closed their doors, but the Verderbar family expanded. They added on a kitchen, a restaurant, and ban-quet rooms, transforming the Oh Henry into an event facility they named the Wil-lowbrook Ballroom. Tastes in music changed, and the next two decades brought such acts as Chubby Checker, the Association, and the Village People to its stage. *Yeah*, thought Jerry, *the dancers who crammed into the ballroom to hear the big bands of yesteryear probably wouldn't even recognize the place today.*

Jerry peered through the dark. Was that a light by the side of the road up ahead? No, it was simply his own headlights reflecting off . . . a dress! Someone was walking out here? Alone? At this time of night?

With the person now in the full beam of his headlights, Jerry could see the back of what appeared to be a slim young woman walking on the right shoulder of the road. Did he say walking? Her feet looked like they were barely touching the ground. She almost seemed to be floating.

Jerry pulled up beside the waiflike figure and rolled down the passenger-side window. He could see the moonlight reflecting off her ivory skin. She was dressed in a plain, white sleeveless dress, and long blond hair fell loosely over her shoulders. And even though it was summer, she was shivering.

"Pardon me. I don't want to bother you," he called out. "But could I be of some assistance? I thought you might need a lift somewhere."

The young woman stopped but didn't look his way.

"I promise I'm not an axe murderer or anything. I won't hurt you." Jerry laughed nervously at his own joke. *Well*, he thought, *if that possibility hadn't already crossed her mind, she was certainly thinking it now*. "Really, I just want to help. You look lost. And cold."

The girl turned to face the open window. She suddenly seemed to wake from a dream, and her face—especially the welcoming blue eyes focused on him—seemed filled with trust.

"Oh," she said, as if surprised to hear her own voice. "A lift. That would be nice."

She quietly opened the front door and slipped into the seat beside Jerry. Without another word, she settled back and stared out at the blackness on the other side of the windshield.

"Where are you headed?"

"Oh, I'm going home. It's just down the road. Straight ahead a few miles." And then, to answer his unspoken question as to what she was doing out there, she added, "I was dancing."

"Dancing? You mean at the Willowbrook?"

"Willowbrook? No, I don't know the Willowbrook. I was at the Oh Henry."

Jerry said nothing. The girl was obviously confused. The ballroom he'd just passed hadn't been called the Oh Henry for more than fifty years.

"It's one of my favorite places," she explained. "There's the music, of course. And the ballroom is full of life. I always have so much fun there." She sat motionless, her eyes wide, as if the scene were replaying in her mind. "I love to dance."

Jerry couldn't help but follow her eyes as she gazed down at her long, slender legs. On each foot was a spotless, soft, comfortable leather flat. The shoes were perfect if you wanted to stay light on your feet for hours at a time on a polished wooden dance floor.

She looked up abruptly. She met Jerry's eyes and smiled.

"I was there all night. The people wouldn't let the band stop playing. I danced and I danced. Sometimes just by myself. But tonight so many men asked me to join them, well, I just couldn't say no."

Tonight? Funny, thought Jerry. The lights had been out when he passed the Willowbrook. Of course, he didn't really know the club, but very few places stayed open this late, way out here in the suburbs. After all, it was after two. By this hour, most things were closed, even on the weekends.

Jerry wondered how long she had been walking. "You know, it's really none of my business. But it's rather unusual to see a woman out here all alone this late at night. Shouldn't you be, well, isn't there some fellow who could have driven you home?"

"Oh, there used to be. But now I like to go to the Oh Henry by myself. I can dance with any man I please. And besides, tonight I don't need him. I have *you* to drop me off."

"Well, whoever the guy was, he must be crazy to have let you out of his sight."

He realized that he was flirting and panicked. He had *promised* her he was not a creep. But he couldn't stop himself. "What's your name?"

"Mary. Just Mary."

"That's a pretty name." *Stop it*, thought Jerry. "I mean, that name, you don't hear it very often these days."

"That's all right," Mary reassured him. "It *is* a pretty name." She was flirting back! "At least my parents didn't name me something awful like Edith or Myrtle."

"Now, wait a minute," Jerry joked, "I have an Aunt Myrtle."

They broke out in a soft laugh. Then, as they both became aware their conversation was becoming a bit too intimate for complete strangers, Mary shyly turned her face to the side window.

"I'm sorry. Where did you say you needed to go?"

"Home," Mary quietly reminded him. "Just on the other side of town."

They were approaching the outskirts of Justice as she spoke. The car crossed Route 12, passed under I-294, and then slipped into the city. The sidewalks were empty as they passed through the center of town.

"Keep going. A little farther. It's just ahead."

Silence fell between them as they drove out of downtown. Businesses thinned out, and they were back in a residential area. *Her place must be coming up soon*, thought Jerry.

"Stop!" Mary's call had come out of the blue. There were no houses nearby, just a park, an open field, a—was that a cemetery? Jerry eased his car to the side of the road and stopped the engine.

"Here. I have to get out here." Mary opened her door and stepped outside.

Jerry jumped out of the car. "But there's nothing here. I can drop you off at your house, even if it's a little out of the way. I mean, I don't mind." Was she afraid to let him know where she lived?

But Jerry's words had fallen on deaf ears. Mary had made a beeline across the field and was standing in front of a set of high greenish metal gates set between tall concrete pillars. Through the bars, Jerry could see a large mausoleum and hundreds of gravestones. To one side of the entrance was a small sign: Resurrection Cemetery.

For what, to Jerry, seemed like forever, Mary stood there in front of the gates. Then she made one small step forward and literally melted through the locked bars. Riveted to the spot, Jerry stared silently in a mixture of wonder and horror. She was now definitely on the other side of closed gates! Mary looked over her shoulder and spotted Jerry. A small, sad smile crossed her lips. She turned back toward the cemetery as her body started to shimmer, then turned translucent. Slowly, her delicate shape began to fade until it completely evaporated into the cool night air.

Mary was home.

Phantom travelers are spectres of a human, a creature, or even a vehicle that appears along a roadway, trail, or pathway, or at a rest stop, tavern, or inn. The haunting is usually associated with a tragedy, an anniversary, a sin or wrongdoing, emotional turmoil, or some other connection with the specific location.

Reports of phantom travelers date back to at least the 1600s, and they were widespread throughout Scandinavia, Russia, and Europe. The tales were certainly popular in the United States by the beginning of the nineteenth century, when they started to appear in American literature.

The myth of the phantom hitchhiker—a spectral figure that enters your vehicle, only to suddenly disappear without warning—is an archetype and the most common of all ghost traveler stories. Spirit hitchhikers have been reported in almost every state of the union and most countries throughout the world.

The basic legend is this: A motorist, usually a male, sees someone walking or hitchhiking on the side of the road after dark. Although details vary from tale to tale, the hitchhiker is usually female and traveling alone. Her clothing sometimes appears to be wet, even though it isn't raining, nor are there any lakes or rivers in the area. In some versions of the story, the driver offers the young lady his jacket so she can get warm. The hitchhiker almost always climbs into the backseat and remains very quiet. Sometimes she doesn't speak at all but writes down the address of her destination for the driver.

In one variation of the tale, she either vanishes from the car or asks the driver to stop far short of her stated destination. She rushes out of the vehicle and hurries off into the distance—often into a cemetery. The most famous of these ghosts in American folklore is Resurrection Mary.

If the driver makes it all the way to the original address he was given, when he turns to the backseat or looks into his rearview mirror, the hitchhiker is gone. Puzzled, the man walks up to the house at that address and knocks on the door.

One or two people come to the door. They tell the driver that they were expecting him, or someone like him. It was the anniversary of the night their loved one was killed in a traffic accident, and it had occurred on the same stretch of highway that the motorist saw her spirit and offered her a ride. Every year on that date, somebody would show up and claim they had just given a lift to the long-dead person.

A coda to this already creepy tale: If the driver loaned the young lady his coat, he finds it lying on the back seat of his car. If not there, he finds the jacket neatly folded and draped over the headstone at the woman's grave.

The legend of Resurrection Mary is supposedly based on a "true" story. According to folklore, around 1939 the ghost of a young female with long blond hair and blue eyes, dressed in white, started appearing along Archer Avenue between Willow Springs and Justice, Illinois. The spectre would either suddenly materialize in the middle of the road or, in times past, jump onto the running board on the side of the car. Some motorists claimed their cars passed right through the girl; others said they struck someone, but when they stopped to look for the injured party, no one was there.

Frequently the ghost would ask to be taken to the ballroom at Oh Henry Park, where she could then be seen dancing throughout the night. Or, when the dance hall was closing, she would ask someone at the ballroom for a ride back to Justice. Sometimes she would get out of the car at Resurrection Cemetery, which is northeast of downtown Justice, and then disappear as she melted through the closed gates. In another variation of the story, she simply vanished from the inside of the vehicle as it neared or passed the cemetery. As a result, at some point the phantom was nicknamed Resurrection Mary. Although there have been regular sightings of her ever since the 1940s, they reached their peak in the 1960s.

Because of her sobriquet, many ghost hunters believe she must be the spirit of an actual person named Mary buried in that graveyard. The Mary legend doesn't match up with the records of any of the cemetery's "residents," however. Nevertheless, she is often misidentified as Mary Bregovy, who *is* interred there. That Mary, however, died in an automobile accident in downtown Chicago in 1934 and had no connection with the Oh Henry. Also, she had short, dark hair and was buried in an orchid-colored dress, not in white.

In another twist to the tale, one night in 1976 police received reports of a woman seen locked behind the cemetery gates. When they investigated, the police couldn't find anyone trapped inside, but they did notice that two of the bars seemed to have been pried apart, and what looked like human handprints were embedded in the metal. Cemetery officials were quick to point out that a truck had accidentally backed into the gates and that the prints were caused by a groundskeeper heating the bars and attempting to bend them into shape with his gloved fists. The later removal of the bars only fueled the legend that a spirit had bent them.

The roads surrounding other cemeteries in the Chicago area are also haunted. The hitchhiking ghost of a girl described as being around twelve to fourteen years old appears near Evergreen Cemetery, and she was even reported to have boarded a CTA bus on one occasion. Another spectral hitchhiker fond of dancing was a young brunette flapper with bobbed hair. She appeared on Des Plaines Avenue between the 2400 block, where a dance hall known as the Melody Hill Ballroom used to stand, and the 1400 block, where Jewish Waldheim Cemetery is located. Sightings of this ghost began in 1933, predating Resurrection Mary, and continued on and off for forty years. And it's not just humans that haunt the cemetery roadways: Phantom cars have been seen passing by the gates of Bachelor Grove Cemetery. (There are said to be dozens of ghosts haunting Bachelor Grove, though none have been reported leaving the grounds.)

A few last words about the ballroom at Oh Henry Park. The name of the park and dance hall are often misspelled as "O'Henry" in ghost literature, because both sites were, in fact, named for the popular Oh Henry candy bar. The Willowbrook Ballroom, as the nightclub later became known, was located at 8900 Archer Avenue in Willow Springs, Illinois. Sadly, fire destroyed it on Friday, October 28, 2016, and there are no plans to rebuild or relocate. As of Summer 2021, new owners of the twelve-acre property were about to begin construction of condominiums and townhouses on the site.

Resurrection Cemetery
7200 Archer Road
Justice, IL 60458
Just northeast of downtown Justice then travel west on the Midlothian Turnpike to the Rubio Woods exit. Entrance to the cemetery is sometimes restricted.

Bachelor Grove Cemetery
Rubio Woods Forest Preserve
Midlothian, IL 60445

The graveyard is on a small, one-acre plot within a forested area west of Midlothian, a southern suburb of Chicago. From Chicago go south on I-294 to Cicero Avenue,

Evergreen Cemetery
3401 West 87th Street (at South Kedzie Avenue)
Evergreen Park, IL 60805

Jewish Waldheim Cemetery
1400 Des Plaines Avenue
Forest Park, IL 60130

Chapter 2

THE PROPHECY

You're out with friends, minding your own business, when a stranger intrudes. What do you do if that uninvited guest begins to predict the future? Especially if ignoring the prophecy could result in your own death? And that spectral visitor is from the Church? Three young men had to face these questions and more when they picked up the wrong hitchhiker in the shadow of a volcano.

"What's black and white and black and white and black and white all over?"

"I don't know, Christopher, what?"

"A nun rolling down a hill."

"Wait! I got one!" Francis chimed in. "What do you call a nun that walks in her sleep? A Roamin' Catholic!"

"Now, that's just stupid!"

"And yours wasn't?"

"Come on, guys," broke in Anthony. "Enough with the nun jokes, or we're all gonna go to . . . well, you know where."

"Where? Mother Superior's office—again? Oh, no! Not the ruler!"

"No," Anthony warned, pointing a finger straight down. "Someplace a little lower."

The three students knew they were alone in the car, but maybe God was listening. Better to be safe than sorry. They cut out the jokes.

As they drove silently on I-5 from Eugene, Oregon, to Tacoma, Washington, the huge mountain loomed off to their right in the distance. Although they had always lived beside the volcano, the boys had never given it much thought. There hadn't been a major rumble from Mount St. Helens since they were born.

The boys had studied the volcano in school. People were living on its slopes, located in the Cascades Mountain Range, at least 6,500 years ago. About 1,500 BC a major eruption buried anyone and anything in the area under a deep deposit of pumice. Native Americans had avoided the volcano for two millennia, but by the time the Lewis and Clark expedition reached the Pacific in 1805, the

Yakama, Upper Chinook, Klickitat, Taidnapam, and Cowlitz tribes had been settling its foothills for about a thousand years.

Although the famous explorers saw the volcano as they floated downstream on the Columbia River, they didn't witness any activity, but Mount St. Helens had erupted only five to ten years earlier. Over the next sixty years, there would be occasional seismic tremors, as well as the so-called Great Eruption of 1842.

But now everyone was safe. It was the early spring of 1980. Although smoke plumes were seen from time to time—in fact, there was one now—the volcano had last erupted in 1854.

Francis, the history buff, knew lots of ancient legends that explained the formation and eruptions at Mount St. Helens. His favorite came from the Klickitat tribe. Their chief god, Tyhee Saghalie, and his two sons, Klickitat (or Paho) and Wy'east, came from the far north to settle at the narrows of the Columbia near the present-day city of The Dalles, Oregon. *What was it about The Dalles that attracted settlers?* thought Francis. *It had also been the end of the land journey of the Oregon Trail.*

In any case, in the volcano creation myth, the sons began to fight for possession of the land. To separate them, their father shot two arrows in opposite directions and told his sons to each follow one and settle where the arrows fell. He built a passage, the Bridge of the Gods, between them.

But that didn't end the family squabbles. Both sons fell in love with a young woman named Loowit, and their violent fights over her devastated the earth, causing earthquakes, leveling forests, and destroying the sky bridge, which tumbled to the ground to form the Cascades.

Finally, to put an end to the destruction, Saghalie turned all three of the others into stone. His son Klickitat became what today is called Mount Adams. To the south, his brother Wy'east became Mount Hood. And beautiful Loowit was transformed into Mount St. Helens, which was called Louwala Clough, or "smoking fire mountain," by the Klickitat.

The guys checked out the peak of the mountain. A little smoke trail today, but nothing to be worried about. Besides, there were scientists up there now, apparently, checking it out. Wouldn't they tell people if it were going to blow?

"Holy Mother of Jesus. Look at that!"

Christopher motioned up ahead. About fifty yards down the highway, standing alone on the shoulder of the road, was a woman. She looked to be about fifty or sixty years old. She was in a black dress, a white collar, and a black and white wimple. The look was unmistakable. She was a nun.

As they watched, the sister smiled gently and then, at the last second, almost comically stuck a curved thumb up into the air. She was hitchhiking!

A hitchhiking nun! Now they'd seen everything!

"Well, do you think we should pick her up?"

"You have to, dude. She's a nun. Isn't there some kind of rule that we have to stop to help her out?"

"Do you think she's really a nun?"

"Do you think we can risk it if she's not? What if we leave her standing there, and then, I don't know, someone finds out?"

"I told you we shouldn't have been telling those jokes!"

"All right, everybody take a deep breath," Christopher warned as he slowed the car. "Best behavior. We're going in."

A slight pause, and then all three burst out laughing.

"A *Star Wars* quote? Nice touch, Chris. How about this one: 'I have a very bad feeling about this'?"

"Luke! Use the force!"

They were still chuckling as the car came to a halt. Polite to a fault, all three boys stepped out of the car. Francis spoke up first. "May we offer you a ride, Sister? We're only going a few miles up the road, just to Tacoma."

When she spoke, they were surprised to hear such a soft voice, not stern like their teachers at school. "Tacoma would be fine. Thank you."

Francis, realizing that he had been riding shotgun, opened the front passenger door for the sister. Once she was inside, he closed the door carefully and hopped in the back with Anthony.

"Where are you boys heading? To Bellarmine Preparatory?"

Bellarmine? the three guys thought. Although that *didn't* happen to be where they were headed, they knew the school well. Bellarmine, in Tacoma, was one of the leading Catholic prep schools in the whole area. How could she know, just by looking at them, that they were Catholic? Were nuns psychic, too?

The sister couldn't help but notice the quizzical expressions on their faces. With a twinkle in her eye, she explained. "Forgive me if I'm wrong—and I doubt if I am—but I knew you must be Catholic. You were so well-mannered that when you stopped to assist me I just assumed you've been raised in Catholic schools."

Her voice was smooth, liquid, calming. Why couldn't she be teaching one of their classes? That voice made you want to listen to her all day.

Before long, she was sharing her story, what had brought her to that spot on the road where they had first spied her. She was on a mission, she said, a sort of assignment she had been instructed—she didn't say by whom—to perform. She was to meet strangers, people in need of help.

But then her tone darkened. Yes, she said, it was like the story in the Old Testament of the young men who appeared at Lot's gate. If her message was well received, goodness would come to the people who heard her words, but if she was met with disbelief or hostility, the offenders would surely suffer the wrath of the Lord.

The boys squirmed in their seats. This was not what they wanted to hear. They were just out having fun. But they couldn't ask a nun to "hold off on the preaching," could they? Was this a test? Was God watching them? Anthony involuntarily looked skyward.

Her voice, once like honey, now was becoming stern and menacing. But they couldn't resist hanging on her words.

"As Jesus said in the Book of St. Matthew, 'If anyone will not welcome you or listen to your words, shake the dust off your feet when you leave that home or town. I tell you the truth, it will be more bearable for Sodom and Gomorrah on the Day of Judgment than for that town.'"

Now the guys were freaked. What was she trying to tell them? They stared into her face, but it was no longer gentle and loving. It had become transfixed, severe. Her voice had become enraptured, messianic, and her whole manner had become detached, as if she were possessed.

Suddenly it occurred to the boys: She was no longer directly addressing them. She was delivering prophecy.

The nun turned her unfathomable face toward the side window. She stared up at the dome of Mount St. Helens. "For I tell you this: The time approaches. Those who do not seek forgiveness for their transgressions and do not change the errors of their ways, they will be consumed by fire and ash."

The clouds parted, and as the last rays of sun burst upon the side of the towering mountain, it became crystal clear. She was telling them the volcano was going to erupt—and soon! If they weren't penitent or didn't seek absolution (were those the right words?), they would die in the explosion.

Then the most incredible thing the boys had ever experienced—and, indeed, ever *would* experience—happened. The nun began to glow and then, with a small pop, vanished.

Startled, Christopher involuntarily slammed on the brakes and veered onto the side of the road. Had that really just happened? Where was she? How could she have just disappeared?

But clearly, the miracle had taken place. The front passenger seat screamed its emptiness.

Struck dumb, the young men continued on to Tacoma without saying a word. The boys never told anyone about their ethereal visitor. If they had, who would have believed them? Besides, they had enough demerits at school; they certainly weren't going to start telling stories about a doomsday nun. Everyone would dismiss it as a tasteless prank or, worse, a drug-induced hallucination.

If the boys had checked in with the Tacoma police, however, they would have found their encounter was not unique. Over the past few years, more than twenty reports had come in from individuals as well as carloads of people who had experienced exactly the same thing. They had all stopped to pick up a middle-aged woman, usually but not always dressed in a nun's habit, who warned the motorists that if they didn't repent of their sins, they would die in an accident on the highway. In the last couple of months, she had changed her apocalyptic story to center on Mount St. Helens.

As it turned out, the nun was right. At least in part.

On May 18, 1980, after several months of underground murmurs, Mount St. Helens erupted. The north side of the mountain blew out, causing a debris avalanche that stripped away everything in its path. Plumes of pumice and steam followed, covering miles around with a layer of ash. Fifty-seven people were killed, and two hundred fifty houses were destroyed. Miles of road and railway were wiped out, as were forty-seven bridges. By far, it was the deadliest and costliest volcanic eruption in US history.

Had the mysterious sister accurately predicted the desolation? Was she describing Mount St. Helens's eruption to her captive audiences at all, or was she receiving a holy vision of Judgment Day? In fact, had she even been a spirit, or was she instead an angel of the Lord?

The 220-mile stretch of I-5 that the phantom nun haunted in the late 1970s and early 1980s is between Eugene, Oregon, and Tacoma, Washington. After Mount St. Helens's eruption, the ghost's prophecy about a fiery apocalypse was widely interpreted as having been a prediction about the volcano. Although the mountain itself is not (and has never been considered to be) haunted, you might still wish to visit it if you are retracing the steps of the spectral sister.

Mount St. Helens Visitor Center
3029 Spirit Lake Highway
Castle Rock, WA 98611
(360) 274-7750
parks.state.wa.us/245/
Mount-St-Helens

The 172-square-mile Mt. St. Helens National Volcanic Monument is managed by the US Forest Service. The visitor center is operated in conjunction with the Washington State Parks and Recreation Commission.

Chapter 3

MADAME PELE PAYS A VISIT

Do spirits of the gods walk among us? And if so, why do they interact with mere mortals? One such deity, Madame Pele, is kind enough to drop by to warn us before her volcanic outbursts. Other times her appearances augur misfortune or are mere mischief. But one thing's certain: She's here, and she's not going away.

There was trouble in Paradise. Pele, the daughter of Kane-hoa-lani and the goddess Haumea, was born in Kahiki, what is today called Tahiti. She had a huge family, and all of her brothers and sisters were gods or goddesses of different aspects of the natural world. Pele's specialty was fire, especially in the way it frequently showed itself throughout Polynesia: She possessed the power to produce the flames and molten lava of the volcano.

But just like in many human families, there was constant quarreling and bickering among these brother and sister dieties. In Pele's case, the thorn in her side was her sister Na-maka-o-ka-ha'i, who was a goddess of the sea. To escape the rivalry, Pele asked her father for permission to leave Kahiki, and eventually he acquiesced. Pele formed a gigantic canoe and crossed the ocean to the northeast, but her troublesome sister followed.

Pele arrived at the chain of islands we call Hawaii, stopping first at the tiny outcrop of Niihau, then moving on to Kauai, followed by Oahu. Every time Pele used her magic digging stick to create a new home for herself deep in the rock, Na-maka-o-ka-ha'i would fill the hole with water, either by having it seep up through the ground or by tossing tidal waves up from the coast.

The monumental battle between the sisters came to a head on the island of Maui, where Pele settled into the crater Haleakala. Fire and water nearly consumed each other in the clash between the titans, and in the end Pele was snuffed out and consumed. Her bones formed the huge cinder cone called Ka Iwi o Pele that can be seen on the road to Hana.

Content in her victory, Na-maka-o-ka-ha'i returned to Kahiki. But Pele lived on in spirit form. She moved to the Big Island of Hawaii, where she was finally able to dig a pit deep enough and far enough inland that it was out of her sister's reach. Her home is in that crater on the 13,680-foot Mauna Loa volcano.

A ridge road, Crater Rim Drive, surrounds the great Kilauea Caldera on the eastern slope of Mauna Loa. For years drivers along the path have reported seeing a woman, usually young but sometimes elderly and often accompanied by a small white dog walking the shoulder of the road. Legend has it that she is Pele, in human form. If she's wearing white, the motorist (or someone he or she knows) is going to fall ill. But if Pele's wearing red, it usually means a volcanic eruption will take place within days!

Madame Pele seldom sits quietly for very long in her home at the bottom of the 280-foot-deep Halema'umau'au Crater, which is located within Kilauea Caldera. She frequently becomes angry if the mortals living on her island don't worship her or leave her tributes, and in her blazing temper she will start a flow of lava or shoot sparks and flames high into the air. So strong is their belief that many locals try to appease Pele by laying offerings of chicken or alcohol along the rim of the crater.

Also according to legend, if you remove pieces of lava from the islands, no matter how small, Pele will curse you. Bad luck will follow you until you return the stones to their native shores.

All quaint stories? Just ancient myths of gods and goddesses? Maybe. And yet the appearances of Madame Pele's ghost on the Hawaiian Islands occur quite frequently, and the sightings are far too numerous to dismiss as the products of mere imagination.

If you're driving anywhere on the island in the middle of the night and you see a woman in a red muumuu on the side of the road asking for a lift, give careful thought before you pass her by. If it's Madame Pele, she'll disappear almost as soon as she steps into your car. But if it's the goddess and you don't offer her a lift, you'll undoubtedly anger her, which could result in your death or set off a new round of volcanic eruptions and devastation to the island. Is it worth taking the risk?

Madame Pele still gives her forewarnings. Residents of Kapoho swear that in 1960 she showed up two days before the 2,600-foot-wide lava flow from Mauna Loa destroyed their town. In fact, many old tales surround the volcanic eruptions that have affected the Kapoho region. In one of the best known, a local chieftain challenged a young lady to race him by sled down the mountainside. He was halfway down the slope when he looked beside him to discover that the woman was actually Madame Pele, and she was riding a river of lava.

Also, in recent years, the spectre of a striking lady in the trademark flaming-red muumuu has been seen roaming the halls of the hotel towers in the Hilton Hawaiian Village in Honolulu, Hawaii. Now, some people think she's the phantom of a woman who was murdered in the hotel, but many locals believe she's the ghostly manifestation of Pele. The spirit certainly isn't warning the visitors about volcanoes, though. If you're in Hawaii on vacation, be careful whom you meet in your hotel hallway. It could be Madame Pele paying a visit.

Kilauea Crater

Mauna Loa and the Kilauea Crater are in the Hawaii Volcanoes National Park. They can be reached via Highway 11, which runs between Hilo and Kailua Kona. At just above four thousand feet, the Crater Rim Road encircles the caldera. For more information, contact:

Hawaii Volcanoes Visitor Center
P.O. Box 52
Hawaii Volcanoes National Park, HI 96718
(808) 985-6011
nps.gov/havo/planyourvisit/kvc
.htm

Kapaho

Located on the coast about thirty miles south of Hilo, Kapaho can be reached by driving down Highway 11 and turning onto Highway 130 at Hea'au. From Pahoa, a ride along a two-mile cinder road allows visitors to see the destruction caused by the 1960 lava flow.

Hilton Hawaiian Village Beach Resort & Spa
2005 Kalia Road
Honolulu, Hawaii 96815
(808) 949-4321
hiltonhawaiianvillage.com

Chapter 4

THE NIGHT MARCHERS

The folklore of Hawaii is filled with stories of spirit orbs; legends of the mysterious Menehune, or "Little People"; and tales of ghosts and apparitions. But none is more amazing than that of the Night Marchers, the parade of spirit warriors that pass over the old trails that crisscross the islands. Just seeing the procession can mean death—unless you're lucky enough to have someone, or something, intervene.

Cutting across the grassy plain of the Nuuanu Valley, Kaimi knew he was late. Where had the time gone? It was already after sundown, and even though streaks of red still lit the western sky, he had promised his mother he would be home hours before this.

Not that he was too young to be out on his own. Heck, he was almost eighteen. But, as his mom had often warned him, "You can't be too careful these days. You never know who you'll run into. Or who will run into you."

Kaimi's mother meant that both figuratively and literally because, these days, drivers seemed to be zooming across the island at top speed. If they were unfamiliar with the roads—and this was the height of tourist season—they could very easily drift just a little too much toward the shoulder and hit someone innocently walking down the side of the highway.

Which is one of the reasons Kaimi was now taking an alternate route, an unpaved hiking trail, toward his home. Walking along the cliffs, Kaimi always felt most in touch with his native Hawaiian roots—something his grandfather Maleko had instilled in him when he was just a little boy.

Maleko had still been a young man when businessmen, led by politician Sanford Dole (a cousin of James Dole, the pineapple magnate), overthrew Queen Liliuokalani in 1893. The queen, hoping to spare her subjects from bloodshed, asked them to be patient while she petitioned Washington, DC, for the return of her throne, but many natives revolted against the new government. The rebellion was squashed, but to his dying day Maleko was proud that he had joined in the struggle.

Liliuokalani was allowed to leave house arrest in the Iolani Palace in Honolulu in 1896, but there was no turning back for the islands. The monarchy had been dissolved forever. Over the years, as mainland people moved to Hawaii, more and more of the natives were forced to assimilate.

But Maleko resisted. As he raised his children he made sure that they learned the language and all the ancient legends of his people. Then, as they had children of their own, Maleko insisted that they be taught the native customs as well.

Now Maleko was gone, but Kaimi treasured the memory of the many lessons he had learned at his grandfather's knee. That was one of the reasons he loved to walk in the Nuuanu Pali. Not only could he catch a panoramic view all the way from the top of the mountains down to the windward beaches of Oahu, but he also knew the area was steeped in Hawaiian history. In fact, the bloodiest battle in the fight for Hawaiian unification took place very close to where he was standing.

In 1795, Kamehameha I (known as King Kamehameha the Great) and ten thousand of his warriors sailed from his base on the island of Hawaii to conquer first Maui and then Molokai before moving to Oahu. In the fierce Battle of Nuuanu, Kamehameha drove the chieftain Kalanikupule and his men across the valley floor, where Kaimi had been earlier that day, up onto the top of the perilous cliff. At the climax of the monumental clash, hundreds of Kalanikupule's warriors were forced over the precipice. In the aftermath, Kamehameha was able to bring all of the Hawaiian Islands under his rule.

The first road over the Nuuanu Pali to connect the windward towns of Kandohe and Kailua with Honolulu was constructed in 1845. When the road was upgraded in 1898, more than eight hundred skulls, no doubt from the warriors who had plummeted to their deaths a hundred years earlier, were uncovered. In the 1950s, the aging motorway was replaced by a new Pali Highway (now State Route 61), with tunnels cut through the mountains to facilitate travel.

Of all the tales his grandfather had told Kaimi about Hawaii's ancient heritage, he liked the ghost stories best. Maleko had warned him to always be on guard when he walked through the Nuuanu Pali because it was haunted.

For instance, they say that if you walk alone out in the fields or woodlands at night without a flashlight, you'll be attacked by a phantom woman dressed in white. Most often she just scares you, but some people claim that if you get too close to her, she'll kill you.

Then, if you drive past the cemetery across from the Kahala Mall with your windows open, an invisible spirit will jump into your car with you. Even though you can't see it, you can feel its presence sitting in the backseat, right behind you. Sometimes you can actually make out the phantom: it's the ghost of a little girl. But as you drive away from the cemetery, the spectral presence evaporates.

Perhaps the strangest legend claims that you should never carry pork in your car if you're driving HI-61. (This was true as well for the original Pali road when it was the main passageway over the mountains.) If you do have any of the taboo food with you, your car will stall or break down somewhere along the road, usually stranding you in a dark, deserted area, until the meat is removed from your car.

In one retelling of the story, a taxi driver crossing the Nuuanu Pali was grabbed from behind by an invisible force as she passed through one of the tunnels. The unseen spectre pushed her body and head into the steering wheel, almost causing her to crash, but it let go as soon as the driver exited the tunnel. When she later cleaned out her car, she found a half-eaten pork sandwich left in the car by a passenger.

In Kaimi's favorite version of the ghost tale, if the spirits stop your car on the highway because you're carrying pork, a phantom white dog will appear next to your car. All you have to do to get your car running again is crack your window and drop out the forbidden meat. As soon as the dog has eaten it, the canine will vanish and, at the same moment, your car engine will start up.

Kaimi loved to strike out on his own to investigate all these old spooky stories. According to Hawaiian tradition, his name meant "seeker," and he knew that people who have the name are said to be able to uncover secrets and hidden truths. Indeed, Kaimi never took what people said at face value. He had to examine what he was told, to make sure for himself before he was able to believe. Yes, "Kaimi" fit him like a glove. How could his parents have known when he was only a few days old that it would be the perfect name for him? Had Grandfather Maleko, who understood such things, told them?

The sun had set, and Kaimi realized he had to be careful. There were no houses in sight, and as he left the Old Pali Highway far behind, there was little light. It was hard to make out the trail.

At first he thought he was imagining it, but rising over the whisper of the grass, he could make out the faint sound of men's voices. Singing. Steady. Soft, but intense. They were accompanied by the rhythm of drums and an *ohe hano ihu*, the bamboo nose flute. The voices seemed to be coming from up ahead, just over the next ridge. They got stronger. The men must be getting closer!

As Kaimi reached the top of the hill, he saw the flickering. Not from flashlights or distant traffic, but from fire. He could make out dozens of separate flames coming from the ends of handheld torches. The shadowy figures carrying them were walking four or six across, drawing toward him on the earthen path.

Kaimi stopped abruptly, puzzled. Who would be out here in the desolate fields in the dark, carrying torches, chanting? And then it struck him: They were Night Marchers!

The Night Marchers, the *huaka'i o ka po,* as they were known in Hawaiian, were ghosts of venerated warriors, chiefs, or even deities that roamed the earth. Although they could materialize anytime, they most often appeared between dusk and dawn on one of the special nights at the end of the month on the Hawaiian calendar that was dedicated to the native gods.

As they traveled from ancient battlefields, the Marchers collected the souls of dead chieftains and warriors, as well as their descendants, both male and female. As they passed, spirits of the dead who were worthy would join their ranks. Then the entire parade would move on, heading either toward the nearest *heiau* (or temple), one of the outcroppings or beach promontories that acted as a jumping-off point to the Next World, or to some other sacred spot.

Kaimi had thought the Night Marchers were only a myth, like all the other ghost stories. But now, here, one of those "myths" had come to life and was about to meet him face-to-face.

He tried desperately to remember everything his grandfather had told him about the Night Marchers. He knew an encounter with them could be deadly. In fact, they *usually* were. Over the years, police had found the bodies of people lying on the ground, face-up, their eyes and mouths wide open, their arms frozen in place in front of them as if they had died trying to fight off assailants. But there were never any marks on the corpses, no signs of assault. Medical examiners always decided that the victims had died of heart attacks, but native Hawaiians, raised on tales of the fearsome Night Marchers, knew what had really happened.

Kaimi's mind raced. What was he supposed to do to survive?

That's right! First of all, don't look any of them in the eye. Don't try to run; you don't want to catch their attention if they haven't seen you yet. Quickly judge which way they're heading and get out of their way. Then stop and drop to the ground.

The warriors seemed to be following the old dirt footpath that had been worn into the hillside long before the Old Pali Highway was made. Kaimi got off the trail and moved swiftly about twenty feet to one side. If the men didn't spread out too wide and he was lucky, they might miss him.

Kaimi got down. He lay there, panting, terrified, as the phantoms grew closer and closer. He knew that, even lying flat on the ground, he wasn't safe. He was supposed to do something else. What was it?

He let his mind drift back. Tell me, Grandfather, he whispered to himself. Tell me, what am I to do? Then, as if in a dream, he could see himself as a young boy. There he was, six years old, sitting by his grandfather, and the old man was talking about the dreaded Night Marchers.

"Some of the elders say that when you see them you are to lie on the ground with your eyes closed, say nothing, and breathe as little as possible until long after the spirits have passed by. Some say that it helps if you take off all of your clothing and lay face upward."

"But why would I do that, *kupunakane*? They would see . . . everything."

"Yes, that is the point, my little *mo'opuna*. But that is what may save you. As the warriors and the chief's guards pass you by, they will see you there, undressed, and cry, 'Shame. Shame on you for being uncovered.' They will feel you have dishonored yourself and your ancestors, so they will leave you behind without stopping. There is no guarantee that it will work. But it could possibly save your life."

Without a thought, Kaimi ripped off his shirt. Soon he was down to his underwear—even in the legends, you only had to strip to your loincloth—when he realized that it was too late. They were upon him. He kept his head down. He didn't dare look directly at them. It would mean instant death. But Kaimi couldn't resist taking a peek. He lifted his eyes just as two warriors raised their spears.

"Strike him!"

"No, stop! He is mine!"

From behind the guards, a third warrior stepped forward. "The boy is my flesh and my blood, of my family. You will not harm him." He pushed past the spectres that were just about to kill Kaimi, turned toward them, and planted his feet in front of the boy, shielding him. The two guards hesitated for only a moment, then moved back to join the procession.

Kaimi sat there—how long? Five minutes? A half hour? The glimmer of torch-light disappeared as the ranks of the Night Marchers moved over the next ridge. The sounds of their chanting, the drums, the flutes, faded in the wind.

Still, the lone guardian stood over him. Kaimi didn't move. Then he remembered: Only an *aumakua,* the spirit of some ancestor that marched with the phantom warriors, could protect you once they had turned against you. Who was his savior?

The warrior looked down at the boy, who was now shivering, nearly naked, under the moonlit sky.

"You may open your eyes, my grandson. You learned well. You are safe."

Kaimi stared up at the spirit hovering over him. The warrior was young, powerful, handsome. The passage into the Other World had changed his appearance, back to a time long before Kaimi had been born, yet the man was unmistakable. The protector standing before him was his grandfather Maleko.

Of course! Maleko. His grandfather's name was Hawaiian for "warlike." His grandfather, who had chosen to take part in the native uprising all those years ago, was descended from warriors! No wonder he was now one of the Night Marchers.

Kaimi was going to live! He had never felt such love for his grandfather.

"Yes, you are safe now, my foolish, reckless grandson. I could not let them hurt you. One day, if you wish, you may join us, for you come from a long line of warriors. But for now, my little Kaimi, aloha." And with that, the apparition dissolved. He had gone to join his fellow Night Marchers.

Mahalo, Grandfather, thought Kaimi. *Thank you. Mahalo nui loa.*

Chapter 5

THE FUNERAL CORTEGE OF BAYNARD PLANTATION

While there are stories of phantom stagecoaches and wagons galore, the sighting of a spectral horse-drawn funeral carriage is a rare sight indeed. For more than a hundred years, that's what some local residents of one South Carolina seaside resort claimed to have seen. And it turns out the cortege is more than just a trip to the graveyard: It's also a search for a missing cadaver.

Today, Hilton Head Island is a dream vacation getaway. Located in South Carolina along the Georgia border, the Atlantic Ocean retreat is just twenty miles outside of Savannah. With all the multimillion-dollar resorts, twelve miles of snow-white sand, and more than two dozen premier golf courses—Hilton Head is a stop on the PGA Tour—it's hard to believe the first bridge onto the island opening it to automobile traffic wasn't constructed until 1956.

But the story of the Baynard Plantation ghost dates back much further, to when cotton was king and the island found itself trapped in the struggle between the Union and Confederate forces during the Civil War.

Spanish explorers led by Francisco Gordillo were the first Europeans to make contact with the natives living on the island in 1521. By the 1600s the land had become English territory, and in 1663 Charles II granted a wide swath of land in the Americas to eight men known as the Lord Proprietors. That same year, Captain William Hilton sailed from Barbados on the *Adventure* and visited the region on their behalf. Off the coast of the Carolinas, he gave his name to a particularly attractive small islet located at the "head" of Port Royal Sound, dubbing it Hilton Head.

In 1776 a sea captain named John Stoney bought a thousand acres known as Braddock's Point (named for Captain David Cutler Braddock of the half-galley ship *Beaufort*), located at the southern end of the island. About seventeen years later, he began to build a house on the site, and by 1820 it was completed. Today most of the existing ruins of the Baynard Plantation are from that mansion.

The Stoney plantation passed by inheritance to a number of heirs until in 1840 "Saucy Jack" Stoney lost the property to William Eddings Baynard in an all-night poker game.

Baynard was already a successful planter on Edisto Island about thirty miles up the coast from Hilton Head, and he owned two other island plantations as well. He introduced Sea Island cotton, which he brought from Barbados, onto his Braddock Point property. It soon flourished.

Baynard and his wife, Catherine, raised four children in the great house. In 1849, at the age of forty-nine, Baynard died of yellow fever. He was buried in an antebellum aboveground mausoleum in the cemetery of Zion Chapel of Ease, a tiny wooden Episcopal church that had been built for the plantation owners in 1788.

In December 1860 South Carolina was the first state to secede from the United States. By the time the war broke out, more than twenty working plantations were on Hilton Head Island, and the Baynard Plantation was one of the finest. Fortifications were built on the island in July 1861 to protect the area from Union forces, but that November, Northern troops gained control over the region after winning the Battle of Port Royal.

More than ten thousand Yankee troops poured onto the island, but by then the Baynard family had fled. Union troops moved into their plantation house without a struggle, and they remained there, using the property as a headquarters until the end of the war.

Thinking that the Baynards might have hidden some of their treasure in the family mausoleum to recover later, looters broke into their tomb at Zion. No valuables were discovered—that is, unless you count the corpse of William Baynard. They emptied the sepulcher, even removing Baynard's body. His remains have never been recovered.

Sometime between August and December 1867 the manor went up in flames. Some think it was torched by a band of ex-Confederate raiders. Regardless, by the time Hilton Head Island was resettled after the Civil War, there was nothing left standing on the Baynard property, and there was no reason for the family to return. (They did go to court to regain legal title to the land about fifteen years later, but they never moved back onto the island.)

Today little more than a few foundations of the mansion remain. There are ruins of a few outbuildings (probably the quarters for the slaves who acted as servants in the main house), part of the chimney from the overseer's lodgings, and a small structure that most likely acted as a reinforcement for Union tents. There's not much more to see. But that hasn't stopped the ghost of William Baynard from returning home.

In 1956 developer Charles Fraser opened Sea Pines Resort, a master-planned enclave designed as a family holiday destination. Hilton Head Island has grown in leaps and bounds ever since. It has become subdivided into private residential gated communities called "plantations" (not to be confused with the Civil War–era plantation estates), each offering its own blend of spas, golf facilities, beaches, and oceanfront views.

More than two million tourists now visit Hilton Head annually, and over the past half century, quite a few have been shocked to witness a most unusual sight: the ghostly funeral cortege of William Baynard.

According to the stories, on moonlit nights his ghost can be seen riding in a black-draped horse-drawn coach at the front of a funeral procession. His carriage is followed by the phantoms of his slaves, dressed in plush red velvet, grieving for their master. The sad parade travels the old roads from the plantation ruins to Highway 278, heading toward the family mausoleum, which is near the intersection with Matthews Drive.

The Zion Chapel itself is gone, but the small cemetery remains. The Baynard mausoleum, built in 1846, is still there. In fact, it's the oldest intact building and the largest antebellum structure on Hilton Head Island.

The cortege stops at each plantation along the route. Baynard's ghost steps out of his coach, walks slowly to the gate, pauses briefly, and then returns to the carriage. It's said his spirit is searching for his body so he can return it to the family crypt.

If you see the ethereal parade go by, please give way. The restless spectre of William Baynard has been disturbed more than enough for one lifetime—and the next.

Baynard Ruins

Located on Baynard Park Road within Sea Pines Plantation
Baynard Park Road and Plantation Drive
Hilton Head Island, SC 29938

The Sea Pines Resort

P.O. Box 7000
Hilton Head Island, SC 29938
(866) 561-8802
seapines.com

The Baynard Plantation ruins are about eight miles from the entrance to the Sea Pines Plantation. They are open to the public and tours are offered occasionally. Ask locally for directions and schedules.

The foundations at the ruins are the only tabby structures (buildings constructed of materials consisting of equal parts sand, oyster shells, lime, and water) left on the island. The site was listed on the National Register of Historic Places in 1994.

Baynard Mausoleum; Old Zion Cemetery

Near the intersection of Highway 278 and Matthews Drive
Hilton Head Island, SC 29938

The Baynard Mausoleum is just as important to historians as ghost hunters because it's the oldest extant complete structure on Hilton Head Island. The crypt is also an outstanding representative example of nineteenth-century antebellum architecture. Matthews Drive, near the old cemetery, crosses the William Hilton Parkway section of Highway 278.

Hilton Head Island is located on the Atlantic Coast in South Carolina, very close to the Georgia border. To get there take Highway 278 off I-95. Once on the island, Highway 278 essentially forms a loop. The Greenwood Drive exit will take you toward the southern end of the island and Sea Pines Plantation. There is a day-use fee, payable at the gate, to enter the Sea Pines Resort.

Chapter 6

OCCURRENCE AT THE CREEK ROAD BRIDGE

If you put five skeptics on a ghost hunt out in the middle of nowhere, you can be sure nothing supernatural is going to show up. Or will it? Imagine the shock when the men in our tale discover that someone may have been trying to deliver a message from the Beyond after all—just not in the way they expected it.

The other four guys in the van weren't really sure what they were doing there, but Shawn had talked them into it. And, well, whenever he cooked up some hare-brained scheme it usually turned out to be worth doing—if only for laughs.

This time they weren't so sure. Standing on the Creek Road Bridge in the crisp autumn air at 11:00 p.m., with their teeth chattering and their toes going numb, they wondered whether this might have been an expedition better taken in the middle of summer.

The whole area surrounding Camp Comfort County Park, just south of Ojai, California, has a reputation for being a hotbed of haunted activity. More than a dozen ghosts are said to appear on that stretch of Creek Road between Oak View and Ojai.

First of all, there are three ghost riders. One is a woman on horseback who appears each year on the anniversary of the day her horse got spooked by a snake on the trail and threw her to her death. The next phantom rider is a black-clothed headless horseman. The third is a motorcycle rider, also missing his head, who chases unlucky drivers down the lonely road.

The most famous Creek Road bogeyman, the Char Man, might not be a ghost at all—at least he wasn't at first. According to legend, a farmer and his son were trapped in their burning house in the hills just south of town during a massive brush fire that swept through Ojai Valley in 1948. The father was killed, but the boy managed to survive. Horribly burned by the flames, he was driven mad from the pain of his injuries. For some reason—perhaps an insane attempt to try to save his dad's life?—he literally peeled the skin off his father's cadaver and hung him from a tree by the heels.

The boy, hideously charred, escaped into the forest. Before long he began to rush out of the woods and jump into the road, scaring or even attacking motorists.

And woe to anyone who was stupid enough to call out his name! Some believe the Char Man, deformed, repulsive, and deranged, is still alive. Others say, after so many years, that the young man has certainly died and that it's his ghost haunting passersby on Creek Road.

There are also spectres that haunt the concrete bridge spanning San Antonio Creek just about fifty yards north of the park's campground. One, the spirit of a murdered bride, still in her wedding dress, appears by the side of the road. The spectres of two young children dressed in 1800s clothing walk the bridge balancing on the rail before falling to their "deaths" in the stream. There's a disembodied ghostly hand of a child that scampers along the same railing. And on rainy nights you can hear the screams from a school bus full of children that skidded off the bridge in the 1930s and plunged into the creek below.

But it wasn't one of those phantoms the five young men sought that unnaturally chilly fall night. They were hoping to meet, or at least contact, the ghost of an unhappy woman who, deciding she had no other way to escape her abusive husband, tied one end of a rope around her neck, the other around the bridge railing, and then jumped off. Ever since, her melancholy ghost has been spotted walking the bridge or dangling by a rope over its side.

Shawn, a professional magician and author, had first heard her tragic story at a lecture by the well-known Ventura-based paranormal investigator Richard Senate. In fact, as part of the session the participants had visited the very bridge on which the five guys were now standing.

After that first ghost hunt, Shawn wanted to learn more. To help him on his nocturnal pursuit, he wanted people who had some knowledge, or at least an interest, in the supernatural, so he enlisted the help of some semi-reluctant friends who were fellow magicians. One of them, Scott—whom he had convinced to drive—was an innovative tinkerer and could find a novel way to solve just about any magical problem posed to him. David was the intellectual, as well as the youngest of the bunch. Bill was generally acknowledged by his peers to have the best control of any of them over a deck of playing cards, and the last of the fearless foursome was Bill's friend, Richard. Out of the entire group, Richard was the only one who wasn't a magician. He was more of what you might call a "party dude" and was along primarily to have a good time: Hey, being out with buds beats sitting at home watching late-night TV any day of the week. And what if they actually found a ghost? Wouldn't that be cool?

So there they were, holding flashlights, a ouija board, and a tape recorder (well, actually it was a "boom box"—it was 1985, after all), about to stand on a haunted bridge. Getting there had been no easy task. The six miles of Creek Road in question run through one of the most out-of-the-way stretches of the Ojai Valley. The path's two lanes, often overhung with the low-hanging branches of ancient oaks, cut through a rural landscape of broad fields and pastureland that's crisscrossed by small streams gurgling their way along the sides of the road. A few solitary ranches and homes dot the low hills.

When it's dark, a drive along Creek Road can be especially unnerving. The lack of streetlights makes the environs jet-black, pierced only by the beams of car headlights, which cast deep, creepy shadows along both sides of the highway. Above your head, the stars and moon are so intense that they seem close enough to touch.

Scott had pulled his van to the side of the road, just a few feet from the bridge near an empty campground, closed for the season. The five men got out and were immediately immersed in inky darkness and a surreal stillness. Rather than provide comfort, the calm added a feeling of apprehension to the adventure. They turned on their flashlights, made a quick sweep of the surroundings, switched on the boom box's recorder, and stepped onto the bridge.

And . . . nothing. No sudden apparitions, no banshee wailing in the darkness. Nothing at all.

There was a collective sigh of relief. As much as the guys didn't want to admit it, they were just as happy *not* to run into some crazy entity. Ghost hunting is all well and good in theory, but who knows how you'll react if you're actually confronted by something from the Other Side?

Now confident they weren't going to be attacked without warning, they moved farther out onto the bridge. There was nothing special about it. It was a typical back-road, two-lane country bridge, just wide enough for traffic to safely pass.

Then Shawn felt it. The temperature around him suddenly dropped by at least ten degrees. It was if he had stepped into a small, circular shaft of icy air. But there was no draft, no wind. It was just a column of cold air over a precise spot about halfway across the bridge. One by one, each member of his crew felt the ice-cold air for himself. It was there all right. Shawn hadn't imagined it. After a bit of investigation, they discovered that the cold spot didn't start on the pavement above the bridge. It was actually a vertical shaft of frigid air that extended all the way from the brook far below, up and through the bridge.

A common paranormal phenomenon, cold spots are thought to be either evidence of a ghostly presence or perhaps a portal through which spirits pass from one plane of existence to another. *But if that's the case*, thought Shawn, *and this was where the suicidal wife had hanged herself, why was the cold spot located six to eight feet away from the railing?*

Then it struck him: The bridge had been widened. The woman had lived in the area when the most common transportation was on horseback. To accommodate cars and the ever-increasing truck traffic in the valley, several feet had been added to each side of the onetime narrow road when it was paved. The cold spot where the side of the bridge and railing would have been when the woman was alive; it still marked the precise location where she hanged herself.

It was time to go to work. They put down the heavy tape recorder and set up the ouija board on the pavement inside the cold circle. Two of them rested their fingertips lightly on the planchette, which had been carefully placed in the center of the board, and waited.

"Is there anyone here?"

No reply. Complete silence, and no movement on the board.

"If there is anyone here that can hear my voice, we would like to talk to you."

Slowly at first, then with increasing speed, the planchette began to move. As the pointer shifted from one letter to the next, the men jotted them down on a piece of paper.

The disappointment was obvious on the faces of the group, however, even dimly lit as they were beneath the overhead glow of the flashlights' beams. The letters the planchette were pointing to didn't spell out anything; even a true believer in the occult would have to admit that the sequence was pure gibberish.

Time and again they tried, with different questions and different people manning the planchette. But it was always with the same result: a short, excited burst of incomprehensible nonsense, then nothing. For more than an hour and a half they tried. Then, frustrated, weary, and chilled to the bone, they reluctantly decided to call it a night.

Their mood was downcast as they walked back to the van. For all of the hope with which they had started the evening, their quest had been a failure. True, they *had* encountered a cold spot (which may or may not have had a natural explanation), but otherwise they had made no contact with the Spirit World. There were no voices, no messages, and certainly no ghosts. Scott started up the van, turned off Creek Road back onto the main highway out of Ojai, and before long the bridge was far behind them.

The next day Shawn started thinking about their nocturnal exploits. He had worked with ouija boards before, and this was the first time that virtually nothing had been spelled out by the planchette moving from letter to letter. True, in previous sessions the "answers" he received often had no correlation to the questions he had asked the spirits, but this time all they'd gotten was a jumbled mess. He checked and rechecked the letters they had marked down, but no matter how he split the letters into groups, he couldn't form a single recognizable word. There were no hidden messages.

Perhaps the problem was with the questions, he thought. Maybe if he checked the audiotape. He rewound the tape, donned a set of headphones, and hunkered down to listen to two hours of nothing.

As he expected, there were no surprises—at least at first. There was the small talk and banter, the guys' glee at finding the cold spot, the busy sounds of setting up the ouija board, the unanswered questions. But then Shawn realized that, for whatever reason, he hadn't turned off the boom box's recorder when they finished the session with the ouija board. He had kept it running the whole time they were packing up and setting off for the van. He could hear the gravel crunching under their feet as they left the bridge and headed down to the foot of the hill where Scott had parked. He heard them joking about why the spirits hadn't shown up.

"Maybe they were too busy tearing the van apart to talk to us."

"Yeah, maybe when we get there, the tires will be gone, and there'll be big red letters sprayed on the windshield, saying, 'You're not leaving.'"

"*What!*"

Stunned, Shawn stopped the tape. What was that? He quickly rewound the tape and listened again. A hoarse voice, definitely not one of the five men's, whispered, "*What!*" Not a question, exactly; just a simple, strong declaration.

"*What!*"

Shawn's mind started to race. The voice on the recording was unquestionably female, but there had been no women with them the night before. In fact, they hadn't run into anyone the entire time they were at the bridge. The place had been deserted. He replayed the tape again and again. The voice was definitely there!

Had there already been something on the tape that the recorder failed to record over? Or had noise bled through from the other side of the tape? No, he distinctly remembered: Halfway through the night he had opened a brand-new tape on the bridge and put it into the recorder, and the boom box had never left his sight. Had he carried it in some way that he accidentally brushed the microphone and created what sounded like a person talking? Could someone have coughed or sneezed in such a way that it could be mistaken for a voice? Popping in a new tape, Shawn tried to re-create the sound, but to no avail.

He was startled by a hard, loud rap on the door and looked up. It was Scott.

"What's up, Shawn? You look like you've seen a ghost."

"Not funny, Scott. Listen to this."

Shawn told his friend about the unusual voice, placed the old tape back into the recorder, handed Scott the headset, and hit play. Though Scott was the hard-core cynic of the bunch, he dutifully put on the headphones. After just a few moments, a shocked expression appeared on his face. Scott pulled off the earphones and threw them across the room.

"Man, what was that?! Don't ever play that tape for me again!"

"You mean you heard the voice?"

"Sure, I heard the voice. And the breathing too!"

Huh? Shawn realized he had never listened to the tape all the way through. He had always shut it off as soon as he had heard the voice. He plugged the headset back in, rewound the tape, and listened. Sure enough, there it was: "*What!*" followed a few moments later by the low but distinct sound of a person exhaling three times, one exhale right after the other. And the most frightening part of all was that the three breaths sounded much closer to the microphone than the voice had been. Whatever had made that sound had been standing in the middle of the five guys, right next to Shawn!

With an almost fanatic fervor, Shawn began to rethink the exact conditions of the night before. Richard had a slight cold. Could the breaths have been his? No. The boom box had two sensitive mikes that recorded in stereo. By listening carefully, Shawn could position each of the five men, identify their voices as well as their breathing, and tell how far they had been from the tape recorder. The exhaling that followed the mysterious "*What!*" had definitely not come from any of them.

Over the next few days, Shawn visited the other three friends who had accompanied him to the haunted bridge. All of them heard the voice on the tape; all of them heard the deep breaths. All of them were dumbfounded. None of them had heard anything out of the ordinary that night, but they had to admit: They had captured something extraordinary on tape.

An electronic voice phenomenon, or EVP, is defined as a form of paranormal activity in which the voice of a deceased person is picked up on electronic equipment, most often on magnetic audiotape. Almost without fail, no one hears the ghost voices when the recording is being made. They aren't noticed until the tape is played back. EVP is very, very rare, so some say that it is definitive proof of a world beyond our own.

Disbelievers say there is always some natural explanation for such sounds, for example, background noises people didn't notice at the time of the recording and, therefore, couldn't recognize later. But for Shawn and the other four men who went on a ghost hunt that night almost forty years ago, there wasn't any doubt. The occurrence was real. They were visited by one of the spirits of the Creek Road Bridge.

Creek Road
Ojai, CA 93023

The haunted six-mile stretch of Creek Road runs between Ojai Avenue (State Route 150) in Ojai and Ventura Avenue (State Route 33) in Oak View in Ventura County, California. To get there from Ojai, turn south from Ojai Avenue onto South Ventura Street, which will become Creek Road. The concrete bridge at the epicenter of the ghostly activity crosses the San Antonio Creek just north of Camp Comfort County Park, which is about a mile and a half south of downtown Ojai.

This story about Creek Road Bridge is based on the experiences of Shawn McMaster, who conducted a ghost hunt on Creek Road outside Ojai, California. His own account originally appeared in the summer 2005 issue of the magazine *Mind Over Magic* (volume 1, issue 3), published by TC Tahoe. Those who accompanied McMaster that night were Scott Miller, David Arnold, Bill Goodwin, and Richard Small.

Chapter 7

THE LONG RIDE HOME OF PETER RUGG

Getting home after a short trip shouldn't have been a problem. But so far Peter Rugg has taken 275 years and counting trying to do just that. Get out of the way if you see storm clouds forming in the middle of the road ahead of you: It just might be Peter Rugg coming through.

In 1820 it was no easy feat to make the long, difficult journey from New York City to Boston. Jonathan Dunwall, who was traveling on business, decided not to take the risky loop around Cape Cod at that time of year and instead settled on a quick packet ship transit to Providence. From there a two-day trip by stagecoach would set him safely in the Massachusetts capital.

Upon arriving in Providence, however, he discovered—much to his dismay—that every seat in the next carriage out was taken, so it was either wait until the following day for another conveyance or sit up front with the driver. Gratefully he accepted the proffered seat, and before long the group was on its way.

The ride and view were exhilarating, and within minutes Dunwall had fallen into animated conversation with the man holding the reins. The coach had carried on for several miles, bouncing down the well-traveled highway to Boston, when suddenly the horses started to falter.

"What's the matter?" asked Dunwall. "Your horses haven't seemed skittish up to now. I don't see any trouble on the road."

"Ah, not yet, my friend. But just you wait. When the horses start to act up like that, there's a storm coming."

"And that's not all," he added. "In a few minutes' time, you'll be seeing something—or someone—that, well, that might not be of this world."

Dunwall scanned the skies. It wasn't yet dusk, although a few shadows from the trees lining the road were starting to stretch across the path in front of them. Still, it was bright enough for him to see that there wasn't a cloud overhead.

"I know what you're thinking," broke in the horseman. "But the man who's coming always brings a cloud of misfortune with him. He's what I call a storm breeder."

And with that, an extraordinary sight appeared on the horizon. A small, worn, open carriage pulled by a mammoth black bay horse came into view. Driving the chaise was a stout man, about thirty-five years old, dressed in the wardrobe of a colonial Dutchman of fifty years earlier—complete with breeches, several waist-coats, and a voluminous jacket with long cuffed sleeves. Sitting beside him was a young girl, about ten years of age, clutching her father's arm.

The mysterious driver was holding the reins tightly as his horse hurried for-ward at a steady pace. As the father and daughter passed the stagecoach, Dun-wall noticed an anxious despair on the man's face. His eyes darted back and forth as if he were desperately trying to recognize his surroundings. Oddly, he and his daughter's clothing and hair were soaked, as if they had just emerged from a fierce rainstorm. The strange coach didn't pause, and its occupants barely looked in Dunwall's direction. Then, just as suddenly as the carriage had pulled up, it was gone, falling back and disappearing in the dust behind them.

"You've seen that man before?" asked Dunwall. "Under what circumstances?"

But before the coachman could answer, Dunwall felt something sprinkle on his brow. He looked up in astonishment. Despite the rest of the sky being abso-lutely clear, a black cloud was hovering above him, following quickly in the wake of the coach that had passed them. Before long, lightning was flashing, peals of thunder were booming in their ears, and then, all of a sudden, there was rain. A cloudburst. It only lasted a few seconds. Perhaps a minute, but no more. The cloud then moved on, as if chasing the enigmatic wagon that had passed them.

"What did I tell you?" the driver murmured ominously. "A storm breeder."

Dunwall was astounded. In all of his travels, he'd never run into anything that fantastic. "If what you say is true, and you've seen this man and encountered such a bizarre storm before, you *must* tell me his story."

The driver confessed that he knew little about the peculiar man and the little girl. But he had seen them dozens of times while making his regular runs between Providence and Boston. Usually the coach simply rushed by. But the stranger *had* stopped to talk to him on a few occasions.

"He would always ask me the same thing. He needed directions to Boston. But he barely listened, instead grumbling in disbelief that he was so far from his destination. Then he'd take up his reins and rush off—more often than not in the wrong direction.

"I've asked people about him all along the route. Others have seen him, too. Many others. And talked to him. He always asks the same thing, and no matter how much he's entreated to stop to eat, to take time to dry off, or to rest for the sake of his daughter, he always curtly replies that he must be on his way, that he has to reach Boston that very night."

It was getting quite dark. Taking a break for the night about halfway to Boston, the stagecoach pulled up in front of Polly's Tavern. Soon the company had settled into the inn and found themselves seated at a long, narrow table, enjoying drinks, a fine repast, and a crackling fire to ward off the early autumn air. In short order, several pitchers of ale had been consumed, and talk among the travelers turned to the unusual man who had crossed their path earlier that day.

"Oh, yes, I've seen him several times," offered one of the local residents who had insinuated himself into the conversation. "The Dutchman always asked me the quickest way to get back to Boston. As best as I can tell, he's never made it."

"In the course of a month, I ran into the man and his little girl in four different states," added a peddler.

"The poor lost souls," lamented a third. He didn't know how right he was.

More than three years passed before Jonathan Dunwall was to think about the "storm breeder" again. He was standing in front of Bennett's Hotel in Hartford, Connecticut, when he heard a man close to him call out in hushed tones, "There he goes again. It's Peter Rugg and little Jenny. He's nowhere closer to Boston. And he looks like he's seen a ghost."

"Perhaps," whispered a man next to him, "it's because he is one himself."

Dunwall looked out into the main street, disbelieving. The very same man and little girl he'd seen so long before, looking exactly the same, passed in front of his eyes. And over their heads floated a low, tight, dark thundercloud surrounded by streaks of lightning.

Dunwall could barely contain his excitement. "Forgive me for accidentally eavesdropping, my friends, but do you mean to say that you know who that man is?"

"Of course," they replied. "Everyone in these parts knows the sad story of Peter Rugg. But you won't believe it even if we tell you."

And if Dunwall hadn't viewed the ghostly phenomenon himself, he might not have.

One morning in the late autumn of 1769, just months before the massacre in Boston that presaged the first battles of the Revolutionary War, Peter Rugg, a wealthy cattle and horse trader, left his comfortable home on Middle Street in Boston's North End for a short visit to nearby Concord. It promised to be a clear, sunlit day, so he asked his ten-year-old daughter, Jenny, to join him. Peter's wife, Catherine, waved goodbye to them as the light carriage pulled by Rugg's favorite horse, Lightfoot, made its way down the cobblestone road. That was the last time the unfortunate Mrs. Rugg would see her husband and child.

Rugg was respected, or at least tolerated, by his colleagues and neighbors. Yes, he was clearheaded, sober, and known for his good manners, decorum, and allegiance to the Crown, but he was also infamous for his short temper and obstinacy. When his mind was made up, he was intractable, and he was more than willing to share his opinions— quite vocally. In fact, once he got into a rage, he often blustered himself into a red-faced fury. And the language! But just as unpredictably as his anger would appear, so too it would instantly and inexplicably evaporate, leaving him a composed, good-natured comrade and friend.

That day, with his business completed in Concord, Rugg started the seventeen miles back to Boston with his daughter. He was making good time when a late afternoon storm unexpectedly kicked up. Before he could find cover, the rain was upon them. Soaked to the skin, with the darkening sky slowing his passage, Rugg decided to stop briefly to rest at the home of a friend, a Mr. Cutter, in the village of Menotomy, just west of what is today Cambridge.

"Peter, you *must* stay the night!" Cutter implored. "It's now pitch-black outside, and you'll hardly be able to see your way. The rain is even stronger than when you arrived, so it's no doubt making parts of the road impassable. If nothing else, think of the comfort and safety of your little girl."

But for whatever reason—pride? arrogance?—Rugg became stubborn and even more determined. *The tempest cannot and will not stop me*, he thought. *No!* And then, daring the fates, he swore the oath that would seal his doom: "Let the rains increase! I will see home tonight, despite this storm, or may I never see it again!" With that, Rugg gathered up his cloak, and with his fearful, dumbstruck daughter at his side, he was out the door.

Back in the chaise, he whipped his horse with a hard flick. Startled, the bay jumped and began to force its way through the downpour. *How terrible could the ride be?* thought Rugg. It was only two more miles to the warmth and shelter of his manor on Middle Street.

But he never arrived.

Peter Rugg didn't make it home that night, or the next, or even the night after that. Although all of the likely routes out of Menotomy were searched, no trace of Peter Rugg, his daughter, Lightfoot, or the coach was ever found.

For many months after that, whenever the night turned stormy, Mrs. Rugg imagined that she could hear her husband's cracking whip, the hoofbeats of the horse, and the carriage wheels clattering down the cobbled street. Sometimes the neighbors, too, heard the commotion; it began to happen with such frequency that they would rush to the windows whenever the distinctive noise was heard.

Then one night some of them saw it: Through the blanket of rain they could just make out the form of a large, black horse, then a carriage, and finally the outline of a man and a girl. It was Peter and Jenny Rugg! But they didn't seem to be slowing down. If anything, his horse was picking up speed. There was a look of horror on Rugg's face as he realized he was unable to stop at his house. Within moments, the spectres disappeared back into the blinding rain and out of sight.

The next day, with the skies cleared, friends of Mrs. Rugg began to make inquiries at all the public houses and stables in the area. Had anyone seen Rugg? Had he been able to bring his horse to rest at any of their establishments the night before? But no. There was no sign of their missing neighbor.

Before long the familiar sounds stopped being heard, and residents of the district gave up any hope of seeing Peter Rugg again.

A few convinced themselves it had been someone else in the coach that wild and turbulent evening. Many decided the merchant had simply deserted his loving wife and home. Still others knew the truth: They had seen a ghost.

Soon rumors began to circulate that Peter Rugg's apparition had been spotted in New Hampshire, Connecticut, Rhode Island, and even as far away as Delaware and Virginia. But never again in Boston.

Listening to the tale there at Bennett's Hotel, Jonathan Dunwall blinked. It couldn't be the same man in front of his eyes at that moment, could it? If the story was true, more than fifty years had passed since Peter Rugg lost his way along the road from Menotomy to Boston. Rugg would have to be more than eighty years old. And what about that little girl? It couldn't be his daughter. Why, she would be over sixty!

Dunwall could contain his curiosity no more. He had to know! He ran into the street and leapt in front of the carriage. The driver reined in the horse as Dunwall cried out, "Pardon me, kind sir. But are you the man they call Peter Rugg? Because I think I have seen you before on the road to Providence."

The man looked Dunwall over, considered for a moment, and then carefully spoke. "Yes, I am Rugg. And this is my daughter, Jenny. Indeed, you may have seen me near Providence. I seem to have become lost. We are headed to Boston. Can you please give me the most direct route?"

"Of course. But first, forgive me for being so forward, Mr. Rugg. You seem quite weary from your travels. When did you leave home?"

"To be honest, I cannot say. It seems to have been a long time ago, but I've lost track of the days. But please detain me no further. I must be on my way. I will see my home tonight."

"Tonight?" exclaimed Dunwall in surprise. "But that's impossible. It's more than a hundred miles to Boston."

"Please don't try to deceive me, sir. Newburyport here is no more than forty miles from Boston."

There was a long pause. "I'm sorry, Mr. Rugg, but this isn't Newburyport. It's Hartford."

Peter Rugg was stunned, even though he had heard such news a hundred times before. How could it be? the spectre wondered. If this was Hartford, then that river he'd been following all day had been the Connecticut, not the Merrimack. How could cities, rivers, landmarks change their places overnight? Why could he never get back to his wife and home in Boston? Was he condemned to haunt these byways for all eternity? What demon had cursed him?

"Damn that oath!" And with that, Rugg shook the reins, and the phantom horse and carriage were off once more. The ghost of Peter Rugg turned the corner, back on his never-ending ride home.

Over the next century the legend of Peter Rugg was told in the pubs and hotels all along the main routes between New York and Boston. Occasionally there would be a burst of excitement when a toll collector on one of the local highways would burst into an inn, claiming the notorious spectre had just passed through his gate, or some traveler would profess to have given directions to a bewildered Knickerbocker desperately trying to get to Boston. But mostly, over time, as the number of sightings grew fewer and fewer, Peter Rugg was more or less forgotten.

It's said, however, that the spectral carriage has never really disappeared. When the coach does show up, it's usually on the main highways between Boston and Hartford, Connecticut, including the Massachusetts Turnpike, or on the Wilbur Cross Parkway between Milford and Meriden, Connecticut. Even if you're traveling the back roads late at night, you might still cross paths with a weathered eighteenth-century wagon carrying a father and child. Pity them, tell them their journey is almost at an end, and give them directions to Boston.

This legend was wildly popularized in "Peter Rugg, the Missing Man," a story written by William Austin (1778–1841) that was first published in the *New England Galaxy* on September 10, 1824. There's some debate as to whether it was based on New England folklore of the time or is a complete fiction.

The story of a traveler doomed to wander for eternity is similar to the famous account of the *Flying Dutchman*, in which the ship was caught in a tempest off the coast of South Africa while rounding the Cape of Good Hope. When the captain rebuffed a spectral visitor that materalized and offered to help him, the spirit cursed the boat and its crew, dooming them to sail forever and never reach harbor.

Chapter 8

THE RETURN OF MAD ANTHONY WAYNE

Some people just won't allow themselves to fade into the pages of history. They keep reliving their heroic deeds throughout eternity. Such is the case with that heroic Revolutionary rider in the storm, General Mad Anthony Wayne.

History? What could be more boring than that? Todd hated history class! Who cares about a bunch of old dead guys?

It was all just memorizing a bunch of names and dates long enough to pass the test, right? And this course, American history, had to be the worst. The country's only two hundred years old. How much history worth talking about could there be?

1492: Columbus rediscovers America after everyone forgets the Vikings got there first. Check. 1620: Pilgrims land on Plymouth Rock. Check. 1776: Duh. When it came to history, Todd really didn't care much about anything that had happened further back than the date with his girlfriend on Saturday night.

"Class, open your books to page seventy-two," droned the teacher. "The Revolutionary War. Todd?"

Hearing his name, Todd stopped daydreaming and was back in the classroom. He squirmed nervously in his seat. Why did the teacher have to call on him?

"So, Todd, other than George Washington, who do you think was the most fascinating military figure in the war?" Todd stared blankly. Was he supposed to have read something about the Revolutionary War? When was *that* homework given?

"Anyone?" asked the teacher without much hope.

A hand sprang up. Everyone groaned good-naturedly. Ashley. Of course, Ashley. *She* had an answer. She *always* had an answer. Her hand was the first to go up no matter what a teacher asked; she was always the first to want to offer an opinion, to discuss, to finish a term paper. What was wrong with that girl?

"Anyone *but* Ashley?" The teacher surveyed the room. She didn't know why she bothered. She knew that her prize pupil—even though she wasn't supposed to have favorites—was probably the only one who had done the assignment. With a well-worn sigh, the teacher gave in. "All right, Ashley."

What was she doing, wasting her life with eighth-graders? the teacher asked herself. She had been just like Ashley when she was in school: enthusiastic about learning, always eager to debate. She loved staying after class, talking to the teachers. They seemed to be the only ones intelligent enough to carry on a conversation. Had she mistaken that passion for wanting to go into education herself? But then, there was Ashley and the one or two other students each year who seemed to make it all worthwhile.

Whom would Ashley select? the teacher wondered. Maybe Lafayette, the flamboyant Frenchman who decided to serve with the Americans. Maybe John Paul Jones, the dashing naval commander: "I have not yet begun to fight!" Or better yet, Benedict Arnold. Now there was a complicated man. Why had he turned traitor? She would love to hear what Ashley had to say about him!

Ashley beamed. She knew she would be called on, but somehow it still always seemed to surprise her when it actually happened. "I think I would have to pick General Wayne."

Silence. No one in the class seemed to have a clue who she was talking about. "You know: General Anthony Wayne. *Mad* Anthony Wayne."

Suddenly Ashley had Todd's attention. *We had a nutcase for a general in the Revolutionary War?* he thought. *This has to be good.*

Almost as if she could read Todd's mind, Ashley quickly added, "Of course, he wasn't really crazy. He got the nickname because when he fought, he used risky, unusual tactics that none of the other generals would have even considered. And, instead of staying safely in the back behind his troops, Wayne always led the charge himself."

Todd had been had! So this Wayne character wasn't nuts after all. Pity. At least that would have made the class interesting.

"But that's not why I picked him," Ashley added. "It's because of his ghost."

You could almost hear the entire class take a giant, collective breath. A ghost? There was a Revolutionary War general who has a real, honest-to-goodness ghost running around? And people have seen it?

This was what the teacher prayed for more and more each day: some small, insignificant detail, some hook that would grab the students and hold their interest. And if it came from a student, all the better. Ashley started her tale.

Wayne was born in 1745 just outside of what is today Paoli, Pennsylvania. He was trained to be a surveyor, worked in his father's tannery, then later served in the Pennsylvania legislature.

Wayne signed on with the Revolutionary cause from the very beginning, raising a militia in 1775. Just a year later he was made the colonel of the Fourth Pennsylvania Regiment and fought with the Continental Army in its unsuccessful attempt to invade Canada. It was during this time that he commanded the troops at Fort Ticonderoga, service that resulted in his being promoted to brigadier general.

He would go on to fight throughout Pennsylvania, and he and his forces were holed up with George Washington's troops that bitter winter in Valley Forge. Afterward, Wayne was victorious in the Battle of Monmouth against the British, continuing to fight even though his army was far outnumbered.

Perhaps his most famous exploit during the war was his 1779 raid on the British fort at Stony Point, New York. The stronghold was built high on the side of a cliff overlooking the Hudson River in a seemingly impregnable position. Nevertheless, on the night of July 15, using only bayonets, Wayne and his men stormed the bastions and overtook the fortress. It was exactly the type of daring attack that earned Wayne his reputation for being "mad."

After the British surrender at Yorktown, Wayne was sent to Georgia to nullify the treaties between the British and the Native Americans and to convince the tribes to forge new alliances with the United States. Though promoted to major general, Wayne left the military in 1784 and served another a year in the Pennsylvania legislature before moving to Georgia, which had given him a sizable plantation to thank him for his peace negotiations with the Creek and Cherokee.

The general returned to military life at the request of then President Washington to help fight the American Indians in the frontier territory of Ohio. To ready his troops, Wayne established the first regular training camp for American soldiers. He was returning from a command in Michigan in 1796 when he died from gout. Wayne was buried in Erie, then later reinterred in the family plot at St. David's Episcopal Church in Radnor, Pennsylvania.

Nice, succinct biography, thought the teacher. *Short, concise. All the major points.* "Good work, Ashley. But what about the ghost?"

Ashley knew that's what everyone in the class was waiting for. She could see it in their eyes—especially Todd's. He was, she suddenly realized, kinda cute—that is, in a goofy, dumb-jock kind of way, if you liked that sort of thing.

Oh, right: the ghost.

Mad Anthony Wayne may have died, she told them, but his spirit apparently won't stay in the ground. Take that burial in Pennsylvania, for example. Originally, Wayne was laid to rest at Fort Presque Isle, where the Wayne Blockhouse, named after the general, stands today. In 1809, Wayne's son Isaac asked to have his father's remains moved back to the family plot in Radnor. Wayne's corpse was dug up and, at a doctor's recommendation to prevent disease, was boiled to remove any lingering pieces of flesh from the bones. The soupy mix of tissue and fluid was then returned to Wayne's grave in Erie, and the bones were loaded onto a cart to make the 180-mile journey across the dusty, bumpy path over the Alleghenies to Philadelphia. Along the way, many of the bones fell off the carriage and were lost. Today much of the route they took forms US Highway 322, and according to legend, every January 1 (which happens to be Wayne's birthday), his spectre walks the roadway trying to find his missing bones.

Cool, thought Todd. He could almost picture the poor ghost, half human, half skeleton, trolling his way along the highway looking for part of his skull or maybe his elbow.

But wait! Was that the whole story? He had to hear that stuff about the Revolutionary War just to find out about one day a year that some guy supposedly shows up as a spook? Why, it was almost like he had been tricked into learning!

Fortunately for Todd, Ashley wasn't through. "That's not all," she continued. "Since he was in the army, Wayne spent years of his life on the move. So it's not surprising that his ghost shows up all sorts of other places. Remember that time he spent at Fort Ticonderoga?"

It seemed the bachelor Wayne had quite an eye for the ladies, and they for him. As the commander of the fort, he naturally had a lot of young women competing for his attention and affection. He met two such ladies at the same private dinner at the fort: Penelope Haynes, the daughter of a wealthy Vermont landowner, and Nancy Coates, a local girl.

Despite Penelope's higher status and her well-connected father, Nancy won out, and she and Wayne were soon a couple. Before long, it became apparent that Nancy wanted Wayne to marry her, but the matter had to be put off because the

British were closing in. Nearby colonists were asking for protection, so George Washington ordered Wayne to bring all the area women into the shelter of the fort.

Wayne set off to gather them, but rumor soon had it that the commander was in actuality going off to bring back Penelope Haynes to marry her. Indeed, Wayne soon returned with many women and young girls from the immediate surroundings, including Penelope. She was the only one Nancy noticed. Were the gossip true? That night Nancy stole down to the shores of Ticonderoga. She tortured herself, crying, berating herself for not being pretty, or witty, or charming enough. Then, just before dawn, as the first rays of light were starting to gleam across the surface of the lake, Nancy strode out into the dark waters and took her own life.

Ever since, Nancy's ghost has walked the paths along the lake, reliving that horrible night. She's also been seen floating above the lake itself and inside the fort. Wayne's ghost, meanwhile, has appeared in his old quarters in the garrison quarters, either in the dining room or by the fire.

Although Wayne doesn't walk the trails around Fort Ticonderoga, he does visit another lakeside. During the Canadian campaign in 1776, Wayne captured two baby eaglets along the banks of Lake Memphremagog, which is located near Newport, Vermont, on the border with Quebec. His hope was to train them for hunting, and, indeed, from then on he traveled with the birds almost everywhere he went. He was so devoted to them that his ghost has now come back to the shores of Memphremagog. He's seen strolling along the path at the water's edge, dressed as a frontier scout and holding the otherworldly eagles, falconer-like, one on each wrist.

But perhaps the most terrifying manifestation of Mad Anthony takes place on the mountain road through Storm King Pass outside Cornwall, New York. He appears as a phantom horseman, re-creating one of the most courageous and audacious rides of his career.

In 1779 George Washington ordered Wayne to issue warnings to the American soldiers located along the Hudson River about British forces in the area. Wayne, who was familiar with the trails, set out on horseback under cover of night in a turbulent rainstorm, passing through Storm King Pass to alert the troops. He returned safely, only to immediately turn around and lead his men against the barricades at Stony Point.

"And to this day," Ashley said, finishing her tale, "just before a big rain hits, the ghost of Mad Anthony Wayne appears on the windswept mountain roads of Storm King State Park. The spectre, wearing a full cape that whips behind him, is on horseback. The hooves of his spirit steed shoot sparks as they pound against the pavement. The pair rushes down the road, dashing through the highway tunnels that now pass through the hills. If you see them coming, move aside. The general is on his secret mission—a mission that he now repeats, over and over for all time."

Wow, thought Todd. *Secret missions. Ghost stories. Girls killing themselves over you. Maybe history isn't so bad after all.* Lost in his thoughts, he let a small grin cross his lips. The teacher saw it and smiled.

US Route 322

The highway, once nicknamed the Lakes to Sea Highway, is a 494-mile east–west road that stretches from Atlantic City, New Jersey, to Cleveland, Ohio. Along the way it overlaps several other highways. Its longest section passes through Pennsylvania, crossing the state line at Chester (ten miles south of Philadelphia), traveling northeast through State College (which is at the exact center of the Commonwealth), and continuing to Meadville (thirty-four miles south of Erie) before turning southwest into Ohio.

Although the exact route taken to transfer General Wayne's bones from Erie to Radnor is unknown, the wagon probably would have entered the road near Meadville and continued along what is today Route 322 at least as far as Harrisburg before heading toward Radnor (which is about ten miles north of Philly). This gives at least two hundred miles of haunted highway from Meadville to Harrisburg for ghost hunters to explore.

Fort Ticonderoga

102 Fort Ti Road
Ticonderoga, NY 12883
(518) 585-2821
fort-ticonderoga.org

Located on Lake Champlain at the New York–Vermont border.

Lake Memphremagog

Newport, Vermont

The lake straddles the Quebec–Vermont border at Newport, Vermont. Newport, at the southernmost end of the lake, is on US Highway 5/State Highway 105, about three miles off I-91.

Storm King Pass

Storm King State Park

US Route 9W

Cornwall, NY 12518

(845) 786-2701

parks.ny.gov/parks/stormking

The park, administered by the Palisades Interstate Park Commission, is on the west bank of the Hudson River between Cornwall-on-Hudson and West Point, New York. It can be accessed either by US Highway 9W, which runs through the center of the park, or State Route 218 (also known as Storm King Highway), on its eastern boundary along the river. General Wayne's exact route through the area is unknown.

Chapter 9

THE GHOST TRAIN

It's not just the souls of the dearly departed that haunt our nation's highways. Drive along any of the roads next to the deserted tracks of the old New York Central Railroad on April 27 and you may catch a glimpse of a ghost train—the funeral train that bore the casket of Abraham Lincoln from Washington, DC, back to Springfield, Illinois, for burial.

"The president is dead."

The words reverberated in Jim's head as he drove westward along the lonely stretch of old State Highway 5 in central New York. What must it have been like in 1865 to hear such startling news: that our nation's president, the man who had fought so hard to keep our country united, had been struck by an assassin's bullet? Such a thing had never happened in our young nation's history. The shock must have shaken our war-weary country to its core.

Today many Americans believe Abraham Lincoln was the greatest president the United States has ever produced. But on the evening of Good Friday, April 14, 1865, when Lincoln was shot at Ford's Theatre, that wasn't necessarily the case. Like the nation at the time, citizens' sentiments were deeply divided, with many admiring the sixteenth president's vision, courage, and strength, and just as many reviling him.

Lincoln had just led the country through the most troubled part of its history. In the aftermath of the Civil War, many people believed it was Lincoln who had saved the United States during its bitter struggle. But others, like his assassin John Wilkes Booth, blamed Lincoln for destroying their very way of life.

Jim was keenly aware of all this as he drove that night outside of Schenectady. In fact, he knew he was following almost the identical path that had taken the president to his final resting place in Springfield.

After his tragic murder Lincoln became the first president to lie in state in the White House. His body was then carried by a train dubbed the Lincoln Special in a 1,700-mile grand funeral procession from the nation's capital to Springfield, Illinois, for burial. A cadre of soldiers escorted the president's body, and three hundred mourners accompanied his coffin. Also on the train was the casket of Lincoln's son Willie, who had died in Washington in 1862 at the age of eleven and was disinterred for reburial with his father.

Although not widely publicized, an undertaker and an embalmer were on board, and their only job was to keep the president's remains looking presentable during the journey. In addition, the casket was surrounded by flowers, with an increasing number of floral bouquets as the trip wore on, in large part to cover the smell of decomposition.

The entire train was draped in black. The coffin, carried in a specially designed hearse railroad car, rested on a dais draped in black and covered overhead by a canopy held up by four columns decorated in black feathers, flags, and crepe. The mahogany coffin was lined in satin and silk and trimmed with black-and-white braid.

The upper third of the coffin's lid could be thrown back to reveal the president in his final repose. In death his ashen face was not diminished. His unmistakable features the deep wrinkles carved into his countenance, the heavy, furled eyebrows—were merely frozen into immortality.

During its trip, the Lincoln Special took an unusually long route, with several out-of-the-way stops so the maximum number of Americans could pay their respects as the cortege rolled by, paused in a train station, or stopped for a few hours in one of the larger cities to allow the casket to be removed and lie in state. The train passed through 445 communities along the way, and residents turned out by the tens of thousands—all total, about a third of the people living along the track's route viewed the funeral train.

From the beginning there were supernatural manifestations surrounding the funeral cortege. Many people claimed that as the train traveled through a town all the clocks in the station came to a standstill, and several individuals said their own pocket watches stopped as well.

Jim had heard the more recent stories, that in the years since the train made its fateful journey in 1865, people driving along the roads that parallel the rails on which the procession traveled had claimed to see a ghost train on the tracks every year on April 27. And if they listened closely, they could hear the faraway whistle of the train or the sad strains of the military band on board drifting through the night air.

The ghost train had been seen at various spots along the original route, all the way from Washington across New York, Pennsylvania, Ohio (especially between Urbana and Piqua, where the train passed on April 29 and 30), Indiana, and into Illinois. This April 27, however, Jim was driving along the most actively haunted stretch of the route, the section between Albany and Schenectady, New York. He wondered, would he see the train tonight?

Back in 1865 the funeral train had departed the District of Columbia on April 21 and made stops in such major cities as Baltimore, Philadelphia, and New York City before moving on to Albany. It arrived in Albany sometime after midnight on April 25, and it remained there until the next afternoon. For the next two days, the train slowly made its way across New York, passing through Syracuse, Palmyra, and Rochester before arriving in Buffalo in the early morning of April 27.

So here Jim was, tracing the path of the funeral train on the anniversary of its passage. If he was going to see its ghost, tonight had to be the night. Consulting the road map he had lying open on the passenger seat beside him, he wondered where the best place would be to stake out the tracks.

Today the entire route can more or less be driven on the modern I-90 from Albany to Buffalo. But it's possible to get even closer to the old tracks, because before the Interstate Highway System was established, the rails were paralleled by a series of smaller highways and roads, including State Routes 5, 5S, 20, 31, 33, 63, 69, and 365.

The details of all these highways were important to Jim, because he knew most of the sightings had occurred on these smaller roads. He decided to try somewhere along the fifty miles of Route 5 between Schenectady and Utica, where the rails ran along the banks of the Mohawk River.

Jim had been attempting to catch a glimpse of the ghost train for years, ever since he first ran across a description of the haunting in the archives of the *Albany Times*:

> It passes noiselessly. If it is moonlight, clouds cover over the
> moon as the phantom train goes by. After the pilot engine
> passes, the funeral train itself with flags and streamers
> rushes past. The track seems covered with black carpet and
> the coffin is seen in the center of the car, while all about it
> in the air and on the train behind are vast numbers of blue

coated men, some with coffins on their backs, others leaning
onto them.

At exactly midnight, Jim pulled his car into a turnoff by the side of the road.
Here on Route 5, far from the city lights of Schenectady, he could just make out
a piece of the old tracks that lay between the road and the nearby Mohawk River.
He rolled down his car windows, tilted the seat back just a bit, and waited. The
night's vigil had begun.

It was already spring, but the April night air was still crisp. There was a
moon, but lazy clouds kept drifting across its face so the night scene was bathed
alternatively in light and shadows. All seemed to be at peace.

Perhaps too much peace, thought Jim. *Odd.* He noticed that all of the insects
had suddenly become quiet. He got out of the car, leaned against the door, and
immediately felt overwhelmed by an eerie stillness.

And then he saw it: At first a hazy mist seemed to hover above the train tracks
far off to his right, just where the rails met the horizon. Then the fog seemed to
take shape. Was it possible? Incredibly, he could make out a large nineteenth-
century-style locomotive steam engine emerging from the haze, billowing out
puffs of smoke from its stack. But there was no sound of wheels rattling against
the iron rails. It was the ghost train!

Softly, the sorrowful sound from the train's whistle cut through the air. Then
the engine passed directly in front of him. Jim could clearly make out the crew in
the open compartment: The train was being manned by skeletons.

Before he could react, the strains of a somber dirge floated to Jim's ears. It
was the saddest, most melancholy melody he had ever heard. Where was it coming from? There: Just a few cars behind the engine was a compartment in which
a spectral uniformed concert band sat, all skeletal musicians playing the solemn
requiem on phantom instruments. As he watched, transfixed, mesmerized, the
other cars passed by, filled with the spectres of hundreds of Union soldiers.

On one of the last cars of the funeral train, Lincoln's casket was clearly visible through the black-curtained windows. An honor guard of skeletons, wearing
their Union dress blues, surrounded the coffin. The only thing missing was Lincoln's ghost. *Then one of the most interesting parts of the legend was true*, thought
Jim: Despite the countless times over the past century the funeral train has been

spotted, no apparition of the president himself has ever been seen on any of the coaches.

With one last cry of its whistle, the train hurtled on, disappearing into a vapor that hung over the tracks. It was gone.

Jim remained speechless, spellbound and unmoving as he reflected on the miracle that had just occurred. He glanced down at his watch. It was still midnight. How could that be? Had time simply stopped to allow the ghostly train to pass through the world of the living? Although he knew he could never fully understand the phenomenon he had witnessed, Jim felt satisfied. He stepped back into his car, fastened the seat belt, and pointed his car west. He still had a long drive to Buffalo.

Does the phantom funeral train still materialize today? According to folklore, as long as there is anyone alive who grieves for the fallen president, the ghost train will continue to appear.

Lincoln Funeral Train Route

The path of the train that bore Abraham Lincoln's casket from Washington to Springfield stretches seventeen hundred miles over seven states and the District of Columbia. Although the phantom train has been reported on almost every stretch of the track at one time or another, the most active section seems to be between Albany and Buffalo in New York.

At the time of Lincoln's death, the New York Central Railroad was one of the most important rail links in the United States. It ran all the way across the state of New York, bordering several bodies of water along its route. By checking a state map, you'll be able to locate the roads that most likely parallel the old tracks. I-90 runs all the way from Albany to Buffalo, approximating the Lincoln train route, but you'll be able to get much closer to the tracks by staying on state roads, such as Highways 5, 5S, 69, 365, 31, 33, 63, and 20.

Chapter 10

TELLY'S PHANTOM

The most famous highway ghost story of all is that of the phantom hitchhiker. But what would you say if you found out the person who gave you a lift turned out to be a ghost? Maybe in the Spirit World, turnabout is fair play.

"Who loves ya, baby?"

That phrase, heard everywhere in the 1970s, was the trademark of Kojak, TV's bald, lollypop-licking New York City police detective, portrayed by charismatic actor Telly Savalas.

Born Aristotelis Savalas on January 22, 1922, in Garden City, Long Island, New York, the popular TV and film actor was the son of Greek Americans. His father owned a restaurant, and his mother was an artist. Young Telly served as a soldier in World War II, then worked in a variety of jobs—as a lifeguard, a newspaper vendor, and, for a time, a journalist for ABC News. All down-to-earth, real-world jobs. It was this background that Savalas was able to bring so effectively to his signature role as Lieutenant Theo Kojak.

Telly's first acting experience was in episodic television, but by 1962 he had also begun to branch out into movies, appearing in such films as *Cape Fear* and giving an Oscar-nominated supporting performance in *Birdman of Alcatraz*. He shaved his head for his standout role as Pontius Pilate in 1965's *The Greatest Story Ever Told*, and it was such a strong, distinctive look that he kept it throughout his long career. He became known for playing tough guys with a soft streak or an edgy sense of humor, so the role of Kojak was an easy fit. Little wonder he was identified with it for the remainder of his life.

Even for actors, there's always a definitive line between reality and the world of make-believe. But all that changed for Savalas when he had a life-altering brush with the Unknown. The encounter haunted the actor until he died in 1994, one day after his seventy-second birthday. His experience was one of the rarest of ghost phenomena: He was actually a passenger in a phantom car!

When you think of Long Island, the first thing that comes to mind usually isn't a dark, deserted highway. After all, the island's western boundary is just across the narrow band of the East River from downtown Manhattan, home to more than 1.5 million souls. On Long Island itself, you'll find another 4 million people living in just the Bronx and Brooklyn. But as you move farther out on the island, away from the New York City limits, the cities shrink into towns and small communities. Some are little more than villages. By the time you reach Montauk, at the island's easternmost shore, you'll find a mere four thousand local residents living there year-round.

It was near one of these unexpected rural enclaves in early 1957 that our story takes place. Driving home from a cousin's house on Long Island late one night—or, more accurately, early one morning—Savalas noticed that his gas tank was almost empty. *Please*, he thought, *don't run out of gas!* It was 3 a.m., long after sensible people on that part of the island were in bed. And it was pouring down rain. If only he could make it the last few miles home! But then the engine started to sputter. He was riding on fumes.

Slowly he eased his car onto the shoulder of the road as the engine died. Pulling his shirt collar up over his head, he got out into the downpour. His eyes searched down the lonely stretch, first one way, then the other. As he'd feared, nothing. Except for that light.

Although he could hardly make it out through the rain, way off in the distance was a red neon sign. Then he remembered: He had passed a diner on the way to his cousin's. That must be it! He started out on a soggy jog toward the glow.

When he got to the diner, his heart sank. In those days many roadside stores had gas pumps out front, and he had hoped he might find one standing by the diner. But no such luck. Worse yet: There were no cars out front. Sure, the lights were on, but was the place open?

Shaking his clothes, Savalas stepped inside onto the linoleum floor. It was a typical 1950s diner: There was a long counter with stools across from the entrance and the usual line of red-backed booths. Through the small window to the kitchen, Telly could see a man at the grill wearing a small white paper hat and a grease-soaked apron. A lone waiter stood behind the counter reading. Otherwise the diner was completely empty. *Of course it's deserted*, thought Savalas. *Who in his right mind would be out at this time of night in this weather?*

"Can I help you?"

"Yes," Savalas said, and, without going into detail he asked if there was an all-night gas station anywhere in the area. The waiter gave Savalas directions to a garage less than a mile down the road.

"I'd be happy to give you a lift myself," the counter kid offered, "but as you can see, it's just me and the guy in back. Good luck, though." With that, having decided that the soaked man standing in front of him wasn't going to stay long enough even for a hot cup of coffee, the waiter turned back to his magazine.

Savalas walked back into the rain. Already soaked, he started to run in the direction the young man had pointed. He had gotten only a few yards, however, when a long, sleek black Cadillac pulled up beside him, slowed, and stopped.

With all the rain streaming down the car's windows, Savalas could barely tell that anyone was inside. But then the driver slowly rolled down the window and shouted, "Do you need a lift?"

Telly wasn't used to hitchhiking, and he wasn't really in the mood to deal with a stranger. But under the circumstances, he figured, beggars couldn't be choosers. He opened the door and got in.

Immediately he felt the warmth inside the car envelop him, and he was glad to be somewhere he could start to dry off. The driver had a calm, reassuring voice as he asked, "Where are you heading?"

Savalas explained what had happened, and as they quietly rode toward the gas station, Telly let his eyes take in the driver. He was immaculately dressed in a slightly dated black tuxedo, with a crisply pressed white shirt and bow tie. His hair was neatly combed back, and he wore a perfectly trimmed mustache. *With that getup*, thought Savalas, *he could easily have been a stand-in for Clifton Webb in any of those old movies.*

Finally Telly's curiosity got the better of him. "You're dressed up pretty swanky for this time of night. If you don't mind my asking, where are *you* heading?"

In a low monotone, and with just the slightest hint of sorrow, the driver simply stated, "To the crossroads."

Involuntarily, Savalas shivered. The crossroads? What was *that* supposed to mean? Was this guy loony? Telly was beginning to have second thoughts about having gotten into the car when, much to his relief, the service station came into sight. The stranger pulled his car into the lot.

Savalas reached into his pocket to offer the accommodating driver some money for his trouble and panicked. His wallet was missing! Mentally retracing the events of the evening, he quickly realized that he had left the billfold back at his cousin's house. Not only couldn't he give the stranger any money to thank him, he couldn't even pay for gas for his own car.

Oh, well, that was *his* problem, not the stranger's. Savalas apologized for not being able to offer him anything. "But give me your name and address, and I promise I'll put something in the mail."

The man hesitated. "Just happy to help get you out of the rain. And I'm glad the gas station is open. In fact"—the driver reached into his coat, pulled out a dollar bill, and handed it to Savalas—"perhaps you can use this for some gas."

Now Savalas really felt stuck. He needed the money, or he'd be trapped at the garage until morning when he could call someone to get a lift home. But he couldn't accept money from a complete stranger. Telly agreed to take the cash, but only, he insisted, if the driver would let him repay him. Reluctantly, the man agreed. He said his name was Harry Agannis, and he hastily scribbled down his address and phone number and handed it to Savalas.

Without another word Telly dashed to the door of the service station. He turned to wave goodbye to the man who had come to his aid, but the Cadillac was gone. It was almost as if the car had disappeared into thin air.

It wasn't until a few days later that Savalas found the paper with the phone number stuffed into the bottom of his pocket. When he called, it wasn't Harry's voice that answered, however, but a woman's.

"Hello? Is this, uh, Mrs. Agannis? May I speak with Harry?"

There was silence on the other end for what seemed like an eternity. Then a clearly agitated voice rang out. "Is this some kind of joke? Who is this?"

Taken aback, Telly rushed to explain that he had met her husband a few nights before and that Harry had helped him out. "He wrote down his name and number on a piece of paper, and . . . "

"That's impossible," she said curtly. "My husband, Harry, is dead. He's been dead for three years." Then a dial tone: She had hung up.

Dead? For three years?

Savalas mulled over what he had just heard. How could that be true? And if it was, who had picked him up? Maybe that would explain why the man hadn't wanted to give Telly his name. After all, the guy was all dressed up, driving out there alone in the middle of the night. And heading to "the crossroads?" Who knows where he was actually heading or why he wanted to keep his identity a secret.

As the days went on, Savalas began to feel guilty. Clearly he had upset the woman who had answered the phone, but they had both been the victims of a tasteless prank. He didn't want to call her back, figuring it would only distress her more getting another unwanted phone call, so, as awkward as the confrontation would be, Telly resolved to meet Mrs. Agannis face-to-face to say he was sorry.

He drove to the address the man had written down, and with some trepidation he walked up the sidewalk to the front door of her home and knocked. As soon as Mrs. Agannis opened the door, he rushed into the speech he had prepared. His name was Telly Savalas. He was the one who had called the other day. He wasn't trying to be funny or cruel. He thought they might both be the butt of a nasty practical joke.

She looked at the actor for a moment and could see the sincerity in his eyes. She widened the door and invited him inside. As they sat down, Telly handed her the paper the mysterious driver had given him.

Mrs. Agannis's hands started to shake, and tears welled up into her eyes. "Where did you . . . ? How could you have gotten this?"

Savalas was puzzled. Hadn't he just explained?

"You don't understand, Mr. Savalas. This is Harry's handwriting."

Stunned, Telly objected. That couldn't be possible. Then, as Savalas described the man who had given him a lift, his wardrobe, and the car, Mrs. Agannis stood. Without a word, almost as if in a trance, she walked across the room and removed a well-worn album from a weathered bookcase. She sat down next to Savalas and started to flip through the pictures. "This was my Harry."

Savalas recognized him instantly. It was the same man, proudly standing next to a black, shiny Cadillac.

In a soft, dreamlike voice, she told her story:

"Harry died in that car three years ago. He had been at a party, wearing that musty old tuxedo of his, and he was driving home around three in the morning. Out at the crossroads, about a mile down the road from where that gas station is that you mentioned, his car was hit by a truck, and my Harry was killed."

The two then sat speechless, considering the implications of what she had just told him. The conclusion was inescapable: For at least one night, Harry had returned. A phantom driver had paused just long enough to give a hitchhiker a hand before returning to his destiny at the crossroads.

Had it happened before? And would Harry ever return to help anyone else? Savalas was never to find out, for he swore to himself at that moment—and kept his promise—never to accept a ride on that haunted highway again.

Some sources give the night of Telly Savalas's brush with the Other Side as February 27, 1957. One version of the story, however, mentions that Savalas was just about to appear on an episode of *The Twilight Zone* that aired in November 1962. Regardless of the exact date of the ethereal encounter, it occurred very early in the actor's career, sometime when he was in his mid-thirties to early forties.

Chapter 11

THE CURSE OF LITTLE BASTARD

It was just another celebrity death. But is it possible that the car in which James Dean was fatally injured was actually responsible for the accident? Could the car have been cursed or even, as some suggest, possessed by an evil spirit? After Dean died, the car was involved in several other deaths and injuries. Is it possible that they weren't all merely accidents? You be the judge.

Flat. Flat for as far as the eye could see. Fresh off filming his last scenes for *Giant*, the twenty-four-year-old movie star was finally free—free to drive as fast as he dared and his wheels could carry him.

Here, over the Grapevine through the narrow mountainous pass north of Los Angeles, California's Central Valley lay wide out in front of James Dean. This was migrant-worker territory: Dean could see them out sweating in the fields as they picked crops under the unforgiving midday sun. *Not for me*, thought Dean. He wanted his life to be full and fast.

He zoomed past the dusty farming community of Bakersfield. In the passenger seat beside him, Dean's mechanic Rolf Wutherich smiled. The silver Porsche 550 Spyder was only one of ninety made. Wutherich knew what the machine was capable of and was eager to see Dean test its limits. Wutherich had just finished checking out the Porsche that morning back at Competition Motors, readying it for the racing event in Salinas to which they were headed.

"Should we load it on the trailer, then?" the mechanic had asked. The engine had been fine-tuned, and he didn't want to risk overheating it with a long drive up the coast.

"Nah," said Dean. "I want a little more time to get used to her before the race. I have to see what she can do."

Dean had always had a fascination with speed. As soon as he had landed his breakout role of Cal Trask, the rebellious son of a domineering, disapproving father in *East of Eden*, Dean bought his first sports car, a bright red MG TD. He also bought a station wagon, the white Ford Country Squire Woody that was now bringing up his rear. Normally the wagon would have been towing the Spyder to

Salinas instead of pulling the empty flatbed. But Bill Hickman, a friend and stunt-man from *Giant*, had agreed to drive it to the speedway, and Sanford Roth, who was there to do a photo spread on Dean and the race, was along for the ride.

Dean's car had been customized by George Barris, who would become famous for his modifications of racing cars and hot rods (as well as his design for TV's Batmobile). The silver body of Dean's Spyder was set off with red stripes over its rear wheel wells, the seats were Scottish tartan, and a large 130 was numbered in black on the front, sides, and back. The car looked so hot that Dean had the car's nickname, "Little Bastard," lettered underneath the license plate.

Little Bastard indeed. From the start, Barris thought the vehicle had a "weird feeling of impending doom." Nick Adams, who had appeared with Dean in *Rebel Without a Cause* and would later go on to star in TV's *The Rebel*, was also uneasy about the car. So, too, was Dean's uncle, Charlie Nolan. Then, just a few days before leaving for Salinas, Dean met Alec Guinness and couldn't help but show off his new racer. He was surprised by the renowned British actor's reaction.

"So, what do you think, Mr. Guinness? She's a beauty, isn't she?"

"That car is sinister, my boy. Sinister. Mark my words: If you get in that car, you will be found dead in it in less than a week."

That had been September 23, 1955. Now, just seven days later, Dean was tearing northward up Highway 99. He had come a long way from his modest beginnings. When he was just a boy, his father had moved his family from Indiana, where Dean was born, to Santa Monica, California. There, Dean's mother died of cancer when he was only nine. His father, feeling incapable of raising his son himself, sent him back to Fairmount, Indiana, to be reared by the young boy's aunt and her husband. Despite being brought up in their conservative household, Dean dreamed of fast cars and acting in the theater.

After graduating from high school, Dean traveled back to California, where he wound up majoring in drama at UCLA—a move that would further alienate him from his father. But Dean had decided on his life's course, and in 1951 he dropped out of college to become an actor full-time. A few bit roles on television and some small parts in movies followed, but it wasn't until he moved to New York later that year that Dean's career really began to take off.

He was accepted into the prestigious Actors Studio, studying "method act-ing"—the same naturalistic technique employed by such actors as Marlon Brando and Montgomery Clift. In 1954, after appearing on several live television dramas,

Dean got a role in the Broadway adaptation of André Gide's book *The Immoralist*. He won a 1954 Theatre World Award for his portrayal of Bachir, a blackmailing Arab houseboy—and Hollywood took notice.

So it was back to California for Dean. But this time it wasn't for a mere walk-on. Instead, he was to star in the screen version of John Steinbeck's novel *East of Eden*. The part seemed written with Dean in mind: a disobedient outsider yearning for the love of his father. Under the direction of Elia Kazan, Dean turned in a performance that was to win him an Academy Award nomination.

(No one at the time could have predicted that Dean would receive two back-to-back Oscar nominations, in 1956 for *Eden* and in 1957 for his supporting role in *Giant*—or that he would receive the nominations posthumously because both films wouldn't be released until after his death.)

Even before *Eden* came out, Dean had given in completely to his passion for sports cars. He traded up from his high speed MG to an even faster 1500cc Porsche Speedster. And by 1955 he was driving in racing competitions in Palm Springs, Santa Monica, and Bakersfield.

Meanwhile, Dean was filming his second movie in what was to become his signature role, the brooding, troubled teen hero of *Rebel Without a Cause*. But even while the film was being shot, Dean's obsession with speed and automobiles continued unabated. He traded in his Speedster for the vehicle that would eventually be his last: the 550 Spyder.

I'm not out of control, thought Dean as he barreled toward Salinas. *And maybe if I am—a little—it's the studio's fault. Didn't they stop me from racing while I was filming* Giant*? I'm just making up for lost time.*

But Warner Bros. knew what they had, and they were protecting their investment. Dean was a valuable commodity; they didn't want him hurt. Now, with work on *Giant* complete, Dean was free to let off a little steam. Besides, what harm could it do? Salinas was just another race, like all the others, and the trip there was a piece of cake.

Crossing into Kern County around 3:30 that afternoon, Dean knew he was driving over the speed limit, but so what—65 in a 55 mph zone? Everyone does that. But that didn't stop a highway patrol officer from pulling over both the Spyder and the wagon, which was still following closely on Dean's tail.

Once the patrolman was finished and out of sight, Dean shrugged off the ticket and revved up his engine. This time he really let loose, leaving the wagon far behind—much to the frustration of Roth, who had hoped to get some action photos of the young star cruising out on the open highway.

Dean stopped briefly to gas up at Blackwell's Corner, where he ran into fellow sports car driver Lance Reventlow. He then turned west on US Route 466 (now 46) toward Cholame. From there it would be a straight shot to US Route 1. Then he'd take the Pacific Coast Highway on the last leg up to Salinas. They were only a few hours away, so Dean slowed down a bit and settled in for the remainder of the drive. No need to hurry now. If he stayed at the speed limit, maybe Hickman would catch up to them before they hit the ocean.

Twenty-three-year-old Cal Poly student Donald Turnupseed was traveling home to Tulare, going east on the same highway as Dean, driving his 1950 black-and-white Ford Custom Tudor coupe. So far his drive had proved uneventful, and the road ahead seemed perfectly clear.

Even with the setting sun in his eyes—it was about 5:30 p.m.—Dean could see the Ford coupe coming toward him. But the Porsche was slung low, and its silver color blended into the shimmering roadway. To Turnupseed, the Spyder was invisible.

The student cut sharply to the left, forking onto State Road 41, and at the last moment he saw the Porsche. But it was too late. The two cars met at full speed. Wutherich was flung out of Dean's car, breaking his jaw and sustaining other injuries in the collision. Turnupseed amazingly also survived the crash with only a slash on his forehead and a battered nose. But Dean was not so lucky.

The Spyder was crushed, with Dean incurring a broken neck and massive internal injuries. When help finally arrived, Dean was removed from the twisted wreckage, transferred to an ambulance, and taken to Paso Robles War Memorial Hospital, where he was pronounced dead on arrival at 5:59 p.m.

How ironic that just a couple of weeks earlier, Dean had filmed a thirty-second commercial for the National Highway Safety Committee. Interviewed by actor Gig Young, Dean made a play on words of the then-popular phrase "The life you save may be your own." He looked directly into the camera and quipped, "Take it easy driving. The life you save may be *mine*." The words had just come back to haunt him.

With his life cut short at such an early age, Dean instantly become a cult icon, forever young.

Yes, the body may have perished, but his fame lives on. And so, too, may his ghost. Dean was interred in the family plot at Park Cemetery back in Fairmount. Ever since, visitors have claimed to sense Dean's spirit hovering around his grave.

Soon, motorists passing through the intersection of Highways 46 and 41 outside of Cholame began to report hearing screeching tires, crunching metal, and shattering glass. (The crossroads was officially named the James Dean Memorial Junction in 2005.)

But there's much more to the story. The "spirit" of Little Bastard may live on as well—and, if so, the vehicle is definitely wicked. At least two other people would die and several more be maimed before the haunted car was through.

George Barris bought the crumpled Spyder. He had no illusions about ever reconstructing it, but he knew any undamaged parts would still be quite valuable. It was under his ownership that Little Bastard claimed its next victims. While the car was being loaded onto a trailer to take it back to Los Angeles, the Porsche slipped and broke a mechanic's leg. Little Bastard was just getting started.

The first salvage had tragic results. Barris sold the refurbished engine and powertrain to two doctors, Troy McHenry and William F. Eschrid, respectively, who installed them in their personal street rods. While racing at the speedway in Pomona on October 2, 1956, Eschrid misread the banking on a curve and was seriously hurt when his car rolled over. The vehicle McHenry was driving spun completely out of control and crashed into a tree, killing him instantly. Little Bastard's two undamaged tires were sold and placed on another car, but they blew out simultaneously, nearly causing the driver to crash.

The next victims of the curse were thieves trying to strip the car. While attempting to steal the steering wheel from the flattened Porsche, one young man had his arm slashed open by a piece of jagged metal. Later, another robber was hurt when he tried to make off with the bloodstained driver's seat.

Enough was enough! Barris decided to put the wreckage into permanent storage before anyone else could be hurt. But the California Highway Patrol had other plans.

The CHP was about to send a highway safety exhibit around the state, and with Dean's death still fresh in the public's mind, they asked permission to put his car on display. How could Barris refuse?

From the start the exhibition had problems. The garage in which the mangled Porsche was being stored burned to the ground, destroying everything inside—except the "remains" of the Spyder, which was barely hurt by the flames. At the display's second showing, at a high school in Sacramento, the car slipped off its tracks and broke a student's hip.

Moving the Porsche from one town to another became a nightmare all its own. En route to Salinas, the truck carrying the car went out of control, and the driver, George Barkuis, spilled out. Little Bastard rolled off the truck and crushed him before he could get out of the way. Other incidents continued to occur: In 1958 a different truck carrying the Spyder was parked on a hillside when it fell out of gear and rolled down into a car. While on display in New Orleans in 1959, the Porsche broke apart into several pieces for seemingly no reason. At least two other times the car slipped off its mountings while being carried on the back of other vehicles. Shards flying off the trucks transporting Little Bastard smashed windshields on a highway in Oregon. Were all of these incidents accidents?

Perhaps the strangest part of the Little Bastard legend is its disappearance. In 1960 the wreck was placed on display by the Florida Highway Patrol. Afterward, it was shipped back to Los Angeles. But when the enclosed carrier truck arrived, the car was gone!

Whether Little Bastard had never been loaded onto the truck or was stolen on the way remains a mystery. But even after it vanished, Little Bastard may have claimed more victims. Some say its curse extended to several of Dean's associates who died in violence, unusually young, or both.

Perhaps consumed by the memories of that afternoon in 1955, Wutherich attempted suicide several times before being killed in a car accident himself in 1981. Reventlow died in a plane crash. Then there were Dean's fellow actors in *Rebel Without a Cause*: Natalie Wood died in a boating incident at the age of forty-three, Sal Mineo was thirty-seven when he was stabbed to death in a West Hollywood alley, and Nick Adams died of a drug overdose at thirty-six.

Was the car actually cursed, inhabited (as some believe) by some sort of malevolent being—much like the Chrysler Fury in Stephen King's horror novel *Christine*? Perhaps we'll never know. That is, unless Little Bastard is still out there somewhere, waiting and watching, biding its time until it makes its nightmarish return.

James Dean Crash Site

Located about a half mile east of Cholame, California, near the intersection of Routes 41 and 46 (which was 466 at the time of the accident). For all practical purposes, the town is nothing more than a roadside restaurant, the Jack Ranch Cafe. Outside the coffee shop stands the James Dean Memorial, an aluminum and stainless-steel sculpture inscribed with quotes about the actor, including some from Dean himself.

As you leave Cholame, the actual crash site now lies about two hundred yards to the right of Highway 46 in the middle of a field because the road was realigned in 1973. The old intersection and the last eight miles of the original Route 466 leading up to it are owned by the State Water Department and Jack Ranch. It's private property, and you have to get special permission to walk or drive on it. You can inquire at the Jack Ranch Cafe.

Park Cemetery

8008 S. 150 E.
Fairmount, IN 46928

James Dean's grave is in Fairmount, Indiana, which is just west of I-69 about forty miles northwest of Indianapolis.

Chapter 12

THE GALLOPING GHOST OF LARAMIE

It's the 1840s. Would you be crazy enough to ride out on your own across the sweeping plains, far from your outpost, without a guide, without a gun? Well, yes, if you were a headstrong thirteen-year-old. The only problem is, sometimes the only way to get back to where you started is by making a detour through the Other Side.

"Take someone with you, someone with a rifle," she thought as she laced up the saddle. *That's all my father ever says. Doesn't he realize that I'm almost fourteen and I can take care of myself? I'm not a little girl anymore.*

And just to prove it, look at how I'm dressed. I'm in my Sunday dress, like a lady. No one will mistake me for some grubby tomboy—or even a cowgirl.

The young woman—let's call her Annie—was, indeed, quite independent, just like her late mother had been. Her father was well aware that his move out west had deprived his daughter of the "normal" childhood she would have had growing up back east, so he often made allowances for her behavior, but not when she wanted to go out on these rides solo. It was just too risky.

Besides, in just a few short years, too few by his reckoning, she *would* be a woman. She would fall in love—would it be with one of the army regulars at the fort, a trader like himself, or one of the immigrants passing through?—and he would lose her forever. He knew that out here in the wilderness, once you've said your goodbyes to people they were usually gone for good.

So when he found out that Annie had disobeyed his orders and taken off on her own, just to see some of the countryside, he couldn't be angry. Sure, he was upset, but mostly he was just concerned for her safety. Things had been quiet, and the traders were at peace with the Sioux, but there were plenty of dangers out there in the wilderness, even for grown men with years of experience, much less for a little girl alone.

Annie's father thought back to how they had found themselves in Fort Laramie.

"Westward ho!" had become the cry for countless nineteenth-century settlers who wanted to set out into the unknown, to try for a better life. To that end the pioneers struggled across the vast, open territories from the Atlantic to the Pacific.

Their path was blazed by the early fur traders. In fact, by the time of the famous Lewis & Clark Expedition (1804–1806), there were already non-native settlers on the Oregon Coast working for the British Hudson's Bay Company, which controlled all the fur trading in the territory.

The early routes across the continent weren't practical for mass travel for a number of reasons. Some passed through the lands of the hostile Blackfoot tribe. Others ran into the Rocky Mountains, which made it next to impossible for settlers to move their wagons farther west. But in 1810 two groups sent out by John Jacob Astor, America's foremost fur trader (and the namesake of Astoria, Oregon), discovered a pathway that traveled through what is now Wyoming before hitting the Snake and Columbia Rivers. Dubbed the Oregon Trail, this became the most popular route for those heading to the Pacific Northwest.

By the 1830s, this trail was being used by traders, missionaries, and the military, as well as hardy individuals and families. It was during this period, in 1834, that a fur trader named William Sublette built a wooden structure on the trail, about a hundred miles north of modern Cheyenne, Wyoming. The great westward expansion hadn't started yet, so the fort was used primarily as a trading post with the Sioux Indians, who exchanged buffalo hides and garments for tobacco and alcohol from the East.

The American Fur Company soon bought out Sublette. The outpost was profitable enough that in 1841 an adobe building replaced the original wooden fort. And it was there that Annie's father had brought the family to seek his fortune.

He was a fine hunter and an even better negotiator with the tribes and chieftains. Originally his plan was to stay for just a year, two at the most. He would feather his nest egg, then his family would continue to the West Coast. There, he could homestead. He knew how to farm, but in the early years, until he knew the soil and was able to bring in abundant crops, he could also trade for the Hudson's Bay people.

But then, during their first winter at the trading post, his wife had taken ill with pneumonia. After she died, his spirit was broken. All he had left in the world was little Annie—she looked so much like her mother—but he couldn't bring himself to either head back toward St. Louis and "civilization" or pick up stakes and continue the hazardous trail westward. Here, Annie was safe, at least as safe as was possible in the middle of the wide prairies.

Although it wasn't yet apparent, the fur trade was already in decline, and most traders, including Annie's father, would move out by the time the army took over Fort Laramie in 1849 as a base to fight the increasing Native American insurgency.

The first organized wagon train of the westward migration wouldn't even embark until 1842. From then until 1869 (when the transcontinental railroad was completed), the Oregon Trail would become one of the main routes for pioneers. It would stretch for more than two thousand miles across what would eventually become six states—Missouri, Kansas, Nebraska, Wyoming, Idaho, and Oregon.

Settlers traveled by horse and oxen, pulling their wagons across the open plains. The trail was not kind to the common Conestoga wagon, which at the time was one of the primary vehicles for transport back east. The big wagons, though sturdy, were so heavy that out west the oxen that pulled them usually died of exhaustion before completing the arduous journey. So a new form of transportation—popularly known as the prairie schooner—would be designed. Also a covered wagon, it would be about half the size (and therefore half the weight) of its Conestoga cousin.

Annie's father scanned the horizon. She had been gone several hours. All anyone remembered was that she had headed east. She would be gone for only half an hour, maybe an hour at most, she had said. Don't worry. She probably wouldn't even get out of sight of the fort. But she had. And young Annie, her father's heart and soul, was never seen again—at least not while she was still in the land of the living.

The Oregon Trail, which passed by Fort Laramie, was still being used into the 1890s, long after Annie and her father had breathed their last, and modern roads, including almost the entire length of Highway 26, either follow or parallel large parts of it. Several sections of the original trail have been listed on the National Register of Historic Places and are maintained in their original condition. So heavy was the traffic over the trail that in some places it's still possible today to make out wagon tracks worn into the earth.

The sad story of the little girl who rode out of the trading post at Fort Laramie has not been forgotten, because she finally *did* return home. The youngster came back as a phantom rider. But it was long after her father and everyone else who had known her or remembered her real name had moved on.

Beginning in the late 1890s, the ghost of a girl on horseback began to appear outside of Fort Laramie, riding eastward toward modern Torrington, Wyoming, on what was a part of the Oregon Trail. Because none of the scores of people who have spotted her know who she was, she has been nicknamed simply the Galloping Ghost of Laramie.

The spectre is always seen dressed in green velvet, wearing a feathered hat, carrying a bejeweled riding crop, and perched on a black stallion. She seems to manifest on the trails near the old fort every seven years, so check your calendar: If everything goes according to schedule, she should materialize next in 2025.

Powerful emotions accompanied those making the trek in search of a new, better life: hope, anxiety, and, of course, fear. Considering the pain, the sorrow, and the inevitable deaths that faced the brave and hardy individuals who undertook the mind-boggling migration, it's only natural that the Oregon Trail has its share of heartbreaking tales. The story of the little girl known as the Galloping Ghost of Laramie is one of its most poignant.

The Galloping Ghost of Laramie appears along sections of the old Oregon Trail near Fort Laramie, but several other ghosts haunt the garrison itself. Over the years, they've been seen by visitors and staff alike. A cavalry officer in uniform appears in the bachelor officers' quarters known as Old Bedlam, and he is sometimes heard to tell people to quiet down. An invisible phantom who opens and shuts doors and whose footsteps are heard in Quarters A (once the captain's living area) has been nicknamed George. Heavy boots are also heard pacing the wooden walkway in front of the enlisted men's barracks. Some mornings, an entire company of spectral soldiers can be heard assembling for reveille.

Fort Laramie National Historic Site
Park Headquarters
965 Gray Rocks Road
Fort Laramie, WY 82212
(307) 837-2221
nps.gov/fola

To visit the fort, travel north out of Cheyenne on I-25 for just over eighty miles. At Dwyer Junction, turn east/south onto US Route 26. Travel for about twenty-eight miles until you reach the town of Fort Laramie. Turn south onto WY 160. In a little over two miles, you will see a signposted entrance on your left and the well-maintained gravel road leading to the old fort.

Alternately, head north on I-25 out of Cheyenne. Just outside of town, exit onto US Route 85. Travel for about eighty-four miles to Torrington, where US 85 meets US Route 26. Turn west/north onto US 26, and travel about twenty miles to Fort Laramie. Turn south onto WY 160. In a little over two miles, you will see the signposted entrance on the left and the well-maintained gravel road leading to the old fort.

Chapter 13

HEADLESS HAUNTERS

Everyone's heard of the Headless Horseman in the classic ghost story by Washington Irving, but old wives' tales about headless phantoms have been around for centuries. Encounters with such spirits today, however, suggest there's more to the legends than meets the eye.

"The Legend of Sleepy Hollow," written by Washington Irving, is one of America's most beloved ghost stories. It was first published in 1820 in *The Sketch Book of Geoffrey Crayon, Gent.*, a collection of the author's essays and short stories. Irving may have based the ghastly Headless Horseman character on a popular folktale being told at the time. Supposedly, a Hessian fighter was decapitated by a cannonball at the Battle of White Plains and was subsequently buried in the Old Dutch Church cemetery of Sleepy Hollow. What remained of the soldier's smashed skull was left behind on the battlefield, however, so the mercenary was never able to rest in peace. Instead, his angry apparition would rise from the grave, mount an ethereal horse, and gallop across the countryside in search of his missing noggin.

Headless spirits have a long tradition in Western legend and literature. For example, in "Gawain and the Green Knight," a fourteenth-century English poem, Sir Gawain of the Round Table beheads the Green Knight, but, rather than dying, the Green Knight scoops up his head and leaves, vowing to return in a year.

The spectre of Ewan, a Scottish clansman, haunts the Isle of Mull, where he was killed in battle at Glen Cainnir. The warrior fought even though he had been visited by a banshee in human form the night before the skirmish and told of his fate. When the ghosts of Ewan and his horse appear, they are both headless.

In Irish tradition, an entity called the *dullahan*, or "dark man," is a death omen, and it carries its head under its arm while riding about choosing victims. In a variation of the myth, the otherworldly being is a headless coachman whose black carriage gathers up those who are doomed to die.

Immigrants to the New World brought their old wives' tales with them, and, over time, versions of their favorite stories found their way into American mythology. There are more modern claims that decapitated phantoms haunt US highways and byways. The headless horseman and motorcyclist on Creek Road in Ojai, California, are just two contemporary examples. (See chapter 6.)

A headless horseman sometimes appears at night in the area of West 49th Street and Loomis Street on the South Side of Chicago. During the Pullman Strike of 1894, an Illinois National Guard command post was set up at the intersection to suppress union labor rioters organized by Eugene V. Debs against the Pullman Railway Company. There's no record of anyone being decapitated in the clashes, but the site of the hauntings nevertheless links the ghost horseback rider with the workers' revolt.

You have a chance to see some phantom equestrians with their heads intact at the intersection of 95th Street and Kean Avenue in nearby Hickory Hills. The junction is located at the edge of the Cook County Forest Preserves, which has numerous hiking and riding paths. One of them, the Palos Trail, parallels Kean Avenue, and at one point it crosses 95th Street. Several horses and riders have been struck and killed by motorists speeding down 95th Street. People have spotted the apparitions of horseback riders in the crosswalk, only to see them fade into nothingness.

Tales of headless riders can be found all across America. For example, the ghost of a headless cowboy on horseback has been seen for more than a century down in Texas. It's said that the phantom rider was Vidal, a known Mexican bandito in the 1850s. When Vidal foolishly stole some mustangs belonging to Creed Taylor, a hero from the Texas Revolution, Taylor gave chase along with a fellow rancher named Flores and "Bigfoot" Wallace, a Texas Ranger and fellow Texas war veteran. The trio soon captured and killed the horse thieves, but, as a warning to future would-be robbers, Taylor and Wallace decapitated Vidal. They set his corpse upright on the back of a wild horse, tied his head (complete with sombrero) at his side, and set the bronco free. The corporeal headless horseman, seen far and wide, became known as El Muerto, the Dead One. Ultimately the horse was caught and what was left of Vidal's body was buried. But that didn't stop El Muerto's nighttime rides. Vidal's decapitated revenant and steed continue to roam the plains of southern Texas, from San Antonio down to Corpus Christi.

There are also plenty of ghost stories about headless horses without anyone in the saddle. One such apparition haunts the road between Doylestown and Clinton, Ohio in a forested area known as Rogues' Hollow. According to local lore, the horse was accidentally beheaded as it galloped under a low tree branch. The whole oak was later removed, but from time to time a spectral tree is spotted in its old location.

And, of course, there are headless ghosts that don't appear on horseback or in a vehicle. For much of May 1974, a female phantom with a glowing blue aura drifted along the 500 block of Charlotte Street in Fredericksburg, Virginia. Nicknamed the Headless Blue Girl, she would pause in front of certain houses, but the locations gave no clue as to her name or why she returned from the Other Side.

The shadow of a head-free figure walks along the shoulder of US Highway 113 as the road passes through Ellendale State Forest, just north of Redden, Delaware. The identity of the spook is unknown, but rumor has it the apparition died in a car crash on that stretch of road. The curiously large number of accidents on that portion of the highway has given it a reputation of being cursed.

You even find decapitated ghosts as far north as Ketchikan, Alaska. Bayview Cemetery is located just off Sledman Street, which is the main route through town. Motorists driving past the graveyard at night have spotted the spirit of a headless woman walking or standing on the side of the road. Seconds later, the apparition's head momentarily appears on the street. Then, just as suddenly, both the cranium and its ghostly owner instantly disappear.

Chapter 14

THE GHOST LIGHTS

The flatland of West Texas spread out under a canvas of stars. Ten miles from the closest town, a solitary visitor peered up into the inky sky. He watched and waited, alone in the dark. It had taken him forever to get this far. Was it worth it? Would the celebrated ghost lights materialize for him that night?

There they are! Standing on the side of Highway 90 outside Marfa, Texas, Ben could see reddish-yellow orbs rise from the prairie flats. They were far off to the southwest, out in the direction of Chinati Peak. Some nights, especially around Labor Day when the town held its annual Marfa Lights Festival, this place was swarming with people hoping to catch a glimpse of the baffling spheres. But tonight, remarkably, he was alone.

Ben was lucky. The Marfa lights didn't appear every night. But there they were, clusters of glowing orbs floating maybe five feet above the desert floor. As he stared, entranced, the balls of shimmering light moved horizontally along the ground. Then suddenly they separated and shot in different directions.

From where Ben was on Mitchell Flat, it was hard to judge their size, since there was no real frame of reference out there. Most of the globes seemed to be about the size of basketballs, but they were at such a distance they could just as well have been ten feet or more in diameter. He watched spellbound as the sparkling spheres grouped into pairs, or merged, only to break apart again. For a time they'd glow brightly, then fade almost into nothing. Some would suddenly vanish, only to reappear a few moments later.

The viewing stand where Ben stood was nine miles east of Marfa, about a third of the way to Alpine. It hadn't been easy to get there. The nearest major airport was in El Paso, two hundred miles to the west. From there, it was a seemingly endless drive across the deserted high Chihuahuan Desert plateau until he reached Marfa.

The town wasn't known just for the mystery lights, of course. In 1955 the classic movie *Giant*, starring Rock Hudson, Elizabeth Taylor, and James Dean, was shot there. (Dean is the subject of his own ghost story. See chapter 11.) More recently, *There Will Be Blood* was filmed in and around Marfa. But the town's origin was much more humble.

Founded as a water stop for the Southern Pacific Railroad in the 1880s, Marfa has always depended on cattle and farming. During World War II, a military base was established there to train Army Air Corps pilots. In fact, the viewing stand from which Ben was watching the ghost lights was very close to the old base at Fort Russell, which had closed in 1945. Marfa was also a gateway to Big Bend National Park, located along the Rio Grande about a hundred miles south. But with each passing year the fame of the Marfa lights brought more and more tourists interested in the supernatural to the small town.

Ben had researched as much as he could about the lights before he arrived.

Supposedly, wagon trains had seen odd, unexplainable lights along the Chihuahua Trail heading into the Big Bend area in the 1840s, but there were so many unfriendly Apache Indians there that no one dared leave the path to investigate.

The first written report of a sighting north of the Rio Grande dates back to 1883. A young ranch hand named Robert Reed Ellison was driving his cattle about eight miles west from Alpine toward the Paisano Pass when he saw glistening lights far ahead. He assumed at the time that he was seeing the campfires of Apaches, but when he and his friends checked out the area the next morning they couldn't find any evidence of anyone having recently camped or even traveled through the area.

Over the next several years, more and more cowboys caught sight of the ghost lights all along the high desert and up into the Chinati Mountains between Marfa and Presidio. As Marfa grew, especially in the first decades of the twentieth century, hundreds of Presidio County residents saw them. The lights appeared throughout the year, in all sorts of weather conditions.

As tempted as Ben was to take his four-wheel drive out across the flats to try to get closer to the orbs, he knew how reckless that would be. The terrain was unpredictable, and at night, with only two headlights cutting through the pitch darkness, chances were good that he'd fall into a gulley, hit a boulder, or break an axle. Besides, these days everything for miles around was private property, and the owners could get pretty disagreeable if people wandered out there without their permission. The local ranchers had gotten tired of trespassers, which is why, at their request, the Texas Highway Department built the viewing stand.

Over the years many people *had* ventured across the desert at night, both by land and air, trying to capture—or at least get close to—the Marfa lights, and the glowing orbs had been photographed and filmed on numerous occasions. In the end, all the scientific studies resulted in the usual explanations for that kind of phenomenon: swamp gas (even though there has never been swampland in the dry deserts of West Texas in recorded history), phosphorescent rocks, ball lightning, air traffic, mirages caused by temperature variations, static emissions from quartz on the ground, and reflections from faraway but unseen light sources (such as flashlights or headlights from cars over on Highway 67).

Regardless of what others thought caused the Marfa lights, Ben preferred the old Native American legends. His favorite claimed that the light is really the ghost of the great Apache chief Alsate, who was denied entrance into the Afterlife after somehow offending the Great Spirit. His spectre was said to haunt the Chisos Mountains in the heart of Big Bend National Park. (In fact, one translation of "Los Chisos" is "the ghosts.") Many think the lights seen outside Marfa are from the great chief's spirit simply wandering farther afield.

All right, thought Ben, *maybe it's all hogwash, but the folklore does have some basis in fact.* Back in the 1850s and 1860s, the Mescalero Apaches hid in the Chisos Mountains while raiding small Spanish villages south of the Rio Grande. Among the Mescalero (also called the Chinati and Rio Grande Apaches) was the great leader Chief Alsate.

Eventually a detachment of mounted police from Mexico known as the Rurales managed to capture Alsate along with his tribe, and they were taken to Mexico City for trial. Through the help of a relative, all of the Apache were set free, and they made their way back to the Chisos. But the tribe soon fell back into robbing the border towns, and when the Rurales captured them again they were taken to Presidio, one of the villages they had been looting. Alsate was executed by firing squad and the rest of the tribe was separated and sold into slavery.

Soon after, glowing lights began appearing in the Chisos Mountains and on the mesas along Big Bend. Almost immediately the luminous orbs were associated with the recent death of Alsate, and the legend arose that the shimmering spheres were the incarnation of the chief's ghost.

Ben knew that the Marfa area has a number of "traditional" ghosts in addition to its mysterious lights. The canyons of Big Bend National Park, for example, are said to be haunted by the cries of an Indian maiden who drowned herself rather than be ravaged by marauding pioneers. People have spotted the phantom of a black bull named Murderer wandering the foothills of the Chisos Mountains. The animal was at the center of an 1891 dispute between two cowboys. One of the men, Fine Gilliland, shot the other, Henry Powe, and escaped into the mountains, only to be later tracked down and killed by Texas Rangers. The bull was allowed to roam free, but its apparition was later said to show up whenever there was a shoot-out in the Alpine area.

Ben wasn't interested in those ghost tales, however. His lifelong dream had been to see the ghost lights, and it had been fulfilled. He kept watch all night. The last of the lights had flickered out long before, and he knew that dawn was just over the horizon. Exhausted after his long drive from El Paso and the nightlong vigil, he was ready to return to the welcoming motel bed waiting for him back in Marfa. He was content.

Spectral lights such as those near Marfa have been seen and reported for centuries throughout the world. According to folklore, ghost lights (also known as *ignis fatuus*, or "foolish fire") are the souls of people who are doomed to wander the earth.

In addition to Marfa, there are numerous places ghost lights pop up in the United States. For example, the so-called Joplin Light is visible almost every night about twenty miles southwest of Joplin, Missouri. Ironically, the phenomenon actually occurs in neighboring Oklahoma, but it's clearly visible across the border. (See the Quapaw listing on pages 164–5.)

Over in the Brown Mountains of North Carolina, spectral orbs have been reported regularly since 1913. They appear most often in the Linville Gorge Wilderness area north of Morganton and can best be seen from Highway 181. Some folklorists say the glowing spheres are the soul of a runaway slave. According to Native American tradition, however, the flickering lights are the spirit of a young maiden looking for her lost brave.

A reddish-orange orb flits about Cole Mountain south of Moorefield, West Virginia. Supposedly the phantom light comes from the lantern of a slave from the nearby Charles Jones plantation who got lost in the hills while hunting raccoons.

The ghost lights of Oriflamme Mountain occur along Highway S2 about four miles outside Butterfield Ranch in Julian, California. Since at least the 1880s, the yellowish glowing spots have been seen hovering over the side of the mountain. Some say the spectral illumination marks the location of gold deposits hidden in the hills below.

The ghost light of Gurdon, Arkansas, appears off a road outside of town along a set of railroad tracks. Many years back, a railway worker fell into the path of an oncoming train. He was decapitated, and his head was never found. According to local myth, the phantom light comes from the lantern of the railroad man's ghost as it walks the rails looking for his head.

Compare that to the Bragg Road Light, also called the Big Thicket Light. Bragg Road is an eight-mile dirt trail that lies about five miles outside Saratoga, Texas. The walkway used to be a track bed for the old Santa Fe Railroad. As you walk along the path at night, a flickering yellow light changes to white and then red as it comes toward you. Legend says it is from the phantom lantern of Jake Murphy, a railroad brakeman who fell under a train and was decapitated. A different version of the tale claims it comes from a hunter who died after getting lost in the nearby forest. Yet another suggests it's the combined spirits of four Mexican day laborers who were robbed and killed in the area by their boss. (For more details about the spirit light, see the Bragg Road listing on pages 177–8.)

A similar railroad legend surrounds the Paulding Light (also called the Dog Meadow Light), a strange, intense single light that frequently appears in the night sky above a cleared power line right-of-way between Paulding and Watersmett on Michigan's Upper Peninsula. The light hovers, moves, and changes color, usually between white and red but also sometimes green, yellow, and blue. Its first documented sighting was by teenagers in 1966. According to legend, the light is the ghost of either a railway engineer or brakeman who died on the tracks that once lay there and who is waving his signal lamp to warn away others. Skeptics and researchers say the Paulding Light is actually a reflection from car headlights on the adjacent US Route 45. The best place to witness the light is facing north along Robbins Lake Road. A signpost erected by the Michigan Forest Service marks the general location.

Chapter 15

CHILDREN ON THE TRACKS

The tragedy occurred more than fifty years ago along an unremarkable railway line in southern Texas. Ever since, a group of spirit children has been at the ready there, twenty-four hours a day, to push your car to safety if you get stuck on the tracks.

The railroad tracks lay in a straight line, set on a slightly raised strip of land in a nondescript rural area just outside San Antonio. They were easy to find. As Gina exited I-410 onto Villamain Road and headed south, she saw the rails to her left, bordered by a line of trees. To her right, empty parcels were covered in shrubs and low grass, without a house or building in sight.

About three-quarters of a mile from the interstate, Villamain made a sharp, ninety-degree bend to the left, and as she crossed the tracks, the name of the street changed to Shane Road. Gina slowed to a stop before crossing the rails and pulled off to the right shoulder.

Gina got out and looked across the tracks. The road was flat, but she could see only a few hundred feet down Shane. There, it curved to the left, and she knew that somewhere just out of sight the street fed directly into a brand-new housing development. The short lanes dividing the homes had names like Laura Lee, Richey Otis, Bobbie Allen, Nancy Carole, and Cindy Sue. If she were to continue on, it was only a hop, skip, and a jump over to I-37, which would take her down to Corpus Christi. But from where she was standing, with no buildings in sight, it was hard to believe she was less than ten miles from downtown San Antonio.

That being said, she was far from alone. About a half dozen vehicles had already queued up on the other side of the rails, waiting without complaint to experience, one at a time, ghostly hands push their cars across the tracks. Gina had come very early in the day. She knew that once darkness fell, especially now in the middle of the hot Texas summer, the line would probably extend back out of sight up Shane Road.

There was also always a squad car or two of bemused policemen sitting off to one side to make sure everything ran smoothly and peacefully. But no one was ever there to cause trouble. Or if they had been, it seemed that once people got there they were hushed into silence, caught up in the spell of the place.

Gina knew only the bare bones of what had taken place all those years ago. Back in the 1930s or 1940s, a busload of children was making its regular run across the tracks. There were no flashing lights, and even to this day warning gates don't lower in front of the tracks when trains speed by. Nothing seemed amiss. But perhaps the sun was in the driver's eyes, or the afternoon heat rising off the tarred railroad ties made it too hazy to see the engine off in the distance. Whatever the reason, the driver couldn't tell that a train was barreling down on them, and the bus started over the tracks—and stalled halfway across.

The impact was fast and catastrophic. The train smashed into the side of the bus, pushing it several hundred yards down the tracks before pushing it off to one side in a tortured mass of crumpled steel. All ten children aboard as well as the bus driver were killed. Today those kids are memorialized nearby. Their names? Laura Lee, Richey Otis, Bobbie Allen . . .

To the community, the tragedy was unforgettable. And to the students on that ill-fated bus, it's also, in a sense, everlasting. It's said that if you stop your car on the tracks, even voluntarily, the ghosts of those children will push your car to the other side to prevent the horror that had killed them from ever happening to anyone else. And if you're brave enough to dust the back of your car with talcum powder before making the crossing, afterward you'll find tiny phantom handprints on your trunk and bumper.

Gina drove across the tracks and got into line. She knew the spectral phenomenon worked only if you were on Shane facing Villamain. Was that the direction the bus was heading when the awful accident occurred?

As she stood outside her car, sprinkling her rear fender with powder, she could see the cars ahead of her getting ready to make their move. Amazingly, you didn't even have to park your car on the tracks for the miracle to transpire. In fact, the sensation was even more dramatic if you stopped your car twenty or thirty feet in front of the tracks and just let the phantom children do the rest.

At last it was her turn. Gina set her car in neutral and waited. At first, nothing happened. Then there was a distinct lurch, as if some huge invisible force had grabbed her car and then given it a single hard shove from behind. Then slowly, ever so slowly, the vehicle started to roll.

It was almost like magic. The 3,500-pound Mustang was moving on its own! She had dutifully stopped the car in front of the railroad tracks. But now, somehow, the car was drifting forward. The front tires rolled up the small incline of the track bed onto the first rail, then inched ahead a bit more, until the two axles were straddling the train tracks.

This must have been the position the stalled bus had been in when the loco-motive plowed into it, Gina thought. Worried, she looked up and down the tracks extending on both sides. Had the ghosts pushed her onto the tracks only to have her repeat their hideous past?

But there was no need to panic. The car continued to advance until, with a satisfying and palpable release, it rolled down off the tracks.

It was over.

Gina sat stunned, overwhelmed for a few seconds. Then, suddenly aware of the people in the vehicle behind her waiting to take their turn, she put her car into drive, made the turn back onto Villamain, and quickly pulled off to the side. She had to check for the prints!

Warily, she walked along the side of her car back to the trunk. She was almost afraid to look down. But there they were: two small sets of palm prints about the size of the hands of ten-year-olds. Had they always been there? Had she somehow just not noticed them when she was shaking out the powder?

She knelt down to examine them closely. No, the prints had been pressed into the talc. Sadly, she ran a finger across them, trying to imagine the terror the children must have experienced as their lives were so brutally snuffed out. She blew lightly on the prints, and a small cloud of powder lifted off. It was caught up in the slight morning breeze and began to drift toward the tracks.

The next car was in place, sitting patiently. It wouldn't have to wait for long. The children were floating back.

The story of phantom children pushing cars to safety on a set of railroad tracks south of San Antonio is one of the most enduring ghost legends in America today. There are several discrepancies in the story, however, that make the tale hard to believe. So if you don't want to have your bubble burst, stop reading now.

Remember, you were warned.

To start off, no railway accident, and certainly no collision between a train and school bus full of children, ever occurred at that particular intersection. However, in December 1938 twenty-six children between the ages of twelve and eighteen lost their lives in a similar incident near Salt Lake City, Utah. The grisly, heartrending story dominated the pages of Texas newspapers for days. It seems likely, or at least very possible, that this was the basis for the myth.

That being said, the anomaly does occur at the San Antonio tracks. It will almost certainly happen to you if you try it. So what makes the car move? There have been numerous inquiries into the "haunting" by paranormal investigators, skeptic societies, reporters, and television journalists. And guess what they all found? Even though the tracks and the surrounding area seem to be level, it's an optical illusion. Starting from the tracks, Shane Road is actually on a slight, imperceptible upward grade of about two degrees. That's right: When your car crosses the tracks, it is simply rolling downhill. It may take a few minutes for gravity to kick in, but you will eventually start to move forward, all the way across the tracks.

But how about the handprints? Those can be explained away, too. In detective work, police routinely dust a seemingly clean surfaces to bring out any latent fingerprints. In the same manner, anyone who touches a car leaves behind indiscernible marks that could show up later if they were dusted with a light covering of powder.

There could be an even more mundane explanation. Jonathan Levit, who hosted an investigation of the site for Discovery Channel's *Miracle Hunters*, talked to people who confessed that, as a joke to fool unsuspecting drivers, they would sometimes secretly press their own handprints into the powder sprinkled on waiting cars. As for the names of the children from the bus accident being used for the nearby streets, the developer of the housing project has said that the names belong to friends and family.

So to sum up, if you do decide to head to San Antonio to try this for yourself, line up on Shane Road facing the tracks so that Villamain curves to the right on the other side. Make sure a train isn't coming before you put your car into neutral and roll out onto the tracks. (If your car does stop halfway across, chances are very slim that the ghostly children are gonna show up to help you out.)

The haunted railroad crossing south of San Antonio is but one example of the phenomenon known as a "gravity hill," a barely inclined stretch of road at which a vehicle parked at the base seems to travel uphill all on its own. Some gravity hills, such as one near New Paris in Bedford County, Pennsylvania, have been heavily promoted as tourist attractions—not as haunted sites but as places in which the laws of physics have somehow gone awry.

But more commonly, gravity hills are connected with ghost myths, usually about people who died or are buried on their slopes. The story most similar to the Texas haunting seems to be the Ghost Hill found in Lewisberry, Pennsylvania. According to legend, a busload of children died there when their vehicle fell over a cliff. Their spirits allegedly will push cars stopped on the hill upward.

Among the other better-known gravity hills are the ones located in the following places:

- Franklin Lakes, New Jersey, located on the Ewing Avenue exit off Route 208 South. The ghost of a little girl who was struck and killed by a car when she ran into the road to chase a ball is supposedly what pushes your car up the grade.
- Lake Wales, Florida, located off Highway 27 between Tampa and Orlando. According to legend, the anomaly on Spook Hill is caused by an Indian chief who died battling an alligator and was buried on the hillside.
- Salt Lake City, Utah, on Gravity Hill a few blocks northeast of the capitol building. The spirit of a person named Emo supposedly buried in the area is said to be responsible for rolling your car up the road inside the canyon. (Although no last name is attached to this ghost, his grave should be easy to recognize. Supposedly his tombstone, wherever it is, glows bright blue at night.)

Chapter 16

THE HIGHWAY TO HELL

Let him who has understanding calculate the number of the
Beast; for his number is that of a man: and his number is 666.
—Revelation 13:18

Jason had no idea how long he'd been driving. It seemed like forever, but looking down at his odometer, he realized he'd gone less than fifty miles. However, he had spent half of that distance negotiating some of the most dangerous mountain curves he'd ever encountered. The switchbacks and hairpin turns on Highway 666 had him traveling at a crawl. Time after time he had seen breaks in the metal railing: Were they grim remnants of fatal miscalculations where cars had crashed through the barricades and tumbled to the valley floor thousands of feet below?

With a sigh of relief, Jason was out of the hills, and he leveled off on the plateau. He saw nothing but wide, empty space in front of him. It should be smooth, uneventful sailing the rest of the way. It was late, but fortunately, he had gotten out of the mountains by nightfall. He couldn't imagine how treacherous that road must be at night.

Glancing in his rearview mirror, Jason noticed the twin beams behind him. From their height, he reckoned they had to be from a tractor-trailer. Odd, though, that he hadn't seen them before. Surely to be this close to him—probably only a mile or so back—the truck must have been tailing him for the past hour or more. Surely an eighteen-wheeler would have to struggle even more than he had to keep from plunging over one of the cliffs.

But then, maybe the truck was farther back than it seemed. They were on a flat mesa. The air was perfectly clear, with no haze, and now, with no lights anywhere except for the full moon and the endless mantle of stars overhead, headlights, especially those from a semi, would cut through the dark for miles.

Suddenly the tractor-trailer was on him, less than a quarter of a mile behind. How had the semi bridged the gap so quickly? But that was the least of Jason's concerns. The truck seemed to be deliberately tailing him.

To Jason's alarm, he saw that there was no shoulder where he could safely pull off the road. The ground on both sides of the highway was strewn with large

98

rocks scattered between the sagebrush. At this speed, without having time to slow first, simply shooting off to one side would be suicidal. He realized that there was nowhere to go but straight ahead. Panicked, he stomped his gas pedal to the floor.

The car leaped forward, kicking into overdrive. He had already been traveling comfortably above the speed limit, but now he had no choice but to go faster. Faster. Seventy-five. Eighty. Still, the semi was rapidly closing in on him. The truck must be going over a hundred miles an hour! In a flash, it was against his bumper. Fear gripped Jason; he was going to die!

Then, about a hundred yards ahead, there seemed to be a slight widening of the road. Someone, some blessed unknown soul, had pulled off the road at some point in the past—to change a tire? to catch a few Zs?—and the car had left behind a narrow but definite space on the right shoulder. Could he possibly make it that far—alive?

With one desperate, last-ditch effort, Jason forced his car to make a final lurch forward, just enough to give some breathing room between the two vehicles. Within seconds he was at the turnout. He spun his wheel to the right, veered off the road, and slammed on the brakes. His tires dug into the loose gravel, and the car slid to a halt.

The Mad Trucker never slowed. The semi zoomed down the highway as if it had never noticed the car at all. Jason gasped as he stared out the windshield. Flames shot out of the truck's diesel stacks, and sparks flew from the tires. The entire tractor-trailer seemed to be engulfed in fire. Then, moments later, the phantom truck was gone. Had it simply passed over the horizon, or had it never been there at all?

They call them Skin Walkers. Like most tribal societies, the Navajo that populated the Southwest had shamans who were able to communicate with the gods and ancestral beings in the Beyond. They were also the healers, and it was thought that they could control the elements and foresee the future. Many believed they had power over life and death.

Most medicine men used their secret wisdom for the benefit of their tribes, but on occasion one of them might embrace dark powers. It was said that once they turned to evil, medicine men became Skin Walkers, shape-shifters who could turn themselves into wolves, coyotes, or crows that would terrorize and attack the natives.

Settlers who moved into the territories took no stock in such superstitions. Nevertheless, they were at a loss to explain the creatures of the night that were haunting the roads that connected their towns. In time, the Navajo were moved onto reservations, and those early trails became highways, but the Skin Walkers never left. On that lonely stretch of Highway 666 between Cortez, Colorado, and Gallup, New Mexico, many a driver has crashed when a spectral animal suddenly appeared directly in front of his car.

And if the Skin Walker doesn't succeed on its first attempt, sometimes the mystic creature will manifest itself over and over. Those motorists who have accidents may be the lucky ones, for it's not unheard of for a Skin Walker to appear inside the car itself.

The Mad Trucker and Skin Walkers are just two of the many apparitions that haunt the sinister route in the Four Corners region of the Southwest that has been nicknamed the Highway to Hell. Other spectres there include a phantom car that, like the deadly tractor-trailer, tries to run motorists off the road. Hordes of spectral yellow-eyed demon dogs with sharp fangs chase after cars and slash the tires of any motorist foolish enough to slow down or stop.

One of the most frequently seen ghosts is that of a young, willowy girl in a full-length nightgown who walks along the side of the road but vanishes when you stop to assist her.

Then there are the stories of people—both living and dead—who will suddenly appear on the highway or become invisible as you pass by. Sometimes a person will dematerialize at one point and reappear farther down the road.

Besides being a home for ghosts and other spectral phenomena, the deserted area has also been a dumping ground for murder victims, and there has been evidence of occult and satanic rituals having been held there. Also, for some unknown reason, a disproportionate number of fatal car accidents and pedestrian deaths seem to occur on the roadway.

Is it possible that some stretches of highway can be just plain evil? There are those who would answer with a resounding yes, and high on their list would be this one—in large part due to the route number it was originally assigned, perhaps the most notorious ever granted: Highway 666.

Many people, especially fundamentalist Christians, say the designation of the highway as US Route 666 is the cause for all the mayhem. After all, it's common knowledge that 666 is the "number of the Beast," the Antichrist prophesied in the Book of Revelation in the New Testament of the Holy Bible. The Navajo were also uneasy with the route number, but in their culture, the number six is thought to be evil and to bring bad luck.

Eventually, due to public outcry, the road's name was changed, and today it is US Route 491. But once the Antichrist, always the Antichrist. If some dark and desolate evening you find yourself driving alone on the Old Route 666, be on the alert. Don't stop to pick up strangers. Look out for any weird or unusual animals. And if you see another vehicle on the road—especially a gleaming tractor-trailer—get out of the way! You don't want to be the next victim of the Highway to Hell.

Highway 666 and the sign of the Beast are totally unrelated, of course. John, the author of the Book of Revelation in the Holy Bible, arrived at the figure through a complex form of numerology in which a value was assigned to each letter of the alphabet. The labeling of "the Devil's Highway" as Route 666 has a much less mystical origin.

In 1925 the route between Gallup, New Mexico, and Cortez, Colorado (informally known up to that time as the Navajo Trail), was established as part of the new federal highway system. Roads that crossed state borders were assigned two-digit numbers, and originally the highway between Chicago and Los Angeles was given the number US 60, but within a year it was changed to the now-familiar Route 66.

Main spurs off of federal highways were given a third digit, so on June 8, 1931, the sixth branch off Route 66, the one from Gallup to Cortez, became the initial section of the soon-to-be-infamous US Route 666.

At the time, the highway was only 141 miles long. But by 1942, US 666 had been extended 415 miles to Douglas, Arizona, to include what had been known as the Coronado Trail (named after Spanish explorer Francisco Vázquez de Coronado, who traveled through the region in 1540).

The addition of this section, more than the "number of the Beast," is probably what has been most responsible for the fatal tragedies along the highway. At places, the Coronado Trail climbs to more than nine thousand feet, and the road descends in hair-raising turns that drop the speed limit at places to as low as ten miles per hour.

In 1970 Route 666 was extended once again, this time north to Monticello, Utah, bringing the full length of the Highway to Hell to 605 miles.

The inauguration of the Interstate Highway System eventually led to 66 being dropped from the federal registry in 1985, but most of the branches (including Route 666) were not renumbered.

Over the years there had been a quiet but rising objection from residents who disliked their main thoroughfare bearing a number with a satanic connection. In 1992 the section of Route 666 between Arizona and Gallup was renamed US Highway 191, but the rest of the route stayed the way it was. It wasn't until 2003 that the New Mexico legislature adopted a resolution calling for a change in the number of the route from Gallup to the Colorado border.

By that time Utah and Colorado had designated their portions of the highway as Route 393. After consideration, to avoid confusion with US Route 93, all four states resolved (and on May 31, 2003, the American Association of State Highway and Transportation Officials approved) changing the name of what had been Route 666 for just under seventy-two years to US Route 491.

PART TWO:
STATE-TO-STATE
SPIRITS

HAUNTED HIGHWAYS, A TO Z

Every state in the United States has at least one highway, city street, or country lane that locals claim is haunted. Some have many, many more. Fortunately, there doesn't seem to be any correlation between a state's size or location and whether its roads have ghosts. As a result, there are plenty of places to explore. What follows are just a few recommendations.

ALABAMA

Double Hill Road
Opelika

Double Hill Road is a narrow, unpaved, tree-lined lane located two miles or so northwest of Opelika. Also known as County Road 161, Double Hill Road is about a mile in length and only runs between West Point Parkway (State Route 29) and Ridge Road (County Road 154). There are no houses along Double Hill Road, so it's very, very dark traveling along it at night.

About a tenth of a mile north of the intersection with County Road 154, Double Hill Road crosses Little Halawaka Creek. Although there may have been a bridge over the stream sometime in the past, these days the creek is a mere trickle, and the water passes under the road through a large-diameter metal pipe culvert.

According to legend, the ghost of a man in a carriage appears on the road close to where the bridge once was. As you watch, he and the wagon abruptly turn onto the shoulder and almost instantly vanish. It's alleged that's he's buried there by the side of the road. Some people claim there used to be a cemetery at that spot before it was relocated, but there's no official record of it. (The closest cemetery is about a half-mile north at Bethel No. 1 Missionary Baptist Church.) Nevertheless, the old wives' tale continues to be told.

Highway 5
Lynn

The ghost of a woman who was struck and killed by a tractor-trailer many years ago haunts a twenty-five-mile stretch of Highway 5 between Jasper and Natural Bridge. It's said her spirit can be seen walking the two-lane, asphalt roadway, searching for the driver who took her life. She sometimes pounds on the doors of eighteen-wheelers as they pass. In fact, she's been known to materialize on (or climb up onto) the step outside the semi's cab and stare at the driver through the side window. Most of the hauntings take place close to the town of Lynn. Enough truckers have been spooked that some now take Highway 13 and I-22 to bypass that section of Highway 5 and avoid any possibility of seeing the spectre.

One variation of this tale has several details in common with the archetypal story of the Phantom Hitchhiker. In this version, the phantom on Highway 5 is a teenage girl. She had argued with her boyfriend, who was driving her home from the prom, and she insisted on getting out of the car and walking the rest of the way. Subsequently, she was struck and killed by a tractor-trailer. Her body was found on the side of the road the next day. Some accounts add that it was raining on the night of the accident, which is a common feature in many haunted hitchhiker tales.

Highway 11
Decatur to Huntsville

Back in 1934, Lonnie Stephens was found guilty of murdering his girlfriend and was sent to prison. He managed to get away from a chain gang while working on the shoulder of Highway 11, but his attempted escape was unsuccessful. He rushed onto the road to flag down a ride and was fatally struck by a car. As it turned out, Stephens didn't commit the murder, but the true killer didn't confess until after the inmate's death. Perhaps Stephens's apparition has returned to seek justice. With his arms waving frantically attempting to get a lift, the phantom materializes on the twenty-five-mile stretch between Decatur and Huntsville in the northbound lanes of Highway 11.

Interstate 65
Greenville to Evergreen

The city of Greenville, Alabama, lies on I-65, about forty miles southwest of Montgomery, the state capital. The next twenty-five miles of the Interstate, from Greenville to Evergreen, has been nicknamed "The Haunted Highway." Although the stretch is rather straight and seldom icy, there's an inordinately high number of traffic accidents on the road, especially close to Murder Creek Bridge.

Dennis William Hauck, author of *Haunted Places: The National Directory*, suggests that the crashes may be caused by vengeful spirits of the Creek Indians who were forced off their lands centuries ago. Even if that's so, Native American souls aren't the only ghosts to torment travelers on that segment of highway. Drivers have swerved to avoid enormous cat-like creatures, similar to jaguars or panthers, which darted across the interstate. It's unknown if the animals are real or apparitions. Also, at least one truck driver has claimed that he smashed into Murder Creek Bridge after a phantom coach suddenly appeared in front of him crossing the highway.

Jack Cole Road
Hayden

Jack Cole Road is a rural, half-mile, unpaved street that cuts west off of Highway 7 about a half-mile southeast of State Route 31. The terrain is heavily forested. There are no houses on that stretch of Highway 7, and only a couple of homes sit along Jack Cole Road before it dead-ends. (There are a few more houses along Julias Lane, a small side street that branches off of Jack Cole Road.)

Since 1890, at least sixty-eight people who lived on Jack Cole Road have died. Sixty of those passed away during a cholera outbreak in 1900. Most of the others died of natural causes, but a few of the others were victims of accidents or murder. A few simply disappeared. And when the mummified remains of a woman were discovered in her house, which was isolated from the rest, superstitious locals branded her a witch.

Some of the dead seem to have returned from the Other Side. Shadowy figures have been seen walking by the side of Jack Cole Road. Unexplained lights glow in the woods, and people sometimes hear loud, unidentifiable noises. Perhaps the most frightening incidents are the sightings of a strange beast—half-human, half-wolf—that roams the surroundings. No one is sure whether the creature is an apparition or a cryptid, one of the enigmatic animals like Bigfoot and the Loch Ness Monster whose very existence is disputed.

ALASKA

Badarka Road
Chugiak

A tragic accident is at the heart of an oft-told tale in Chugiak, a municipality of around four thousand people situated on the Old Glenn Highway twenty-two miles northeast of Anchorage. The legend that's been passed down says that sometime in the distant past a father took his five-year old daughter with him when he went to chop wood outside his cabin. Before taking a break, he stuck his axe into a tree trunk for safety, but the girl, anxious to help her father by chopping some wood herself, reached up and pulled out the axe when his back was turned. It was too heavy and fell on her head, striking her dead. The father, overcome with sorrow, dropped down and cradled the girl in his arms. Despite his wife and another child waiting at home, the grief-stricken man never moved, until finally he froze to death. According to the old wives' tale, if you drive down Badarka Road at about 3:30 a.m., you'll see the apparition of the father sitting on the side of the road, still clasping the ghost of the lifeless child.

This myth is seen frequently in books and on websites about hauntings in Alaska, but there seems to be one detail that has stumped modern ghost hunters. The town doesn't have (and never has had) a street named Badarka Road (or Bardarka Road in the Woods, as some sources call it). There is a Bairdaka Street on the outskirts of town, however, and it's possible the name of the road was accidentally misspelled in some retelling, and the error has simply been repeated. If the haunted Bardarka Road of folklore is the same Bairdaka Street that exists today, it's only 0.1-mile long and runs between South Birchwood Loop Road and Adrian Avenue. The area is still forested, but any cabin that might have been on Bairdaka Street is long gone.

Chena Hot Springs Road
Fairbanks

Chena Hot Springs Road runs from Highway 2 all the way to Chena Hot Springs, about sixty miles northeast of Fairbanks "as the crow flies." (The route by car is longer and passes through Two Rivers and Pleasant Valley.) The small, unincorporated community of Chena Hot Springs is best known for its thermal baths, which were first discovered by non-natives in August 1905. The natural surroundings, unlimited recreational possibilities, and even an ice museum draw visitors throughout the year.

It's said that motorists on Chena Hot Springs Road often mistake a pair of lights tailing them or coming toward them at night as headlights from another car. The drivers change their tune when the orbs change colors, shoot off sparks, zip by them, or merge into a single, giant, luminous ball. The incidents occur most frequently on the road between mile markers eight to twelve outside Chena Hot

Springs. The phenomenon always takes place after 7:00 p.m. and is reported most often in the winter.

As a possible explanation to at least some of the sightings, Chena Hot Springs is considered to be one of the best (and most reliable) spots in Alaska to view the aurora borealis. The Northern Lights are unearthly, but people usually don't mistake them for paranormal activity.

McCarthy Road (Old Copper Railroad)
Chitina to McCarthy

Ghosts from the early twentieth century show up all along McCarthy Road, a sixty-mile gravel route that stretches between the Edgeton Highway in Chitina and McCarthy at the southern end of Kennicott Glacier in Wrangell–St. Elias National Park.

Malachite and chalcocite, two ores used in the production of copper, were discovered on a mountain ridge along the glacier in 1900. Various mining and financial interests merged to form the Kennecott Copper Corporation to extract the ore, and the first load was shipped from Kennecott, the new town built at the head of the mines, in 1911. (Both the company and the mining town used an alternate spelling of the glacier's name.) The village of McCarthy sprang up nearby with stores, bars, and other diversions to service the workers' needs. Before long, the corporation had five separate mines in operation, but over the next two decades the ore was depleted, and the mines closed one by one. The last train filled with ore headed out in 1938, and Kennecott became a ghost town—until around 1980, when the national park was formed, and its glaciers, hiking opportunities, the ruins of Kennecott, the defunct mines, and McCarthy became tourist destinations. Even today, though, McCarthy Road is inaccessible during the winter and not regularly maintained.

The 196-mile Copper River and Northwestern Railway was built between 1907 and 1911 to carry the ore down to the coast, but its construction required thousands of workers. They had to blast through the mountains to clear a pathway as well as build more than a hundred bridges to span canyons and rivers, all under punishing weather conditions. It's unknown how many people perished while completing the near-impossible task. Many of the deceased were undoubtedly buried along the track, close to where they died.

From McCarthy to Chitina, the Copper River and Northwestern Railway more or less followed the Copper River. Today, McCarthy Road shadows the abandoned railbed. At the McCarthy end, the road stops at the Kennicott River, and people take a footbridge over to town. From there, shuttles carry visitors the 4.5 miles to Kennecott.

For years, travelers have reported seeing apparitions wandering among the trees on both sides of McCarthy Road. They also spot phantom grave markers that disappear at a second glance. If folks drive with their windows down, they sometimes hear the eerie voices of unseen adults and the sounds of children laughing and playing. There are also horrific cries from invisible, long-gone miners. When a government housing project was started near the Chitina end of McCarthy Road in 1997, many of the workers also heard the creepy voices and laughter. Even more disconcerting, their tools often went missing or turned up in places other than where they were set down.

Rookies Corner (The Old Kiksaadi Corner)
Sitka

Just east of downtown Sitka, a small coastal town southwest of Juneau, there's a sports bar named Rookies at 1615 Sawmill Creek Road. The tavern has had a ghost story connected to it for as long as anyone can remember. Sometime back when the bar was known as the Kirk or the Kiksaadi Club, a local woman left around closing time, and despite being extremely tipsy, she decided to walk the short distance into town, as she had on many occasions. Tragically, she wandered onto the street, and was struck by a truck at a blind corner in the road. (It didn't help that the driver was also intoxicated.) Despite her fatal injuries, the woman managed to stagger into Sitka, screaming in pain as she went. Dozens of people were leaving the clubs in town, and they saw and heard her as she approached. Too late to be of any help, they watched in horror as she died.

Ever since, there have been claims that her ghost appears back at that blind curve, walking along or drifting onto the road at night. Disembodied cries of pain and loud groans have also been heard at the corner just before dawn, coming from the brush on the side of the road. The phenomenon is so disconcerting that some drivers have stopped, parked their cars, and called for a lift. (As is often the case with ghost stories, even though the woman must have been known by everyone in the neighborhood bar at the time, her name has been lost over the years.)

ARIZONA

51st Avenue and Indian School Road
Phoenix

There have been many reports of the apparition of a woman suddenly appearing in the middle of the road just before a car enters the intersection. The unidentified ghost is "hit" by the vehicle and vanishes upon "impact," but not before people hear the spectre's horrific screams. The spirit also enters nearby houses, sits on the furniture, and knocks objects off shelves. The reason for the hauntings remains unknown.

Slaughterhouse Canyon Road
Kingman

Slaughterhouse Canyon, also known as Luana's Canyon, is about two miles southeast of Kingman, which can be found on Historic US Route 66. Slaughterhouse Canyon Road passes through the ravine that shares its name and can be accessed from the northwest via Topeka Street or from the northeast via Hualapai Mountain Road (County Road 148).

According to legend, in the late 1880s a prospector and his family lived somewhere in the canyon in a small, wooden cabin. The miner would go into the hills for days at a time looking for provisions, and he would always return with fresh food for the family. No one knows what became of him, but one day the man never made it home. The isolated wife and children soon began to starve, and their anguished cries of hunger would bounce off the mountain walls. The mother went insane, killed her children to end their suffering, chopped their bodies into pieces, and threw the remains into a river that flowed nearby. The ethereal screams of the youngsters and their guilt-ridden mother can still be heard echoing through the canyon.

Parts of the Slaughterhouse Canyon ghost story are strikingly similar to a centuries-old myth that originated in Mexico. The tale dates back to the time of the Spanish occupation and involves a phantom mother dubbed La Llorona. ("Llorar" is Spanish for "to weep.") It's said that a nobleman named Don Nuño de Montesclaros took a local village woman, Doña Luisa de Loveros, as his mistress, despite her being from a much lower caste. Over the next two years, Luisa bore Don Nuño two children. He never told her, however, that he had a fiancée back in Spain, and when the woman arrived in Mexico City for the wedding, Luisa went mad.

She took her babies, threw them into a river, and then drowned herself as well. It wasn't long before her ghost began to show up on the streets of Mexico City. The wraith would wail, "Mis hijos, mis hijos" ("My children, my children"). She grabbed at passersby, asking whether they had the infants. She also roamed the pathways alongside nearby rivers and creek beds, looking for small children who may have drowned in the rushing water. La Llorona's spirit still searches for them today, but, cursed by the gods for her horrific actions, she will never find her babies.

In some versions of the story, Luisa killed her children with an ornamental knife given to her by the infants' father. She then ran out onto the streets, shrieking and covered in blood. The police discovered the murdered infants, and Luisa was hanged for her grisly crime. Today, her ghost is often seen wearing a long white bloodstained dress.

The phantom Weeping Woman, or La Llorona, is now also seen in the United States. Her most documented US hauntings have occurred on the banks of the Rio Grande in El Paso, Texas, and Las Cruces, New Mexico; along Coyote Creek and on the streets in Guadalupita, New Mexico; and along the Yellowstone River in Billings, Montana. The appearances of a Woman in White in Gary, Indiana, can almost certainly be attributed to the La Llorona legend, which was transplanted to the city's suburb of Cudahy by Mexican immigrants.

In addition to the allegedly true story of Doña Luisa de Loveros, the La Llorona legend may have its basis in the ancient Greek myth of Medea, who murdered her two sons when she was abandoned by their father Jason (of Argonaut fame). There is also an ancient Aztec tale that the goddess Cihuacoatl appeared in human form in Tenochtitlán just before the Spanish invasion. She manifested as a black-haired woman in a white dress and was heard crying for her lost children.

State Highway 80
Tombstone

Tombstone, Arizona, was a Wild West boomtown from the late 1870s through the mid-1880s—that is, until the nearby silver mines were depleted. Today, it's most remembered as the site of the notorious Gunfight at OK Corral that took place on October 26, 1881. Aficionados of the Old West flock to what remains of the hamlet's historic center, but paranormalists come for its many ghosts. There have been claims of phantom gunfighters appearing in the corral, of course, but cowboy phantoms also show up at Big Nose Kate's, a nearby saloon dating to that era. Some of the bar's spectres have been captured in photographs. Perhaps the most haunted extant building from Tombstone's heyday is the refurbished Bird Cage Theatre. Once called the Bird Cage Opera House Saloon, the "concert hall" had a stage for singers, musicians, and dancing girls, but primarily it was a combination bar, gambling parlor, and bordello. At night, the ghost of Fred White, who preceded the more famous Wyatt Earp as marshall, supposedly walks Allen Street, which was the town's main drag at that time.

Then there's Boot Hill Graveyard, located about a half mile north of Tombstone on State Highway 80 (also known as Tombstone Road). About 250 people were buried there between 1878 and 1884. Tourists to the cemetery occasionally see odd lights and hear unusual sounds. Ghosts sometimes show up in photos taken in the graveyard, and occasionally they materialize in front of visitors. One of the revenants is Billy Clanton, who died in the shootout at the OK Corral. He has been spotted rising out of his grave as well as walking alongside Tombstone Road into town.

Thornton Road
Casa Grande
In 1982, InnerConn Technology, Inc., a California circuit board manufacturer, announced that it was moving its headquarters to a 135-acre site in Casa Grande, Arizona. When the company defaulted on its loan with Union Bank the following year, work on the partially completed buildings stopped, and they now lie empty, in ruins. Their unique appearance is due to their design and unusual method of construction. Enormous balloons were affixed to solid foundations and inflated. They were then covered by layers of polyurethane foam, followed by three inches of concrete. After that, the balloons were deflated and removed, leaving behind the rounded structures now referred to as the Domes. Three of the buildings resemble large Quonset huts, but the one closest to Thornton Road has the stereotypical, disc-like look of a flying saucer.

The whole area is fenced off, but that hasn't stopped curiosity-seekers and vandals. The place has a strange, inexplicable aura about it, and a few people have spied—and heard—shadowy phantoms in the area at night. Drivers passing by have heard unexplained tapping on the outside of their vehicles if they slowed or paused too long. To get to the Domes, take the Thornton Road exit from Interstate 8, and travel south for about a mile. The abandoned buildings will be on the east (left) side of the street.

The Casa Grande Mountains are just south of the intersection between I-8 and I-10, about four or five miles east of the Domes. Dark, hazy figures sometimes appear on the roads and trails in the foothills, and backpackers claim that every now and then, spirits follow them on their hikes.

ARKANSAS

Nine Mile Ridge
Hardy to Saddle

Nine Mile Ridge is the crest of a hill located about two miles north of the Arkansas River and ten miles south of the Missouri border. An old wagon trail on the top of the ridge is now County Route 42, although it's also known as Nine Mile Ridge Road. The closest town is Hardy to the southeast on US Route 63. The unincorporated community of Saddle, on Arkansas Highway 289, lies to the west.

Nine Mile Ridge is best known as the site of the infamous January 1863 Cherokee and Arapaho attack on nine freight wagons that were heading east from Santa Fe, New Mexico. The incident began when the Native Americans approached the wagon master to ask for food and drink. They were turned away, and in the process one of the Indians was shot (perhaps accidentally) and wounded. The warriors retreated, but they returned the next day and slaughtered the entire party, except for one man who managed to escape.

A spectre from the mid-nineteenth century haunts the ridge, but it's not one of the massacre victims. The ghost appears at night carrying a lantern. It's believed he walked the ridge during the Civil War, lamp in hand, hoping to see his son returning home from battle.

Dry Hill Road on Highway 220
Cedarville

Something strange is said to be going on about ten miles north of Cedarville near the junction of State Highway 220 and Dry Hill Loop. There's a small road somewhere off the west side of the highway that was part of the old Butterfield State

Coach route between 1858 and 1861. Folks have reported hearing disembodied whistling when they're near the trail, but it instantly stops if they step onto the road itself. The whistling is almost always followed by the sound of an invisible team of stagecoach horses barreling by.

Highway 365
Little Rock to Pine Bluff
Over the years, dozens of reports have been made of a "Vanishing Hitchhiker" along the forty-five-mile stretch of Highway 365 between Little Rock and Pine Bluff. The area around Woodson is particularly haunted. Almost all of the claims follow the archetypal old wives' tale about a hitchhiking "damsel in distress" that disappears from a Good Samaritan's car. (See chapter 1.)

Redfield Road
Grant County
AR 46, also variously known as Redfield Road and Sheridan Road, runs for seventeen miles between Redfield and Sheridan in south-central Arkansas. Redfield is on the haunted section of Highway 365, but the paranormal activity on Redfield and Sheridan Road seems to be totally unrelated to Highway 365's ghostly hitchhiker. Phenomena include car radios shutting off, hoods popping open on their own, flashlights going dead, and even an apparition or two. Most of the anomalies take place in or near a graveyard along AR 46, the most likely one being Jackson Cemetery, at the intersection of Redfield Road and Country Road 4608.

Primrose Lane
Paragould
Reynolds Park Lake is a small reservoir located about two miles outside the town of Paragould, Arkansas. The water is stocked for fishing, and the park is set up for all kinds of outdoor recreation. There are RV and camping facilities as well. In recent years a modest housing development was built at the southeast corner of the lake, and eight of its homes line a short street named Primrose Lane. A male apparition carrying a rifle and an equally ethereal dog appear at the lakeside end of the drive. According to local lore, the unidentified man shot himself while hunting nearby. People wandering through the neighboring woods sometimes spot the friendly phantom canine, but it always vanishes as it approaches them.

CALIFORNIA

Corner of Octavia and Bush Streets, California Street
San Francisco

Singer Tony Bennett crooned that he left his heart in San Francisco. More than a few folks have left their spirits there as well.

There's a small, fenced park—the smallest in San Francisco—at the southwest corner of Octavia and Bush Streets, dedicated to the memory of Mary Ellen Pleasant, whose house was once located there. Her spectre is supposedly a frequent visitor to the site. The apparition is seen standing among the six eucalyptus trees on the property and, although benign, the spirit has been known to throw nuts at passersby and scare away dogs.

Little is known for certain about Pleasant's early years because her three sets of memoirs contradict each other. The year of her birth is generally agreed to have been 1914. Her true parentage is unknown. Though a person of color, she was able to pass for White, and she adopted the surname Pleasant sometime in her youth. After a period as an indentured servant, she married a wealthy abolitionist, and they became active in the Underground Railroad. After her husband's death, Pleasant moved to New Orleans, where it's probable she met with Marie Laveau, the "Voodoo Queen" of the Crescent City. (There are countless ghost legends about Laveau, whose apparition is still seen regularly throughout the Big Easy.)

Pleasant moved on to San Francisco, and using her late husband's name and inherited fortune, she opened several semiprivate, fashionable men's clubs and restaurants as well as boardinghouses, stores, and laundries. She partnered with Thomas Bell, a White former banker, and armed with their combined business acumen as well as inside information that Pleasant overheard at her upscale establishments, they amassed a $30 million fortune, the equivalent of about $725 million today. She built a lavish mansion with a row of eucalyptus trees at the corner of Octavia and Bush Streets in the Pacific Heights district. She and the Bell family both lived there, and together they gave extravagant parties that helped solidify their place among San Francisco's upper crust.

Pleasant didn't hide her true race from the Black community, and she helped find employment for those who came to the city via the Underground Railroad. From 1857 to 1859 she left San Francisco to encourage John Brown as he planned his attack on Harpers Ferry. She also helped finance the insurrection to the tune of $30,000 (which would now be about $1 million). In fact, a message from Pleasant was found in Brown's pocket at his execution. Fortunately, she had only initialed the note, so the author's identity initially remained a mystery.

That didn't stop rumors about her involvement in the raid, however. Tabloid newspapers spread other gossip as well: Her luxurious mansion was actually a brothel; orgies took place there; witchcraft was practiced on the grounds. Pleasant was dubbed "the Queen of the Voodoos." She supposedly stole babies, was a human trafficker, ate human brains, and murdered at least four people. And there was one more damning accusation—perhaps the worst possible sin of all to polite society: Mary Ellen Pleasant was actually Black.

Then, when Thomas Bell was found dead in the house he and his family shared with Pleasant, *The San Francisco Chronicle* published a scathing full-page article about "Mammy" Pleasant, as the newspaper called her, strongly implying that she was responsible for Bell's death. (The hit piece was written with the full cooperation of Bell's widow.)

Pleasant met the accusations head on, dismissing the ludicrous ones but admitting publicly that she was, indeed, Black—and acknowledging that she had written the infamous letter found on John Brown.

Later, when she was removed from a San Francisco streetcar because of her race, she sued. The case went all the way to the California Supreme Court, where she was vindicated. Although she wasn't awarded damages, segregation was outlawed on the city's public transit.

All of Pleasant's activism was costly, however. With her fortune, home, and reputation gone, she was near destitute when she died in 1904. She was interred in a friend's burial plot in Napa.

Crumbling and neglected, the Pleasant mansion was razed in 1928, but the stately eucalyptus trees were spared. In 1974, the City of San Francisco declared them a Structure of Merit, and they were enclosed within a square christened the Mary Ellen Pleasant Memorial Park. Many of the city's walking ghost tours depart from a commemorative plaque in the plaza that recognizes Pleasant as the "Mother of Civil Rights in California."

Not far away, in the Nob Hill neighborhood, a teenage female apparition in white Victorian garb haunts the sidewalks of California Street between Jones and Powell Streets. Many believe that it's the ghost of Flora Sommerton, who fled the city in 1876 rather than agree to a marriage arranged by her parents. Traveling under the alias "Mrs. Butler," Flora quietly made her way to Montana, where she took a job as a housekeeper. Her true identity wasn't discovered until after her death in 1926. Her body was found in a boarding house in Butte, dressed in a crystal-beaded ballroom gown dating to the time of her unwelcome engagement to be married. (Some sources claim the gown was her unused wedding dress.) Also found in the room were numerous articles about her disappearance that she had clipped forty years earlier from Bay Area newspapers. Flora's remains were returned to San Francisco and buried with members of her family. If the spectre on California Street is Flora Sommerton, she has chosen to materialize at the age she was when she ran away rather than when she died.

Prospectors Road
Lotus and Garden City

The community of Lotus lies on CA 49 in the Sierra Nevada Mountains, just three miles northwest of Sutter's Mill, where gold was discovered in 1848. John W. Marshall's unexpected find sparked the California Gold Rush, and within a year approximately eighty thousand prospectors, nicknamed the "forty-niners," moved West to seek their fortune.

Marshall Road travels northward from Lotus for about nine miles to George-town. About a mile outside of Lotus, Prospectors Road branches to the west. This narrow, two-lane side street runs for about two or three miles, more or less paralleling the main road, before rejoining Marshall.

Prospectors Road is paved, but at a seven-thousand-foot-plus elevation its many twists and turns make travel extremely dangerous even for the most accomplished driver, especially in bad weather. Well over a dozen people have lost their lives in vehicular accidents on the short stretch of highway.

So, yes, Prospectors Road is haunted, but surprisingly the phantom isn't any of the motorists or passengers who died on the treacherous pathway. The anonymous apparition is a crotchety elderly man dressed in attire usually associated with gold miners of the late nineteenth century. The spectre emerges from the scrub on the side of the road and floats into the path of an oncoming vehicle, angrily pointing an accusatory forefinger at its occupants. Perhaps the grizzled prospector thinks the interlopers are trespassing on his claim. Regardless, it's clear the intruders are unwanted, so it's probably best if they simply continue on their way.

COLORADO

County Line Road
Bennett

On November 29, 1864, with no command or approval from superiors, US Army Col. John Chivington led a band of 675 men out of Fort Lyon in an attack on about 750 Cheyenne and Arapaho, whose village was in nearby Sand Creek. Reports varied as to the number of Native Americans killed, but anywhere from 70 to 150 were slaughtered, most of them women and children. Chivington's forces also torched teepees, looted the Indians' possessions, and stole their horses. Many of the soldiers returned the next day to finish off the wounded and desecrate corpses. A military investigation found that Chivington was responsible for the carnage, but by that time he had resigned his commission and was never punished. The National Park Service maintains the location of the Sand Creek Massacre as a National Historic Site (nps.gov/sand).

Almost two hundred miles to the southeast, Colorado's County Line Road (County Road 50/194) stretches in a perfectly straight, east-to-west line near Bennett and Aurora. Motorists along this seventeen-mile route routinely hear what seem to be Native American drumbeats. They also see a ghostly man on horseback. Local folklore says that much of the paranormal activity occurring along County Line Road is somehow connected to the Sand Creek bloodbath.

But not all of it.

There's also a story that in 1864, the same year as the massacre to the north, a settler near today's County Line Road shot a Native American who was trying to steal his horse. Fellow warriors avenged the victim by killing the frontiersman and his family, then mutilating their remains. This incident may be responsible for the apparition of a girl standing by the road, whispered voices, and disembodied screams.

A lot of the spooky stuff on County Line Road takes place around Third Bridge, which is located between CR 129 to the west and CR 53 (Kiowa-Bennett Road) to the east. It was the site of a horrific car crash in the summer of 1977 that resulted in the death of two teens. Also, a 2020 murder allegedly took place at the bridge.

At night, motorists sometimes see a vehicle with only one headlight rapidly approaching them on the road—and in some cases, there's no car, just a single, strong light—but it always vanishes before coming too close.

Gold Camp Road
Colorado Springs

Also known as County Route 8, Gold Camp Road (divided into Lower and Upper Gold Camp Road) runs for about thirty miles between South 8th Street in Colorado Springs up to Lazy S Ranch Road (Route 81) high in the Rockies. The road replaced a railway from the nineteenth century whose tracks were torn up in the 1920s. The road passes through the original tunnels, although some of them have caved in and required detours.

There are many rumors about hauntings all along Gold Camp Road and especially in or around the tunnels. Some of the spectres are believed to be workers who died while building the railroad. Others are the ghosts of school children whose bus was involved in a terrible road accident or, according to another version of the tale, the bus was inside a tunnel when it collapsed. (It should be pointed out that, despite the legends, there's no evidence that either school bus tragedy ever happened.) Oddly, motorists have also spotted apparitions in KKK robes.

Highway 93
Golden

State Highway 93 is a nineteen-mile road between US 6 outside of Golden and SH 119 in Boulder, just east of the Rockies. A sudden, mysterious haze or heavy mist sometimes appears on the route, especially near Van Bibber Creek about a mile north of Golden. In addition, some drivers are overwhelmed with an inexplicable feeling of nervousness or anxiety.

The haunting dates back to long before the highway was a roadway. Originally, it served as the track bed for the Colorado Central Railroad between Ralston and Golden.

On July 20, 1881, one of the CCR's locomotives fatally struck a man walking the track near Van Bibber Creek, throwing his body off into the brush. Nothing of him was ever found, save for his hat. Almost immediately, the dead man's derby-clad ghost started to materialize on the tracks and inside railcars. Over time, the number of sightings decreased, then ceased entirely. Eventually, the rails were torn up and replaced by State Highway 93. Although motorists experience the strange fog and uneasiness on the roadway, the apparition has never reappeared.

CONNECTICUT

Chamberlain Highway
Berlin
Ragged Mountain, peaking at 761 feet, is part of a long, rocky ridge located near Berlin, Connecticut, close to the geographic center of the state. Folklore says that sometime back in the 1800s a local boy wandered off into the dense forest covering the hills and got lost. He was never found, and it's presumed that coyotes, which were plentiful in the region, killed the youngster.

Today, in the spring and then again in the fall, people will sometimes hear the muted howls of coyotes echoing down the mountainside. The baying continues for several minutes, then suddenly cuts off, only to be followed by the barely audible call of a lone trumpet. It's believed that the mysterious sounds are revenants of the coyotes and the lad's futile call for help.

Depending upon the source, the ghostly noises can also be heard along the seven-mile Chamberlain Highway (Connecticut Route 71A), which parallels the eastern face of the ridge, or CT 372, which passes to the northeast of Ragged Mountain Memorial Preserve. There have even been reports that the sounds have reached as far as CT 72, three miles to the northeast near the city of New Britain.

Oak Avenue
Torrington
Oak Avenue is a two-lane, blacktop street through a semirural residential area southeast of downtown Torrington. The road is only about a half mile long, and it more or less parallels Connecticut Route 8, a major north–south highway that lies a mile to the east. Legend has it that, back in the 1950s, a young girl was killed in the woods along Oak Avenue and that her apparition has returned to haunt the roadway. She materializes most often in the winter but only when there's a full moon. The phantom wears a white, torn dress and, for some reason, carries a dog collar. She is usually seen crying. Nothing else is known about the ghost, and if anyone gets too near it disappears.

Velvet Street
Trumbull

Downs Road
Bethany and Hamden

Edmonds Road/Jeremy Swamp Road
Oxford

Marginal Drive
West Haven

Saw Mill City Road
Shelton

Zion Hill Road
Milford

According to fans of the strange, odd, and curious, Connecticut is secretly inhabited by a small group of mysterious people known as Melon Heads. According to which legend you hear, they are the descendants of escapees from Garner Correctional Institute or Fairfield Hills Hospital, a mental institution. An alternate tale suggests that sometime in the forgotten past a family moved into seclusion in the woods, and the Melon Heads' disfigured appearance comes from years of inbreeding.

Though rarely seen, Melon Heads are instantly recognizable. They're short—only about three feet tall—but they have gigantic heads with bulging veins. Their eyes are huge, ranging in color from a pale pink to orange, and they have gnarled, yellowed teeth, pallid skin, and unusually long, reedy arms. Although there have been no confirmed reports of Melon Heads attacking humans, folks nevertheless consider them dangerous.

One of the places Melon Heads supposedly turn up with some regularity is along Velvet Street, an unpaved, 1.2-mile road in a forested area just north of Trumbull. Located near the northern end of Easton Reservoir, the lane runs between Judd Road and Tashua Road to the south. The creatures live in the surrounding woods and are seen only at night. (It's thought they may be albinos and stay hidden during the day because they're sensitive to sunlight.)

There are also sightings of a phantom car traveling Velvet Street: a 1970s-era Ford Granada. According to local lore, about forty years ago, six girls went in search of Melon Heads, driving the Granada. They stopped on a lonely stretch of Velvet Street and stepped out of the car. Rather than harm or confront the curiosity-seekers, several Melon Heads sneaked up behind them, jumped in the vehicle, and drove off, leaving the girls stranded. The car itself was never recovered, but not too long after the incident the ghost of a Ford Granada with Melon Heads behind the wheel began to frequent Velvet Street.

Downs Road in Hamden is separated into two sections. The upper stretch runs for about a mile between the Quinnipiac Trailhead southward to Gaylor Mountain Road. From that point the car-free, unpaved Quinnipiac Trail continues for about a mile, almost as far as Hoadley Road. Then, Downs Road picks up again and continues south to State Road 69 (the Linchfield Turnpike) in Bethany. The entire length passes through deep forest. Menacing Melon Heads are seen on the upper stretch of road, including the path that's closed to vehicular traffic. Apparitions of children have also been spotted. A spectral, high-spirited-but-skittish beast resembling an albino horse has shown up often enough that it's acquired a nickname: the Downs Road Monster.

Edmonds Road in Oxford runs north from State Route 188 (Quaker Farms Road) for about 1.5 miles. Near Plaster House Road, Edmonds Road takes on the name Jeremy Swamp Road, and the street continues northward for about three more miles, eventually hitting State Route 67 (Southford Road). Both Edmonds and Jeremy Swamp Roads are "haunted" by Melon Heads.

Marginal Drive is located just south of the Yale Bowl at Yale University. The road parallels the West River and runs for about a mile between State Route 34 (Derby Avenue) and US 1 (Boston Post Road) to the south. For most of the way, the paved, narrow lane is tree-lined, and the upper two-thirds (from Derby Avenue to Westfield Street) is gated to form a cycling path and pedestrian walkway. Recently there have been tented encampments along the wooded passages, and the accidental death of a homeless man was reported there in 2013. Student lore says that Melon Heads live in the patchy forests and should be avoided at all costs.

Saw Mill City Road cuts through a sylvan region outside Shelton, Connecticut. It stretches for 1.5 miles, east-to-west, from Birds Eye Road to Walnut Tree Hill Road. Travelers down this quiet, paved lane sometimes hear disembodied voices coming from the woods and, now and then, spot a Melon Head or two trying to keep out of sight.

Finally, Zion Hill Road runs westward for about a mile from Wheelers Farm Road to West Rutland Road in Milford. The curved, paved street passes through a semirural neighborhood dotted with upscale houses. In addition to a reportedly nasty band of Melon Heads hiding somewhere in the vicinity, glowing light orbs are known to dart through the trees.

DELAWARE

Highway 12
Frederica

Delaware's Highway 12 is a paved, two-lane road that runs northeast for about nine miles from the Maryland–Delaware state line to Felton, Delaware. From there it turns to the east, crosses US Route 13, and continues to Frederica, Delaware, thirteen miles south of Dover.

People swear that they've encountered a gigantic phantom dog with fiery red eyes on the section of Highway 12 between Felton and Frederica. He's been spotted since the turn of the twentieth century. An old wives' tale says that the humongous canine once belonged to a tenant in a farmhouse somewhere along that stretch of road. The man murdered his landlord and, in an attempt to conceal his crime, ground up the corpse and fed the "meat" to his dog. The story doesn't say whether the ghostly dog is dangerous, but people stay as far away from it as possible just to be safe.

The sudden appearance of an enormous black dog with burning red eyes has been a mainstay of paranormal mythology for years. Normally, seeing one of the cursed canines, known as hellhounds, or even hearing its howl is a bad omen—even a harbinger of death. These spooky creatures are said to be watchdogs that protect paranormal entities from the living.

Old Baltimore Pike
Newark

The only significant engagement of the American Revolution to take place on Delaware soil was the Battle of Cooch's Bridge, also known as the Battle of Iron Hill. On September 3, 1777, the Continental Army and local militiamen fought against a regiment approximately twice their size made up of about 450 Hessians and one thousand British Army regulars. The daylong skirmish ended in a draw, casualty-wise, but the American forces retreated enough to allow the British to claim victory. According to tradition, it was the first battle in which the Stars and Stripes was flown.

Cooch's Bridge was situated on what is now called the Old Baltimore Pike. The rustic span didn't survive the war, and no one is sure exactly where it stood. Today, there's a modern, concrete bridge on Old Cooch's Bridge Road near the battlefield, but it may or may not be where the original one was located.

In 2003, descendants of the Thomas Cooch family sold some of their acreage around the battlefield to the State of Delaware; four years later the state also acquired the Cooch farmhouse and surrounding property. Today, the battle site is on the National Register of Historic Places and is part of the Cooch's Bridge Historic District.

A battle memorial stands at the junction of Old Baltimore Pike and Dayett Mills Road. The headless spectre of a British Redcoat is regularly seen on the pike near this intersection, but only on moonless nights. The method of his decapitation is unknown, but most people believe it was from cannon fire.

Salem Church Road
Newark
Salem Church Road, located a few miles southeast of Newark, is a two-lane, north-to-south street that runs from State Route 4 in Ogletown to the north down to US Route 40. The haunted section is between DE 4 and Old Baltimore Pike. Six ghosts are seen crossing the road together as a group. It's believed they were members of the same family and were hanged for witchcraft somewhere along Salem Church Road back in the 1600s. Their angry spirits may have cursed the highway as well: An inordinately large number of car accidents occur on this two-mile stretch.

Despite the similarity in names, the Salem Church Road hangings were not connected to the witchcraft trials that took place in Salem, Massachusetts, between February 1692 and May 1693.

State Route 488
Seaford
Delaware's State Route 488, also known as Airport Road, runs just 2.5 miles between US Route 13 (Sussex Highway) and Fire Tower Road. The silent revenant

of a Confederate soldier is sometimes seen walking on the shoulder of Route 488. The ghost dates back to when Delaware was still technically a slave state despite remaining in the Union during the Civil War. Another spectre that appears on the road is a bride-to-be, all decked out in her wedding gown. She's said to have died in an accident on her way to the ceremony. Perhaps she's returned in the hopes of completing her nuptials.

FLORIDA

Greenbriar Road
Jacksonville

For as long as anyone can remember, a floating, glowing orb has been following cars on Greenbriar Road, which is located in St. Johns County about twenty miles south of Jacksonville. Known as the Greenbriar Light, the shimmering sphere always stays at a distance of twenty-five to thirty feet behind any moving vehicle. The paved road runs for about four miles between Route 13 and Old County Road 210. The light appears most often near the junction of Greenbriar Road and CR 210, but the manifestations have been less frequent since the intersection's layout was modified. Some say the Greenbriar Light has gone away completely.

According to local lore, the radiant ball is the headlight of a phantom motorcycle. Supposedly the driver was speeding on Greenbriar Road when he lost control of the bike and ran into an angled steel wire supporting a telephone pole. He was instantly decapitated.

Highway 98
Lakeland

Since around 1985, a phantom tractor-trailer has been seen heading north on Highway 98 between Highways 50 and 471. The ghost semi is said to be hauling produce to Texas, but there seem to be no stories regarding the origin of the haunting. The truck, or perhaps a similar one, also appears on Highway 47 about fifty miles from Brooksville.

Interstate 4
Daytona Beach to Tampa Bay

Interstate 4 stretches approximately 132 miles between Tampa and Daytona Beach. Although I-4 is signposted as an east–west highway, it mostly travels in a northeast–southwest direction. The freeway's mileage markers begin at the Tampa end, where I-4 meets I-275. (The intersection has been nicknamed "Malfunction Junction.") I-4 is concurrent with State Route 400, but the interstate ends when it hits I-95 in Daytona Beach. SR 400 continues another four miles to the Atlantic shore.

There have been reports of ghost cars and trucks, phantom hitchhikers, sudden bursts of bright light, floating illuminated spheres, and inexplicable cold spots all along the route. Odd noises—including unknown voices, groans, and screams—are picked up on CD radios, car radios, and cell phones.

Some of the phenomena are attributed to the revenants of Native Americans, especially the activity occurring near Tampa. It's thought that an ancient Indian graveyard was discovered during construction of the I-4 in 1959, but the burial ground was quietly paved over. As a result, the angry, aggressive apparitions of those buried there sometimes appear along the highway, frightening motorists.

An inexplicably large number of vehicular accidents occur on I-4 around Sanford, which is located about twenty miles northeast of Orlando. The reason is uncertain, but an old cemetery was found there during construction of the highway. At Sanford, however, the graves were relocated before the roadwork continued. Nevertheless, many of those whose remains were disturbed may have become restless spirits.

Rolling Acres Road
Lady Lake
Rolling Acres Road in Lady Lake, Florida, runs for about four miles in a straight, north-to-south direction. The street's northern terminus is Guthrie Avenue, and it ends in a rural area about a half mile past Lake Ella Road. A white, glowing female phantom, said to be named Julia, walks the forested section of the road. Besides seeing her apparition, people have heard piercing screams coming from the woods.

The story goes that Julia's parents detested her boyfriend (secretly her fiancé), so one night the young couple chose an isolated spot along Rolling Acres Road for a clandestine rendezvous. Unfortunately, while waiting for her suitor to arrive, Julia was killed by a passing stranger. Her spectre now roams the roadway where she perished.

GEORGIA

Omega Road Overpass
Tifton

In the mid-nineteenth century, Captain Henry Harding Tift moved from Mystic, Connecticut, to south-central Georgia to acquire lumber for his family's shipbuilding trade. Tifts Town (as Tifton was known until 1890) grew as folks settled in the area to operate the sawmill, its railway, and the typical businesses that support such a community.

Today, Tifton has a population of about fifteen thousand and is home to Abraham Baldwin Agricultural College as well as a satellite campus of the University of Georgia. The town is located at the intersection of Interstate 75, which skirts the western edge of town, and US Highway 82. Just south of this juncture, Old Omega Road runs under I-75.

It's said that at some indeterminate time in the past, a female student from the agricultural college decided to drive home to Florida for the weekend, but she didn't get away until late Friday night. Not too far into her journey, she had a fatal car accident under the Omega Road Overpass. (Details of the wreck and what caused it are sketchy. She may have been speeding to make up time; perhaps another car was involved.) These days, people coming up to or traveling beneath the overpass occasionally hear the ghostly sounds of whining, screeching tires. There have been similar claims from drivers on I-75 as they passed over Omega Road heading south to Valdosta. The spooky noises vary in pitch and volume.

Robertson Road
Brooklet

Railroad Bed Road (County Road 404, also known as Railroad Street) runs to the southeast from Parker Avenue in Brooklet to Buie Driggers Road in Stilson. About halfway along this stretch, a 0.9-mile, packed-gravel lane called Robertson Road (County Road 403, also nicknamed Old Ghost Road) branches south, connecting CR 404 to US 80.

Rumor has it that if you park your car along Robertson Road late at night and wait for about fifteen minutes, a flickering, dim light will appear off in the distance. Its color varies from orange to red. If you approach the soft glow, you'll discover it's the spectre of a nondescript man digging a ditch on the side of the road. Occasionally the apparition stops what it's doing and walks toward your vehicle, but it always vanishes before it reaches you. It's also claimed that the man, still bathed in a faint luminescence, reappears behind your car as you drive away. There are various other old wives' tales about the spirit. Some say that, in life, the man was a plantation worker. According to one story about him, he's digging his own grave. In another, he's been decapitated and is looking for his head.

Oh, and the revenant may not be alone. According to local lore, people have also seen phantom dogs on Old Ghost Road.

HAWAII

Morgan's Corner, Nuuanu Pali Drive
Oahu

When driving from Honolulu to Kailua and Lanikai Beach on Oahu's east coast, most people take HI 61, the Pali Highway. Many of the highway's ghost legends can be found in chapters 3 and 4.

About three miles of the old road that the modern road replaced still exists, however. If you take the Nuuanu Pali Drive exit off of Route 61, the path will split in about 0.2 miles. Bear left to see what remains of the Old Pali Highway.

If you take the right branch, you'll be on Nuuanu Pali Drive. Almost immediately, the scenery changes. The lane is surrounded by dense foliage, and the trees lining the road create a thick canopy overhead. Like the Pali Highway, Nuuanu Pali Drive has ghosts of its own.

On March 11, 1948, two escaped convicts, James Majors and John Palakiko, broke into the home of Therese Wilder, a sixty-eight-year-old widow, whose house on Nuuanu Pali Drive was located near a dangerous hairpin turn known as Morgan's Corner. (The notorious bend, the scene of many car accidents, took its name from a Dr. James Morgan, who lived in a villa close to the curve from the 1920s through the 1940s.)

Because they were on the run, the prisoners' intent was only to steal a few supplies, a quick in-and-out burglary. They selected Wilder's house because they were hungry and drawn to the scent of her cooking. Once inside, the men immediately attacked Wilder, breaking her jaw in the process. They then bound and gagged her and put her on the bed, not so they could assault her but so she was out of the way. They quickly grabbed what they needed and left. Unfortunately, at some time that night, Therese Wilder died, suffocating from the gag in her mouth due to her broken jaw. It's claimed that motorists navigating Morgan's Corner today often hear the sound of Wilder's disembodied screams, still echoing through the ages from the night of her murder.

There's another ghost story about Nuuanu Pali Drive for fans of the occult. It has many variations, but they all involve a teenage girl. In some versions, she's an unknown runaway; in others, she was from one of the local households. All the variants agree that the young woman hanged herself from a tree, perhaps using her own jump rope. The site of the suicide has been variously reported as Morgan's Corner or one of the ends of the drive. In any case, the girl's body wasn't found for several days after she was reported missing, and by then her weight on the rope coupled with decomposition had caused the teenager's head to separate from the rest of her torso. (Some tales say her head was only partially detached.)

Folks claim the girl's apparition can be seen jump-roping down Nuuanu Pali Drive at night. There's a conflicting urban legend that says the spirit drifts down the road with her head in her hands. Others have seen the revenant of her corpse still hanging from a tree limb. Even more people have spotted a dark, unidentifiable shape among the leaves. Regardless of where the phantom is spotted, those who get a good look at it say that half of its face is rotted away.

Palani Road
Island of Hawaii

For such an enduring ghost story, there are very few details about the haunting on Palani Road. Located on the Island of Hawaii (or, as it's usually called, the Big Island), Palani Road is part of Hawaii Route 190, an inland, cross-island highway that stretches between Waimea and Kailua-Kona. Palani Road is the section between Kailua-Kona on the coast and Route 180 up in the hills.

Sometime in the 1950s, a woman, whose name has been forgotten in time, was flying down Palani Road on a stormy, moonless night. Tears streamed down her cheeks. She was angry and heartbroken, but most of all feeling betrayed, having just caught her boyfriend in the arms of another woman. Completely unaware of the speed she was traveling on such a slick road, she lost control of her vehicle at a hairpin turn. The car flew from the roadway and crashed into a tree, killing her instantly.

There have been numerous similar accidents at that spot over the past sixty years, most of them ending with a collision into that same tree. Almost all of the motorists who survived said that they had swerved to avoid hitting a mysterious woman, who was soaked and sobbing, standing in the middle of the road. Of course, by the time anyone else arrived on the scene, the anonymous apparition was long gone.

IDAHO

Old Highway 30 Bridge
Caldwell

In 1922, the American Bridge Company built a one-lane, three-span, 388-foot-long, through-truss bridge over the Boise River in Caldwell. The official name of the span when it opened was the Boise River and Canal Bridge, but since then it's become known by other names, including the Red Train Bridge and River Road Bridge.

The road crossing the bridge was the Idaho Pacific Highway, which later became US Highway 30. After I-84 was constructed outside of Boise in the 1960s, the portion of the road coming off the west side of the bridge was dubbed River Road, or Old Highway 30. The road heading southeast from the other end of the bridge was renamed Plymouth Street.

Sometime in the 1920s or 1930s, an unidentified woman hanged herself from one of the spans of River Road Bridge. It's claimed that when the sun is just right, her ghostly shadow will appear on one of the trusses.

Sadly, the poor woman is far from the only one who's committed suicide on the bridge, but most if not all of the others have leapt to their deaths. The spectral sound of thrashing water can sometimes be heard while crossing or standing on the bridge, wafting up from the river far below. Paranormalists attribute the splashing to the ghosts of the departed drowning victims.

Finally, area residents frequently see an inexplicable eerie light on a small, uninhabited islet in the river. When it does materialize, the light normally appears at 7:00 p.m. Despite repeated attempts, no one has ever discovered the source of the glowing orb.

Silver City Road
Silver City

Deposits of silver and gold were discovered in the Owynee Mountains in 1863, and prospectors and miners immediately flocked to the area. Silver City was founded the next year to cater to their needs. At its zenith, Silver City had about 2,500 residents and was one of the largest communities in the pre-statehood Idaho Territory. Unfortunately, most of the mines were played out by the 1890s, and the town's population declined rapidly.

Although nominally a ghost town, Silver City has never been completely deserted. About seventy of its original buildings still stand, all privately owned. Some of the structures have been fully restored, and the town has become an off-the-beaten-track tourist destination. The Silver City Historic District was added to the National Register of Historic Places in May 1972.

Located seventy miles south of Boise, Silver City is isolated and sits in the valley of a ridge at an elevation of more than six thousand feet. Almost all of its permanent residents leave town in late fall and return when the snow starts to melt. In fact, the main vehicular route into town, Silver City Road, becomes impassible during the winter and is closed. Even in the summer months driving it is no picnic.

The single-lane road turns southwest off Idaho Highway 78 and is well maintained by Owynee County for such a precipitous route. The first six miles or so are paved, but after that it's dirt and packed gravel all the way to Silver City. The narrow roadway climbs twenty miles up into the mountains, with steep grades, plenty of curves, a few hairpin bends, sheer drop-offs, and elevations topping 6,500 feet. The final descent into Silver City from New York Summit can be a real nail-biter. (You can find video of this last stretch of road at youtube.com/watch?v=eJfzOemGOQE.)

For such a small place, Silver City has more than its share of ghosts. The spectres of unknown workmen have been spotted in some of the abandoned mines, and one of the three cemeteries in town has been haunted by the revenants of Chinese laborers ever since their remains were exhumed and returned to their homeland.

In town, the Idaho Hotel plays host to at least four spectral guests, including a tuxedo-clad owner/manager who committed suicide in the building. Two men who argued over a claim and shot each other on the steps of the hotel have returned to the scene of their demise, and a woman dressed in fancy white lace appears in one of the upstairs rooms as well as on the hotel's balcony. Phantoms are also spied in some of the hotel's mirrors.

Even the streets of Silver City are haunted. The spirits of a little girl and boy are frequently observed playing marbles in the dirt roads through town, especially near the end of autumn and in early spring. Their clothing suggests they're holdovers from the mining town's heyday.

Also, the cries of "Screaming Alice," as the ghost has been nicknamed, sometimes echo down the town's dusty lanes. Legend has it that the young woman decided to leave Silver City after her entire family died from a disease that swept through the area. She booked passage on a stagecoach but it was later learned she never boarded it. Her luggage turned up, but Alice was never found. What happened to her remains a mystery.

For those of you adventurous enough to make the trip, the prospect of negotiating tricky switchbacks—or even running into spooks after you get to town—may not be the most troubling part of driving on Silver City Road. It's the possibility of being attacked by hideous, naked, cannibalistic dwarfs said to inhabit the caves dotting the Owyhee Mountains. The infernal imps, first mentioned in Shoshone and Bannock Native American lore, stand about two feet tall. They possess enormous strength and have extremely long tails, which they are able to coil up and carry wrapped around themselves. The fiends' favorite snack is supposedly small children, so if you take your kids along and have to get out of the car along the way, don't let them out of your sight!

ILLINOIS

Bloods Point Road
Cherry Valley

Bloods Point Road, also designated CR 12, is named for Arthur Blood, a prominent early settler in the township. The highway runs 5.5 miles from Fairdale Road eastward to Pearl Street, where the Bloods Point Cemetery is located. To the west of Fairdale Road, Bloods Point Road becomes River Road, and it turns northward to wrap itself around the eastern edge of the Oak Ridge Forest Preserve.

A phantom tractor-trailer, a spectral police car, and a ghostly pick-up truck allegedly travel Bloods Point Road, and all of them have been known to disappear in the blink of an eye. At night, luminous orbs are seen near the intersection of River Road and Sweeney Road. There's also the spectre of an elderly, shotgun-toting farmer roaming the area, trying to chase people away from what he believes to be his property.

Over the years, several creepy legends have become attached to a nondescript railroad bridge on Bloods River Road located about halfway between Pearl Street and the forest preserve. Sometime in the past, a school bus filled with children supposedly plunged off the bridge. Ever since, their apparitions have materialized on the span, although more often people just hear their screams. (Fact check: There's no historical record of the accident ever having happened.) Also, it's claimed that at least eight people were lynched or hanged themselves from the bridge, allegedly including Arthur Blood, his wife and family, and a witch. This last victim may or may not be the Witch Beulah who features in several local folk tales.

Hauntings reported at the cemetery include the sound of children laughing, an ephemeral barn that appears and disappears, those ubiquitous balls of lights, and a huge black dog-like beast, or hellhound. Also, electrical devices often seem to go haywire in and around the graveyard.

Cuba Road
Barrington

All of the paranormal activity on West Cuba Road seems to take place in the 0.8-mile stretch between Barrington Road (also known as IL 59) and Old Barrington Road, especially in the vicinity of White Cemetery. The phenomena include red or white orbs of light floating from the graveyard at night, phantom cows in the roadway, and the spectre of a woman on horseback who was killed in an accident nearby. There's also a male ghost that suddenly appears on the side of the road and immediately steps in front of an oncoming vehicle. The motorist feels the impact, but when he or she steps out of the car to help the victim, there's no one there.

A romantic daytime haunting takes place on Cuba Road every November close to the cemetery. The shadows of a man and woman walking hand-in-hand appear on the highway—not their ghosts, just their shadows.

Drivers about to cross the railroad tracks at the intersection of West Cuba Road and US 14 (also known as the West Northwest Highway) sometimes see the headlight of a phantom train off in the distance, presumably speeding toward them. Most cars stop to prevent a collision, even if the crossing gates haven't lowered. No matter how long they wait, however, the train never arrives. If the motorist gets out of the car to peer down the tracks, the light disappears.

Dug Hill Road
Jonesboro

The city of Jonesboro in southern Illinois is located on State Route 146, which passes through the town and continues westward until it meets SR 3/34 about two miles shy of the Mississippi River. The ghost story most associated with SR 146 involves a section of the highway about five miles outside of Jonesboro. It's referred to as Dug Hill Road because that portion of the route had to be cut through a small hill during construction.

Allegedly, a Union Army provost marshal by the name of Welch arrested three deserters and had them imprisoned in Jonesboro in April 1865. Following their release at the end of the war, the men tracked down Welch and shot him as he was driving a wagon through a narrow stretch of Dug Hill Road. They left Welsh's blood-soaked body on the ground where it fell.

Almost immediately, folks traveling on that section of the road reported seeing the ghostly body of a man lying facedown in the path in a pool of blood. Sometimes the apparition might be seen walking on the side of the road in bloody clothes instead. In all instances, the ghost looked to be solid flesh and blood, so people were stunned when the phantom would suddenly vanish.

The legend soon expanded to include Welch's cargo wagon, but as the story evolved the cart began to be described as a sinister-looking coach drawn by two black stallions, the sound of their hooves clopping as they passed. To avoid colliding with onlookers, the otherworldly horses and wagon would fly up and over their heads and then drop back to earth far down the road.

As ghost stories go, it's a good one, but there are multiple variations, and a few historical details compromise it. First of all, Welch was indeed gunned down, but it was in the middle of the Civil War in 1863, not 1865. The location of the ambush, if it even occurred, is hard to pinpoint. According to the old wives' tale, the passageway was supposedly called Dug Hill Road long before its state route number was assigned. Today, the only vestige of the name "Dug Hill" is Dug Hill Lane, a short, dead-end side road that branches off of SR 146. Also, several sources mistakenly cite the haunting as occurring on State Route 126, just outside Chicago. Even the number of assailants is disputed: Most retellings say there were three; others, only two; some, as many as a dozen. In one version of the ghost story, Welch's best friend betrayed him and let the attackers know which route Welch would be taking.

Finally, an urban legend having nothing to do with spooks deserves mention. Rumor has it that a terrifying boogeyman prowls the area. The creature is hard to miss: He's eight feet tall and always wears black pants and a white shirt. Most likely there is no monster, and he's a myth created by local parents to help keep their children in line. But then, like the legend of Welch's ghost, more than one fable has at least some basis in fact.

INDIANA

Old Porter Road, Stagecoach Road
Portage

Old Porter Road runs for about 3.5 miles between Willowcreek Road and South Mineral Springs Road in Portage. The street passes through a mix of residential and wooded areas with a few commercial properties thrown in along the way. Although the number of accidents on the street isn't unusual, several of them have been blamed on the sudden appearance of strange dog-like creatures in or alongside the roadway. Motorists describe the cryptids as skinny with unnaturally long legs and piercing yellow eyes. Even when the odd beasts aren't seen, drivers still hear their blood-curdling howls.

The strange animals have also been spotted running beside the railroad tracks that parallel Old Porter Road. In addition to these queer canines, unidentifiable dark figures have been observed walking the rails, but only in the winter months.

A few miles to the northwest of Portage, Stagecoach Road winds its way through a rural area between Dunes Highway (SR 12) and County Line Road. People in the area have reported peculiar lights in the nighttime sky, and motorists on the route have passed ghosts in outdated clothes.

Parke County Route W 40 N
Montezuma

Parke County Route W 40 N is located two miles southeast of Montezuma. It runs between US 36 and CR 600 W for just two miles. Sim Smith Covered Bridge is located on the roadway and is just one of thirty-one covered bridges in Parke County, Indiana. It spans Leatherwood Creek.

Constructed in 1883 by Joseph A. Britton and refurbished in 1973, Sim Smith Bridge is only 101 feet long, 16 feet wide, and 14 feet high. It was put on the National Register of Historic Places in 1978.

It's said that a fatal accident occurred on the bridge just seven years after its completion. A Native American woman, carrying her baby, entered the covered bridge one night while walking home to Montezuma. Unfortunately, before she could finish crossing, a fast-moving horse and buggy hurled onto the bridge. It's unknown whether the mother couldn't be seen in the dark or whether the carriage couldn't stop in time, but she and the baby were stuck and killed.

Not long after the tragic incident, people approaching the one-lane covered bridge began to hear the clomping and rattling of a horse and buggy inside the structure. Naturally, they always pulled off to one side to allow the coach to pass before they entered, but the phantom carriage would never emerge.

It's also been claimed that, if you stand on the Montezuma side of the bridge, sometimes you'll see the ghost of an uncommonly tall Native American woman with her baby on the other side of the creek, walking toward the bridge. She goes in, but never comes out.

It's not just motorists and pedestrians who experience the phenomenon. People fishing in Leatherwood Creek have heard and seen the spectres, too. The sightings occur most often just outside the bridge itself, but the apparitions of the woman and child have been spotted on Park County Route W 40 N as well.

Primrose Road
South Bend

Legends last a long time. (That's one of the things that, by definition, makes them legends.) Most of the ghost stories about South Bend's Primrose Road predate its being paved and the construction of two housing developments.

Local folklore says that if you drive slowly along this 2.3-mile road at night with your headlights off, freaky things may occur, especially in the wooded areas. If you travel at exactly 20 miles per hour, your tires will go flat; your car's engine will die if you stay at exactly 30 miles per hour. Cell phone reception often cuts out. You may hear unseen spirits telling you to turn around and leave. A female ghost occasionally materializes and grants you good luck or bad, depending upon how she sizes you up.

People have claimed that a phantom farmhouse frequently appears in the open fields along the road, and now and then spectral horses are spotted in the pastures of the real farms. Drivers passing through the forested sections of Primrose Road have noticed piercing eyes glaring out at them from between the trees. Finally, Satanic rituals were supposedly carried out in these woods, including human sacrifices, and a few motorists have encountered the ghost of one of the cult's female victims.

To get to Primrose Road, take Exit 72 off of the Indiana Toll Road (I-80/I-90). Turn right (north) onto US 31. Take the Brick Road/Cleveland Road exit. Turn right onto Brick Road. In just over three miles, you will come to a "T" at Primrose Road.

IOWA

Highway 34, Stony Hollow Road
Burlington

The phantom of an African American man carrying a small leather bag walks the north side of Business Highway 34 between Burlington and Danville. (Sightings of the spectre, which always occur between one and two in the morning, long predate the modern four-lane US 34.) Legend says the man was an escaped slave from the 1860s who died of diphtheria and was buried in the basement of a house somewhere along the road.

Stony Hollow Road (County Road H50) is located about fifteen miles north of Burlington, where it meanders through rolling farmland between County Road 99 and US 61. Folklore tells the story of a local woman named Lucinda who made plans to elope with her boyfriend. They were to meet at the top of a high mound next to the rural lane that is now CR H50. Her beau failed to show and, filled with despair, she leapt to her death off the sheer bluff at one end of the knoll. Her troubled spirit now roams Stony Hollow Road at night.

It's claimed that if you stand at the face of the infamous cliff at night and call Lucinda's name three times, her ghost will materialize on top of the hill. (In one variation, you have to be standing on the top of the hill when you say her name.) Be careful what you wish for, however: Supposedly if the apparition places a rose on the ground in front of you, you will die the next day! Another version of the old wives' tale says that Lucinda was married, and she jumped off the cliff because her husband, not her fiancé, had deserted her.

I-80
Des Moines to Mitchellville

I-80 is a 2,900-mile, transcontinental highway that runs east to west, all the way from Teaneck, New Jersey, to San Francisco and was one of the original routes in the Interstate Highway System. Among the many major cities I-80 passes through is Iowa's state capital, Des Moines. Our ghost story concerns a spirit that haunts just eighteen miles of that interstate, the stretch from Des Moines east to Mitchellville.

You see, sections of I-80 follow the historic Oregon Trail and the California Trail. No doubt a Native American footpath existed between the Des Moines and Mitchellville areas prior to pioneer expansion westward and long before cities were established and modern roads constructed. Fur trappers were active in the area no later than 1690 when a series of "forts" (really glorified trading posts) were established along the Mississippi River. Similar structures were built along the Des Moines River.

Judging by the frontier clothing the apparition on I-80 always wears, he was a fur trader from that era. You'll know it's the trapper's ghost when you see it. Besides his telltale garb, the spectre glows. Take a good look while you can: He will vanish the instant your vehicle's headlights fall directly on him.

And to be fair, the phantom probably doesn't know he's on I-80. He's simply following an old hunting trail.

KANSAS

State Highway 243
Hanover

Neither snow nor rain nor heat nor gloom of night stays these couriers from the swift completion of their appointed rounds.

It was the ancient Greek historian, Herodotus, and not the US Postal Service, who coined that memorable phrase. And he wrote it in praise of the fifth century BCE Persians, who had successfully developed a system of horse-mounted messengers to quickly relay information throughout their empire. Herodotus could just as well have been writing about what became the Pony Express.

By 1860, railroad tracks and telegraph wires had only gotten as far west as St. Joseph, Missouri, and travel by stagecoach the rest of the way to the Pacific was slow. The Pony Express was established to speed communication. The company promised to deliver mail, newspapers, or other written messages from St. Joseph to Sacramento, California, in just ten days!

This nearly impossible feat was accomplished by having dozens of riders on horseback at any given time; half of them heading west, the others east. The first part of the approximately two-thousand-mile route followed much of the Oregon Trail, but after that it dipped down through Salt Lake City and Nevada to reach Sacramento. Along the way, riders cut distance—and precious time—by being able to travel across terrain that Conestoga wagons and stagecoaches couldn't.

The Pony Express was set up with relay stations ranging anywhere from five to twenty-five miles apart. The courier would shout as he approached a station so everything would be ready for a smooth, rapid transfer. Horses were changed at every station; riders would cover about seventy-five miles per day.

In addition to being exhausting, the trip was also extremely dangerous, with riders having to endure everything from scorching heat and snowstorms to attacks from wild animals or Native Americans. Also, a rider carried only the mail pouch, which also contained his pistol and water. It took a very special type of man—or sometimes boy—to ride for the Pony Express.

In all, there were 100 to 120 hundred riders hired. Four hundred horses were stabled, and about 190 stations were built or converted from existing structures. The first rider for the Pony Express set out from Missouri on April 3, 1860.

Sadly, the glorious experiment lasted just eighteen months. Starting in the spring of 1861, the Pony Express could only run between Salt Lake City and Sacramento due to the onset of the Civil War. Telegraph lines, though, had continued extending westward, and they delivered information faster, cheaper, and more reliably. The Pony Express announced its closure on October 26, 1861, two days after the first transcontinental telegraph was completed.

Today, a century and a half later, only one of the original Pony Express stations remains unaltered, sitting at its original location. The eponymous Hollenberg Station, located about 125 miles from St. Joseph and just 7 miles south of the Nebraska border, was built by Gerat and Sophia Hollenberg as their residence and a supply station for pioneers traveling west. It contained a store and a bar and acted as the local post office. During the time the building was used by the Pony Express, their riders were housed on the second floor.

After the Hollenbergs' deaths, the station became a farmhouse. To preserve the property, the State of Kansas bought the structure and seven surrounding acres in 1941. Twenty years later it was listed on the National Register of Historic Places, and since 1963 the Kansas Historic Society has maintained and operated the Hollenberg Pony Express Station Historic Site as a museum.

Yes, you can visit the Hollenberg Station, but beware: Several phantoms from the past may still be rooming there. Both guests and staff of the museum have heard the undeniable, unmistakable sound of horse hooves galloping outside on State Road 243. The clopping noises have occurred during the day as well as at night. People have also heard the faraway voice of a young man calling to the station to be ready for his arrival, but no apparition ever appears. No one has ever discovered a source for the disembodied sounds—at least, not a living source.

Though short-lived, the Pony Express was an extraordinary undertaking and a unique part of American history. It still captures the imagination of anyone who's heard its story. Perhaps some of its participants don't wish to be forgotten, or maybe they want the adventure of riding their old trail just one more time.

US 56 and 189th Street
Burlingame

US Route 56 is a 640-mile northeast–southwest highway that runs from Kansas City, Missouri, to Springer City, New Mexico. Much of it follows the old Santa Fe Trail used by pioneers to move westward.

Burlingame, located twenty miles or so south of Topeka, was a regular stop on the trail. The small community, with only about nine hundred residents, is surrounded on all sides by miles of sparsely populated farmland.

US 56 enters Burlingame from the east and then turns ninety degrees to the south in the center of town. Then, after a mile or two, the highway crosses West 189th Street. The intersection is nondescript, surrounded by vacant fields except for a tiny chapel on the southwest corner.

But here's where it gets spooky. At night, the ghost of a man, dressed head to toe in black, appears at or near the intersection. The apparition has been seen walking the roads in all four directions, but if a person or vehicle gets too close, the phantom instantly vanishes. The manifestation is all the more strange because no one has a clue as to the spectral stranger's identity or why any spirit would want to haunt the intersection.

KENTUCKY

Florence Street
Corbin

What could be more terrifying than seeing a ghost? Sometimes it's *not* seeing the spirit, but knowing that it's there waiting. Such is the case when folks travel on Florence Street in Corbin, Kentucky.

Florence Street is narrow and paved, but short. It is less than a half-mile long, and as it snakes its way northward from West Wentworth Street to Byrley Road, it passes through dense woods. Motorists and pedestrians alike have reported feeling anxious or afraid on this stretch, sometimes to the point of panic, or becoming physically ill. Almost everyone who has ventured down Florence Street sensed they were being watched by some unknown, perhaps otherworldly, being the whole time they were there.

South Pope Lick Road
Fisherville

There have been reports since at least the 1940s that Fisherville has been home to a half-man, half-beast creature that locals refer to as the Pope Lick Monster. The beast acquired the name because it's frequently spotted on South Pope Lick Road or in the fields lining Pope Lick Creek.

The cryptid is also sometimes called the Goatman because it walks upright, has the upper body of a man (albeit with a curled horn protruding from each temple), and the lower body of a goat. Unlike the better-known but unrelated Goatman found in Maryland legends, the Kentucky monster is often seen surrounded by a herd of feral goats.

Fisherville is located about ten miles east of Louisville. The stretch of South Pope Lick Road that has the most Goatman sightings is just north of its intersection with Taylorsville Road (State Route 155), especially near an old train trestle for the Norfolk Southern Railway. The mysterious Pope Lick Monster isn't aggressive, but he's been known to lure victims onto the tracks, where they've been struck and killed by oncoming locomotives.

LOUISIANA

Mona Lisa Drive
New Orleans

New Orleans is one of the most haunted cities in the United States. Many of its early ghost stories feature Marie Laveau, the flamboyant Voodoo Queen, who lived in the Big Easy for eighty years back in the nineteenth century. A lesser-known figure, from a tale set in the early 1900s, is a young woman named Mona, and the story involves her affluent father and the girl's beau, a sailor.

Mona and the hearty seaman would take long walks through the city park whenever he was in port, which was a very public display of affection for the time. Her family was not only wealthy but also well regarded in society, so Mona's father insisted she stop seeing the young man. Distraught, the girl committed suicide.

Mona's father doesn't appear in an alternate version of the legend. Instead, the sailor simply breaks up with Mona, telling her his ship is about to sail. She becomes hysterical at the news and angrily throws herself at the young man. In the altercation that follows, the sailor, whether by accident or in a blind rage, kills Mona and, to hide his murderous deed, throws her body into a pool of water.

Regardless of which variation you choose to believe, soon after Mona's death her grieving father gave the city an impressive collection of statues. His only caveat was that one particular bronze, made in her likeness, had to be prominently displayed in remembrance of his daughter. It was decided to place the work in a cul-de-sac at the end of a new, one-mile paved road dubbed Mona Lisa Drive (also called Mona Lisa Lane) within the expansive New Orleans City Park.

Over time, the isolated area became a popular lovers' lane as well as a spot for teens to party. Others came to show off their souped-up cars. Unfortunately, a heated race around Mona's statue ended with one of the vehicles spinning out of control and striking the pedestal. The sculpture was knocked down and shattered.

The site became off-limits for a time, but after several months, people forgot about (or lost interest in) the accident. Young couples began to return to park on Mona Lisa Drive at night. That's when the hauntings began. Over the ensuing weeks, the sound of wails and sighs from Mona's spirit started to be heard, as did her ghostly fingers tapping and scratching on car windows. If the occupants dared to peek out, they were startled to see a female apparition dressed all in white. She would have a crazed, tortured expression on her face and would be trying to force open the door. Talk about breaking the mood!

Word soon circulated and, once again, folks began to avoid Mona Lisa Drive. Before long, the phantom expanded her territory, and her ghost is now encountered all over the park. But, sooner or later, Mona's spirit always returns to the narrow street that bears her name.

MAINE

Brownville Road
Millinocket

Maine State Road 11, a two-lane paved highway, connects the town of Millinocket to Brownville, about forty miles to the southwest. Sections of the route have local names as well. As the street exits Millinocket, ME 11 is also known as Brownville Road. About five miles outside of town, it crosses a narrow channel connecting Elbow Lake and Quakish Lake via an old truss bridge.

Sometime in the 1940s or 1950s—sources vary—a newlywed couple was traveling on Brownville Road. As they came up to the bridge, the husband lost control of the vehicle, and their car plummeted down the embankment. In some versions of the tale, the vehicle fell from the bridge instead. By some miracle, neither of them were killed, but the car was a total loss. The man told his wife to wait there while he went to get help. When the husband returned, she was gone. And she was never seen again.

Now as motorists approach the bridge, they sometimes find their vehicles surrounded by a dense fog, and occasionally the spectre of the missing bride, now called the White Lady, appears in the mist. Her unexpected presence startles and often frightens those who see her, but she has never hurt anyone. It's been suggested, however, that while the woman waited by the wreckage, an assailant descended from the road above and stole her wedding ring. An abduction could explain her mysterious disappearance. Perhaps the bride's ghost returns to search for the thief and her ring—and to exact revenge.

Goose River Bridge
Rockport

Only thirty-five miles southeast of Augusta, Rockport is a picturesque town and art colony. It's located where the Goose River empties into Penobscot Bay, an inlet

of the Atlantic Ocean. The town, settled in 1769, was also known as Goose River until 1852. During the Revolutionary War, the village was frequently raided and ransacked by British soldiers.

In 1779, William Richardson, who was already fighting the British by guerrilla warfare, assisted Samuel Tucker, a privateer, in capturing one of England's supply ships. Richardson's identity was unknown to the British, so he met with their local troops, claiming to be a sympathizer, and offered to guide their next vessel into port. They readily agreed. They were taken by complete surprise when their ship was set upon by Tucker's men and captured. Unfortunately, that didn't end the British army's presence, and the town suffered many more indignities at their hands before the end of the war.

When news of the Treaty of Paris granting America its independence from England finally arrived in Goose River, a spontaneous night of revelry broke out. No one partied more than Richardson, who spent most of the night, a pitcher of beer in hand, wandering up to folks to refill their mugs. In the wee hours he was on the bridge out of town that spanned the Goose River when he came upon three strangers, far away from the other merrymakers. Richardson cheerfully offered them a drink, not realizing they were all Tories, still loyal to the Crown. The men responded by fatally bashing in Richardson's skull with the butts of their rifles.

(In many versions of the story, the three outsiders were on horseback and they trampled Richardson's body as they fled the bridge, ensuring his death. In another variation of the tale, the attack occurred in a back alley near the bridge, and the assailants left Richardson lying in the dark, empty lane to die.)

It wasn't until the bridge was replaced in 1920 that Richardson's ghost began to appear on it, presumably at the spot where he died. His phantom has been nicknamed "the Pitcher Man," because he still carries one, the same way he did on that night so many years ago. He offers passersby a drink, often startling those he approaches from behind. The apparition has one more quirk: He's been known to shove his spectral pitcher of ale through open car windows if the vehicles are driving slowly enough. So if you're in the neighborhood and thirsty, why not try your luck and cross the bridge? It's on Pascal Avenue. And the drinks are on Richardson!

US Route 2A
Haynesville

Haynesville is a small rural town on the Mattawamkeag River in northeastern Maine. The community lies about ten miles from the US border with New Brunswick, Canada. There are just over a hundred full-time residents, and all of them have heard the old wives' tale that a wooded stretch of US Route 2A just outside of town is haunted.

The spectre seen most frequently is a woman standing on the shoulder of the road frantically signaling for a vehicle to stop. Sometimes the driver first notices her running alongside the car; on occasion, she simply appears in the road in front of the vehicle. Regardless, she tells any motorist who pulls over that it's her wedding day. She says that she and her new husband have just been in an accident and that he's still trapped in their car. The driver offers to assist, invites her into the car, and they take off. Imagine the motorist's shock when, just a few minutes down the road, the new bride evaporates into the aether. Now and then, the apparition disappears before she even gets into the stranger's vehicle!

Supposedly, sometime in the unknown past, two newlyweds, names long forgotten, were in a horrendous solo car crash at that very spot on a bitterly cold evening. The husband was killed instantly. The bride managed to escape the wreckage, but she was injured and unable to walk. She froze to death while waiting for someone to find her.

There are claims that there's also the revenant of a young girl walking along part of Route 2A. In some versions of the story, there are two girls! Just like in the tale of the phantom bride, the girls vanish from a rescuer's vehicle if given a lift. This legend seems to have some basis in fact. In August 1967, two young ladies, their identities lost to storytellers, were fatally struck by a passing semi on that section of highway. Some reports say that, instead, the youngsters were hit by two separate tractor-trailers on the same day. Regardless, neither of the spirits seems to be aware they're no longer alive.

Not everyone believes the ghost stories, of course, but no one disputes that there seems to be a disproportionally high number of wrecks on US 2A, also known in that area as Military Road. The spur was constructed between 1828 and 1832 to speed supplies to a military post in Houlton, twenty-four miles to the north. Today, Route 2A is a paved, two-lane highway with several sharp curves. The highway is often covered with snow and ice during the brutal Maine winters, and it's particularly dicey to navigate safely when the weather is bad. Before I-95 was extended past Bangor, however, US 2A was one of only three routes available for vehicles, including big rigs and produce trucks, traveling south toward Boston.

The large number of fatal accidents on US 2A inspired a young composer, Dan Fulkerson, to write a "trucker song" entitled "A Tombstone Every Mile."

Dick Curless recorded it in 1965, and it reached #5 on the *Billboard* country music chart. It's possible to see an old video of Curless singing the tune on an episode of *The Buck Owens Show* posted at youtube.com/watch?v=0g5I5r4XBps.

MARYLAND

Ardwick Ardmore Road, Fletchertown Road, Lottsville Road, Zug Road
Bowie

These four roads, scattered in and around Bowie, Maryland, have one eerie thing in common: They all access areas in Prince George's County where the mythic creature known as the Goatman has been sighted. The man-beast closely resembles the satyr of Greek mythology or the ancient Roman faun, which had the upper torso of a man (except for the two horns on his head) and the lower body of a goat, complete with fur-covered legs, tail, and cloven hooves.

According to an old wives' tale, the Goatman was the tragic result of an experiment on goats gone wrong at the Beltsville Agricultural Research Center. A scientist somehow accidentally contaminated himself during the trials and quickly began to mutate until he completely transformed into a terrifying man-goat hybrid. He fled the lab and was forced to banish himself from society.

Others say the beast is simply a disheveled, hairy hermit who lives alone somewhere in the forests around Bowie. He's rarely spotted, but when he is, it's always late at night. Most often he's seen slowly walking alone on one of the backwoods roads.

In the 1970s, the Goatman was blamed for a series of dog disappearances, mutilations, and killings. He's allegedly attacked couples, especially at a lover's lane on Fletchertown Road, and he's been known to rush onto roads and attack random moving vehicles with an axe.

If a Goatman actually exists, he's a cryptid, one of a class of unusual animals not recognized by zoologists and whose existence is based solely on old wives' tales, eyewitness testimony, or secondary, inconclusive evidence (such as footprints or fuzzy photographs). That would put him in the company of Bigfoot, Mothman, chupacabras, and the Loch Ness Monster, to name just a few. That alone might make someone seek him out, whether it would be dangerous or not.

Shakespeare Street
Baltimore

The town of Fell's Point, also written as Fells Point, was established on the Patapsco River by William Fell around 1763 when he and his son, Edward, began to lay out village streets and sell parcels of land. The Robert Long House, built in Fell's Point in 1765, is the oldest surviving house in Baltimore.

In 1773, the village merged with the nearby community of Baltimore Town, which had already combined with neighboring Jones Town, and together they were officially incorporated as the City of Baltimore in 1797.

Located in the inner Baltimore Harbor, Fell's Point was a major commercial and shipbuilding port up until the Civil War. By the mid-twentieth century the area had fallen into urban decay, but preservationists have since restored or renovated many of the waterfront structures and rows of townhomes to make it a tourist-friendly quarter. The Fell's Point Historic District was added to the National Register of Historic Places in 1969.

Fell's Point is also very walkable, apparently even for the dead. Shakespeare Street, a five-hundred-foot-long lane between South Broadway and South Bond Streets, plays host to a male phantom who strolls the block late at night. Perhaps because the spectre is dressed in eighteenth-century garb, many people think he's the revenant of William or Edward Fell.

MASSACHUSETTS

Battle Road
Lexington

Although the infamous "shot heard round the world" wasn't the cause of the American Revolution, it may well have been the incident that ignited the war. British Lt. Col. Francis Smith had been given orders to disarm the rebels in the Lexington-Concord area and destroy their weapons. He marched down Battle Road, which linked the two communities, on April 19, 1775, with an army of seven hundred men. To his surprise, he found a militia of eighty men under the command of their captain, John Parker, lining the sides of the road in full sight. When the Americans refused to surrender their guns, the British fired, killing eight of the men.

The original Battle Road cannot be driven on today, but a peaceful five-mile pedestrian path called the Battle Road Trail follows much of its route. Hikers have reported feeling frightened or having an inexplicable sense of anxiety when they walk down the wooded lane, especially around 5 a.m.—the same time the confrontation took place in Lexington all those years ago.

Many folks believe that the trauma of that first fight for freedom has echoed down through the centuries and is causing today's hauntings on Battle Road Trail. Or it may be restless spirits of the seventy-three British soldiers who lost their lives at the Battles of Lexington and Concord, some of whom were allegedly buried along Battle Road. Of course, neither of these explanations would account for the ghosts of young children that have also been seen on the path.

US Route 44
Rehoboth

An apparition known as the Redheaded Hitchhiker has been haunting US Route 44 between Rehoboth and Seekonk for as long as anyone can remember. He's been seen all along that five-mile corridor, but the tall spectral man manifests most often at the official boundary between the two small towns. It's hard to miss him if he's around: The ghost is forty to sixty years old, sports a full beard and head of red hair, and wears a red flannel shirt, work pants, and boots.

Your mom always told you when driving not to pick up strangers, and this particular hitchhiker is certainly strange. First of all, once you get a really good look at him, you realize his body is translucent. Also, you might not get a chance to offer him a lift because he's been known to vanish as soon as a motorist slows to a stop. If the hitchhiker does climb into your car, he usually disappears before you've traveled very far, sometimes while giving out an odd laugh. Sometimes you don't have a choice whether to give him a ride: The spectre simply materializes in your back seat, stays for a while, and then dissolves, leaving no trace he was ever there. A few drivers have had the misfortune to run over him when he suddenly popped up in the middle of the road in front of their cars. As is typical in such ghost stories, when the motorist stops to look under his vehicle, no one is there.

MICHIGAN

Hatchet Man Road
Gobles

28th Avenue is a straight, ten-mile, east–west road that runs between Gobles and Kalamazoo. The surface is paved except for a two-mile stretch where the road crosses Campbell's Creek, roughly halfway between Fish Lake Road (County Route 653) and North Van Kal Street. Locals have nicknamed this thickly wooded dirt stretch Hatchet Man Road.

The moniker refers to an incident that legend says took place there in the 1980s. Somewhere along that dusty bit of 28th Avenue, a paranoid survivalist supposedly built a "bomb shelter" on his property to save himself and his family in the event of a major disaster. Already obsessed and suspicious of the world around him, he soon moved in. But he lived there alone, never being able to convince his family to leave their house and join him. Finally, his brain snapped. Perhaps he decided even his family was out to get him. In any case, he took a hatchet and hacked them all to death.

Before long, rumors started to circulate that Hatchet Man Road was haunted, even though none of the paranormal phenomena that reportedly occurred there ever seemed to be connected to the grisly murders in any way. For instance, people's cars change gear or stall out as they approach the creek at night, and sometimes it's impossible to restart the engine. Phantom vehicles materialize and just as suddenly evaporate. Human apparitions float alongside cars or cross the road; other spectres peek out from behind the trees. In addition, weird sounds emanate from the forest, including disembodied footsteps and strange voices. And, of course, there are the inevitable spooky, luminescent orbs, but some folks also encounter flashing streaks of orange, red, and gold.

Morrow Road
Algonac

Morrow Road is a straight, two-lane blacktop north of Algonac, Michigan. It runs for about 2.5 miles from Shea Road southward to Holland Road, crossing the Beaverdam Drain and Swartout Creek. The upper half of the Morrow Road is lined with houses and open fields, but the other end runs through forest.

Morrow Road began as a cattle trail back in the 1800s. The path was later converted into a dirt road for motor vehicles and stayed that way for many years before being paved. The urban legends heard most often about Morrow Road involve a mother and son, both of whom died somewhere on the short stretch.

In the most basic version of the ghost story, the young lad leaves the house to play one winter day without telling his mother. When she notices he's missing, she runs out to search for him, but before she can find him, they both die of hypothermia.

Here a few more variations of the old wives' tale:

- The boy's mother found his lifeless body after he had frozen to death. She then hanged herself in guilt for not having watched her son more closely.
- An unknown assailant murdered the youngster while the boy was playing down by Swartout Creek. The killer then hid nearby, waiting for the boy's mother to come looking for her son. As soon as she showed up, the thug jumped out, grabbed the woman, and killed her, too.
- The boy didn't run off: He was kidnapped. When there was no ransom note or telephone call demanding money, the mom went out on her own to find him. She died in the search.
- The mother and son lived in a two-story house along Morrow Road. Burglars broke in and, whether it was part of their plan or not, wound up killing the two during the robbery.
- Rather than dying by ice and snow, the mom and her boy succumbed in a fire.
- The child was a baby, and the mother had him out of wedlock. She took the infant to the stream and gently placed him on the creek bank under the bridge. Filled with remorse on the way home, she rushed back to bridge to save her child, but by the time she arrived the infant was gone. She spent the rest of her life mournfully pacing Morrow Road, searching for her baby. (In the 1950s there was a short-lived addition to this retelling that an ogre known as the Morrow Road Monster found the abandoned child, carried him off to the woods, and ate him.)

An apparition of the youngster (or baby) has never been seen on Morrow Road, but the same can't be said for the mother. Her ghost is spotted at night, usually close to where the bridge once stood. She's always seen wearing a thin blue night-gown and is often waving her bloodstained hands in the air. Even if she doesn't materialize, motorists can sometimes hear her hysterically calling out to her son. The spectre has been known to leave its bloody handprints on the sides of passing vehicles. Occasionally, people have been chased by unexplainable, colored orbs of light or they see them in the adjacent forest. Ghost folk believe the lights may be the disembodied spirits of the mother and son.

Oh, and there's one final haunting: If you stop your car where the bridge used to be and honk your horn three times, you're often rewarded with the sound of a phantom baby crying, sometimes from far away, sometimes from the culvert that replaced the bridge.

MINNESOTA

Timber Lake Road
New London

Timber Lake Road, a section of 240th Avenue West in Colfax County, is located just north of Sibley State Park in central Minnesota, about an hour's drive southwest of St. Cloud and 130 miles northwest of Minneapolis. The narrow, paved lane passes through forest and farmland and stretches between County Route 121 (5th Street Northwest) to the east and County Route 5 (35th Street Northwest) to the west. Although it would only be about 5 miles long as the crow flies, Timber Lake Road may be almost twice that length because of its many bends and curves, some of which are quite sharp.

At some unknown time in the past, a woman who lived along the country road came home to discover that all of her children had been murdered while she was away. In utter despair, she hanged herself from a tree near the house. Her troubled spirit, dressed in white (or, some say, red) now walks back and forth on Timber Lake Road, hoping to find the killer.

The woman and her offspring were buried in the small Colfax Cemetery, which is located at the intersection of Timber Lake Road and County Route 5. The youngsters' ghosts have been seen running through the graveyard. A howling dog and a shrieking woman have been heard in the area, but an apparition has never materialized of either one.

There are other entities haunting Timber Lake Road, too. Motorists have spotted disembodied, burning red eyes peeking out at them from the woods, and occasionally they catch a glimpse of fully formed phantoms!

MISSISSIPPI

Nash Road
Columbus

Nash Road, also known as Three-Legged Lady Road, got its nickname from a gruesome local legend. In the version heard most often, a young girl was kidnapped, murdered, and dismembered. Her assailant then tossed her body parts into the forest that borders both sides of Nash Road. The youngster's mother searched up and down the street, trying to locate her little girl, but the only thing she ever found was one of her daughter's legs.

Despite there being no chance of ever finding her daughter alive, the anguished mother continued to pace Nash Road on her own two legs, with her child's leg clutched to her bosom. Eventually, the mother died, by then out of her mind. Now it's her apparition, with her daughter's phantom leg in hand, that motorists sometimes encounter on the wooded stretch. Thus, the sobriquet Three-legged Lady Road.

Apparently you can have an ethereal "three-legged race" with the ghost if you happen upon her on Nash Road and she feels in the mood to play. But be forewarned: Not only will she keep up with your car, she will repeatedly throw herself against the side of the vehicle, trying to force you off the road. So far she's never been successful at that, but she only gives up the pursuit when you leave the woods. Oh, and check your car the next day: You may find some very real dents in it.

A coda to the story suggests that the spectre, for some reason, was drawn to an abandoned church on Nash Road. Supposedly, if you parked your car outside the empty church, turned off your headlights, and sounded your horn three times, the "three-legged" phantom would appear. She would come up to your car, bang on the hood, and then chase your vehicle as you sped away. There were also rumors that a Satanic cult sometimes met in the former church to practice human sacrifices. Both tales became moot when the building was eventually razed.

There are several other ghost stories about the road's nickname that are even creepier, but none of them involve a kidnapped girl. One of them dates back to the mid- to late-nineteenth century. When a man discovered his wife was having an affair with a Civil War veteran, he killed the former soldier, dragged his corpse down Nash Road, and dismembered him. After hearing the news, the woman ran down the road looking for her lover's remains. All she found was one of his legs.

She retrieved the limb, brought it back to her house, and sewed it onto her own body. She soon went insane, murdered her husband, and then committed suicide.

In a slight twist, some say it was the husband who was the adulterer, not the wife. When the woman found out she had been betrayed, she flew into a fit of rage. She killed the cheating husband and chopped him into little pieces—except for one his legs, which, for some reason, she sewed onto her body. A memento, perhaps? At least she gave the rest of his remains a decent burial.

In perhaps the strangest version of the tale, the woman developed a rare medical condition that required doctors to stitch her organs together and let them hang outside of her body. Dangling down from her torso, the organs resembled a leg.

Regardless of whether or not any of the many versions of the story actually happened, locals claim the woman's ghost still appears, most often between 2661 and 4548 Nash Road.

MISSOURI

Bloomfield Road
Cape Girardeau

Since the 1830s, Bloomfield Road, in one form or another, has served as a major artery between Cape Girardeau on the Mississippi River and the city of Bloomfield, thirty-six miles away. Over the years, the road's original route has been broken into a hodgepodge of state highways, city streets, and rural lanes.

Hauntings on Bloomfield Road have been reported since at least the late eighteenth to early nineteenth centuries. The first recorded ghost story told of a headless horseman, who may have been a Revolutionary War soldier decapitated by a cannonball. They say the spectre still materializes from time to time, but more often a headless man is seen walking down the road. (Of course, the latter ghost could be the same apparition, simply not on horseback.)

An angry phantom nicknamed Mad Lucy loudly screams as she storms back and forth on the section of Bloomfield Road closest to what was once Mount Tabor Park. (The property, a county-owned recreation area for several years, returned to private ownership in 1983.) Some people believe that Mad Lucy is the revenant of a girl who was murdered in or near the park in the 1970s. Others claim the banshee's been around much longer and is the ghost of a woman who was severely but not fatally injured in a horse-and-buggy accident in the 1800s.

Wilcox Road
Poplar Bluff

Wilcox Road (County Road 554) zigzags its way through Missouri farmland for about two miles, from Main Street in Poplar Bluff to where the Black River passes under I-60. Along the way, the road makes about a half dozen ninety-degree turns; in between the bends, each segment is almost a perfectly straight line. On one of the north–south straightaways close to the river, Wilcox Road passes over a set of Union Pacific Railroad tracks that are in active use.

Urban legend says the crossing is haunted due to a train having derailed there in the early 1900s, killing most of the passengers. The subsequent investigation turned up some strange anomalies. For example, one man had been decapitated, but his head was never found. When another victim, a pregnant woman, was examined further, it was discovered that the baby was missing from her womb.

The most-often heard ghost story about Wilcox Road is that if people drive up to the tracks between 10 p.m. and midnight and turn off their car's engine, the interior windows will rapidly fog up, making it almost impossible to see through the glass. Soon, everyone in the vehicle will hear a faraway train whistle that gets louder and louder as the phantom train gets closer and closer. Many folks also see the train's single front headlight, which increases in intensity as the ghost train approaches. Sometimes the occupants of the car hear tapping on one of the steamed-up windows, and if they look out, they can just barely see the faint apparition of a woman asking for her lost baby.

Then, without warning or explanation, all of the freakish phenomena suddenly stop. The shrieking train whistle, the bright headlight, the fog, the apparition, everything! They all disappear, and then there is nothing but dead silence.

WARNING: NEVER STOP YOUR CAR OR PARK ON A SET OF RAILROAD TRACKS. Although many versions of this legend say you must park your car on the tracks for the paranormal activity to occur, DON'T DO IT! The same goes for any haunted railroad crossing.

Playing "Ghost Train," as Poplar Bluff locals call it, is a dangerous game, and one you could very well lose. Distances are often much shorter than they seem, and a train that looks to be a mile or more away could be upon you in an instant. Although you may want to believe the locomotive is an apparition, it may very well turn out to be all too real.

As recently as June 2012, a fatal collision took place at the Wilcox Road crossing outside Poplar Bluff, killing two of the five people in a Jeep. When an Amtrak train unexpectedly appeared on the horizon, the driver was unable to restart the vehicle. Three of the occupants managed to escape but, in the panic, the other two were unable to unhook their seat belts.

There's a completely different haunting that occurs at the tracks, usually at night, and the spectre looks so real that people don't realize they're looking at a ghost—until she abruptly disappears. The mesmerizing vision is that of a girl or young woman, some say with Native American features, who's seen walking toward cars at the crossing. She has straight, long brown hair that hangs gracefully over the shoulders of her white sleeveless wedding dress. For whatever reason, the spirit always carries a water bucket.

MONTANA

US Route 87
Great Falls to Fort Benton

US Route 87 is a north–south road that stretches for some two thousand miles from northern Montana to southern Texas. A male ghost known as the Black Horse Lake Phantom is frequently seen hitchhiking along forty miles of the highway between Great Falls and Fort Benton, Montana. The spectre is often described as having long, straight black hair and wearing jeans. He got his nickname because most people encounter him near Black Horse Lake, which is usually dry except in the spring and early summer months.

If a motorist slows to pick him up, the spectre unexpectedly leaps onto the vehicle's hood, smashes his body against the windshield, and then rolls off the side of the car out of sight. When the startled driver stops to help the injured stranger, no one is ever there. Nor is there any damage to the vehicle.

Some folks have reported the hitchhiker as being Native American, wearing traditional tribal garb from the time of the American frontier. Regardless of its ethnicity, the ghost is always mistaken as being flesh and blood—up until the time it disappears, of course.

Wallace Street
Virginia City

Nine mining camps grew up almost overnight on a fourteen-mile stretch of Alder Gulch after gold was discovered there in 1863. The largest and most prosperous of these was developed into a full town to service and supply the miners. It took the name Virginia City and was made the first capital of the new Montana Territory.

By the time Montana became a state in 1875, gold in Alder Gulch had become scarce, and most of the area mines had been abandoned. The camps became ghost towns, but somehow Virginia City managed to hang on, even after the state capital was moved to the more-thriving city of Helena.

Virginia City had two subsequent mini booms. The first lasted from 1898 to the early 1930s when dredging was brought in to salvage the last of the gold ore. Quartz mining then sustained the town until America's entry into World War II, when almost all nonessential US industries were shut down or assigned other duties.

Fortunately, throughout all of this, Virginia City and its historic storefronts have changed very little—so little that in 1961 its downtown area was named a National Historic Landmark District. Located just ninety minutes from Yellowstone National Park by car, the town's main business today is tourism. Its year-round population is only about two hundred inhabitants.

State Route 287 runs through the center of Virginia City, and the two-lane paved roadway takes the name Wallace Street as it transits town. Several apparitions walk the main drag at night, but all of their identities are unknown. Two of the more frequently seen ghosts are a lady and a little girl, perhaps a mother and daughter. There's the spectre of a woman on horseback galloping down the street and the phantom of a Civil War soldier dressed in uniform. Perhaps the most unexpected revenant is that of a nun who peeks into windows, especially those of the Bonanza Inn—which itself is very haunted.

Not all of the spirits in Virginia City stick to the streets. Private homes and shops have reported getting phone calls with no one at the other end. Doors open and shut by themselves, there are disembodied voices, and things sometimes fly off the shelves on their own.

Finally, no visit to a "ghost town" is complete without a trip to the graveyard, particularly if it's an Old West–era Boot Hill. Fortunately, Virginia City has one, completely separate from the town's main burial ground. It's located about a half mile above town, but it's an easy walk or a short drive on a dirt lane to get there. If you go at night, don't be surprised if you see an apparition or two roaming among the headstones and wooden markers.

NEBRASKA

Alma City Streets
Alma

Alma is located at the junction of US Routes 136 and 183, close to the Kansas border. The town was founded by Union Pacific Railroad workers in 1873, and it incorporated as a city in 1871. Today there are about 1,200 residents.

The streets of the 1.15-square-mile community are laid out in a more-or-less rectangular grid pattern, and there have been sightings of an unidentified ghost known as the Alma Nightwalker on many of them. Indeed, the female phantom has been spotted strolling in the streets all over town. She doesn't seem to favor any particular road or sidewalk. The unidentified spectre, dressed in a long black robe, appeared with some frequency around the start of the twentieth century, but she shows up much less often today.

L Road/Seven Sisters Road
Nebraska City

L Road is situated about five miles southeast of Nebraska City. Its haunted section runs for about 2.5 miles from the Missouri River west to S. 68th Road. Locals refer to it as Seven Sisters Road due to a horrific event that allegedly occurred there back in the 1800s. The story goes that a farmer, his seven daughters, and a son lived in a house somewhere along the road, and that one of the two men murdered all seven of the sisters.

In the most common version of the tale, the son stormed out of the house after a vicious family fight and, still seething, hid nearby. As soon as his father left to go into town, the young man returned to the house and tied up his siblings. He then took each sister, one at a time, to the top of one of seven different nearby hills and hanged her. (It's unknown where the killings took place—if at all— because there are few hills of any size in the area.)

Nevertheless, motorists on L Road hear the victims' terrified shrieks all along the route, even though their apparitions never manifest. Sometimes vehicles will inexplicably stall or have other electrical problems on Seven Sisters Road, such as headlights dimming or going out entirely. If anything out of the ordinary occurs while you're driving this street, it's probably best not to linger.

NEVADA

Six Mile Canyon Road
Six Mile Canyon

Six Mile Canyon Road (formerly State Route 79) is located about fifteen miles north of Carson City and is named for the mountain pass it traverses through the Flowery Range. The 7.9-mile two-lane blacktop road connects Virginia City (at the western end of the canyon) to US Route 50. Six Mile Canyon saw some of the earliest mining efforts in Nevada, and one of the men drawn to the area was a bandit named Jack Davis.

Davis opened a livery stable in the community of Gold Hill, three miles south of Virginia City on today's State Route 342. The business offered him respectability and masked the fact that he was also secretly robbing trains, stagecoaches, and wagons, primarily those transporting gold and silver from the area mines. Davis set up a secluded bullion mill in Six Mile Canyon to melt down the stolen metals into untraceable bars, which he then sold. To avoid suspicion of his true wealth, Davis buried most of his ill-gotten fortune somewhere in Six Mile Canyon.

His luck ran out in 1870 when he was sent to jail after a bungled train heist. Davis was paroled five years later, but in 1877 he was fatally shot during a failed attempt to hold up a stagecoach. His treasure has never been found.

Nor will it ever be if Davis's ghost has anything to say about it. His shrieking apparition scares away anyone in Six Mile Canyon that he thinks is seeking the hidden cache. If his screams don't work, the phantom has been known to suddenly grow wings, fly into the air, and swoop down on would-be thieves.

There's a video of a drive through Six Mile Canyon posted at youtube.com /watch?v=iRZMy1S8VF8.

Highway 375
Crystal Springs to Warm Springs

Nevada's State Route 375 isn't haunted, but it's of interest to paranormal enthusiasts because motorists have reported a high number of UFO sightings while driving the route. The southern terminus of the two-lane macadam road is at US 93 in Crystal Springs, about a hundred miles north of Las Vegas. The highway stretches to the northwest for about ninety miles until it hits US 6 in Warm Springs. There had been so many claims about flying saucers along SR 375 over the years that in February 1996 the State of Nevada gave it an official nickname: "The Extraterrestrial Highway."

Highway 375 has also long drawn the attention of ufologists because the highly classified US Air Force facility known as Area 51 is located within the Nevada Test and Training Range on the desert flats southwest of SR 375. Area 51 is famously where the remains of one or more alien beings and a "flying disc" were allegedly taken after the saucer (again, allegedly) crashed outside of Roswell, New Mexico, in July 1947.

South Sandhill Road, East Sahara Avenue
Las Vegas

The 0.2-mile stretch of South Sandhill Road between East Charleston Boulevard and East Olive Avenue parallels I-515/US 95, and it's one of the most haunted roadways in Las Vegas. Two of the spooks seen there are a man and woman who died in a motorcycle accident close to where large culverts run under the interstate. The apparition of at least one other woman has been seen standing at the opening of the drainage ducts. The channels are only 3 feet high; nevertheless, the openings have been fenced off so that no animals or people can crawl into them. Nevertheless, folks have reported hearing human groans and voices coming from inside the pipes.

About half of a mile to the south, a phantom car with a female driver chases vehicles on East Sahara Avenue (SR 589). As soon as the ghost car and driver are spotted in the rearview mirror, the spectral pursuer instantly vanishes. Legend has it that the otherworldly woman harasses cars that she thinks drove down a nonexistent private driveway in front of her long-gone house.

NEW HAMPSHIRE

Indian Rock Road
Nashua

Nashua Airport (also known as Nashua Airport at Boire Field) is located three miles northwest of downtown Nashua, not far from the Massachusetts border. It dates back to 1934, when the city of Nashua purchased land containing an existing grass runway to establish a regional airfield. The landing strip was paved, new hangers were added, and in 1943 the property was christened Boire Field to commemorate the city's first casualty in World War II, Ensign Paul Boire.

Tree-lined Indian Rock Road runs northward from Pine Hill Road just a few blocks west of Boire Field. After passing several houses and taking two sharp bends to the left, the half-mile-or-so street comes to a dead end at a meadow. People traveling on Indian Rock Road or hanging out in the open pasture have reported the sensation of being watched by unseen eyes. Others have spotted shadowy, ghostlike figures, and a few folks have observed the apparition of a tall Native American man. Glowing orbs of light flitting over the empty field at the end of Indian Rock Road have also been reported.

It turns out that the original runway and parts of the airport expansion had unknowingly been built over the graves from the Pennacook tribe, which inhabited the region in the 1770s. And any lover of ghost stories knows that nothing good can come of disturbing an "Indian burial ground." Many paranormalists suspect that restless spirits of the Pennacook are responsible for the hauntings along Indian Rock Road.

Island Path
Hampton Beach

Island Path is a 0.75-mile two-lane, paved road in Hampton Beach. It runs between Ashford Avenue, which is a short section of State Route 1A and Ocean Boulevard, and Hampton River Harbor to the southwest. Hampton Beach is the seaside resort district for the town of Hampton, so there are plenty of houses along Island Path, but there are also marshy fields lining much of the road's length. These areas are prone to sudden fogs, and inexplicable, blinking lights often cut through the heavy mist. Travelers on Island Path also sometime see a hazy yet unmistakable female form floating over the meadows. Many folks believe the ghost is Eunice "Goody"

Cole, who lived in Hampton back in the seventeenth century and was accused of witchcraft on three separate occasions.

Goody Cole was born in England in 1590. She and her husband William, a carpenter, came to America in 1637 soon after completing their time as indentured servants for a wealthy London merchant. As part of their contract, they had received passage to the New World. After a brief stay in what is now Quincy, Massachusetts, the Coles moved to present-day New Hampshire, first to Exeter and then to Hampton, where they purchased forty acres.

In 1656, thirty-six years before the famous witchcraft trials in Salem, Massachusetts, Goody Cole was accused of the hellish crime. New Hampshire was still part of Massachusetts at the time, so she was imprisoned in Boston, the colony's capital. She was released in 1660, but the charges were never dropped. Goody was taken back to jail in 1662 to further await trial, and she was finally acquitted sometime between 1668 and 1671. Incredibly, she was charged with witchcraft again in 1673, but she was quickly found not guilty. In 1680, however, Goody Cole was arrested a third time for practicing witchcraft. Although never formally indicted, she was nevertheless sent to prison, where she died before the year was out.

Was Goody Cole really a witch? Almost certainly not. But she was mean, devious, and vindictive—which gave her neighbors more than enough reason to despise and want to get rid of her. The courts also had a vested interest in witchcraft trials: The Crown seized the property of those found guilty.

According to local legend, a stake with an iron horseshoe attached to it was driven through Goody Cole's heart before she was interred. (The belief that horseshoes ward off evil dates to ancient times, perhaps as far back as eighth-century Chaldea. Iron itself was once thought to have magical powers, and it was a particular bane to witches. One old wives' tale suggests that it was because witches so feared iron that they took to broomsticks rather than travel on horseback.)

The site of Eunice Goody Cole's grave remains a mystery. It's thought that she and her husband lived on Winnacunnet Road in Hampton, and a few sources claim she was interred less than half a mile away, close to the intersection of Park Avenue and Landing Road. Popular lore, however, says she was buried somewhere along Island Path in Hampton Beach, which would explain why her phantom haunts that particular roadway.

Ossipee Mountain Road
Ossipee

Ossipee Mountain Road is located between Moultonville Road and Pine High Road just outside the small town of Ossipee. It runs for approximately four miles along the western side of Raccoon Mountain.

For years, a spectral horse, sometimes pulling a coach, was known to travel the forested roadway. The steed purportedly belonged to Adam Brown, a local mill owner, who was ambushed and murdered by an angry neighbor on a narrow stretch of Ossipee Mountain Road bordering a deep ravine. The attacker jumped out from hiding and jerked the startled horse's bridle, causing the animal to rear back, lose its footing, and plunge into the canyon to its death—dragging along Brown and the wagon. Soon afterward, folks traveling on Ossipee Mountain Road began to hear—but never see—the distinctive clip-clopping of a horse and cart coming up behind them. The noise would get louder and louder as they approached the ravine, but the sounds would instantly stop at the exact spot the tragic incident had taken place.

According to Patricia Edwards Clyne in *Ghostly Animals of America*, the hauntings ended for good when Ossipee Mountain Road was paved. A few other paranormal authors report that the horse's phantom still shows up from time to time, alone without coach or driver, and is now clearly visible. The eerie equine will abruptly "appear" behind a vehicle and gallop up to it, always keeping a discreet distance. It will then just as instantly vanish.

There are other oddities in the area as well. The region is dotted with small but "bottomless" lakes left behind as glaciers receded at the end of the last Ice Age. Native Americans considered one of them, Ossipee Lake, to be sacred. One of their massive burial mounds—with no occult associations—was discovered off the western shore of Ossipee Lake around 1800. It contained the skeletons of close to ten thousand tribespeople. They had been buried in a seated position facing outward from the center in a series of tiered, concentric circles.

In modern times, locals have reported seeing UFOs hovering above the lake district, with some of the spacecraft diving into the waters. (This has led to a myth that secret underground passageways connect many of the lakes. If any such tunnels are ever found, however, they would most likely be naturally occurring volcanic vents, not subterranean shafts dug by aliens.)

NEW JERSEY

Clinton Road
West Milford

Clinton Road winds its way northward from State Route 23 to the Warwick Turnpike at Upper Greenwood Lake. The lonely, two-lane blacktop runs through a large forest, and, for several miles, snakes around the 424-acre Clinton Reservoir.

The road crosses Clinton Brook near the southern end of the reservoir, and it's said that if you toss a coin over the creek's bridge at midnight, the ghost of a little boy will throw it back to you. According to the old wives' tale, the youngster was walking across the bridge one night when a fast-moving vehicle sped around the corner leading up to the bridge and struck the lad, sending him flying into the air. The boy was either killed instantly or died shortly after from his injuries. There have been so many fatal vehicular accidents at the bend approaching the bridge that it's been nicknamed "Dead Man's Curve," and several people who lost their lives there have returned as spirits to haunt it.

Motorists on Clinton Road have reported chatting with two park rangers near Terrace Pond, only to later discover they had been talking to a couple of ghosts. There were no rangers on duty the day they drove by, and the ones they saw had died in 1939.

Ghost trucks have been known to appear out of nowhere and chase panicked motorists down Clinton Road before instantly vanishing. Supposedly a phantom Chevy Camaro with its ghostly female driver can be summoned from the Next World by simply talking about her fatal accident, which occurred in 1988.

There are also claims of hellhounds and other weird creatures roaming Clinton Road at night. Some folks believe that the beasts are the hybrid descendants—or the revenants—of animals from a local drive-through safari called Jungle Habitat that closed in 1976. One of the fiends is a wolf-like cryptid with burning red eyes.

And that's just the tip of the iceberg. Motorists have also allegedly sighted UFOs, run into a secret community of albinos in the adjacent woods, and seen evidence of Satanic rituals. A drive down Clinton Road is eerie enough during the day, but it might be downright dangerous at night.

Garden State Parkway
Toms River

Toms River township is located in east-central New Jersey at the junction of the Garden State Parkway and New Jersey State Route 37, about forty miles north of Atlantic City. Of course the community, which was founded in the 1760s, long predates the current parkway, which was built between 1946 and 1955.

At 173 miles in length, the Garden State Parkway extends from the southern tip of New Jersey up to the New York Thruway. It is the longest highway in New Jersey, and it's also one of the busiest toll roads in the United States. The route's most frequently mentioned haunting takes place at night near Exit 82, which is located where the parkway meets US 37 in a giant cloverleaf. The exit is split: Exit 82 heads east toward Island Beach State Park and the beach; 82A takes motorists west toward Lakehurst.

Ever since the road was completed, a male ghost dubbed the Parkway Phantom has been seen trying to cross the highway at Exit 82 and at different spots for about four miles in each direction. No one knows his identity or has a clue what may have sparked his arrival. He's reportedly very tall, wears a nondescript, belted topcoat, and always waves his arms, bent at the elbows, to warn oncoming traffic as he makes his way across. So far there have been no reports of auto-apparitional collisions.

NEW MEXICO

Alto Street
Santa Fe

Santa Fe, New Mexico's capital, is on I-25 in the north-central part of the state. Founded by the Spanish in 1610, it is one the most haunted cities in New Mexico, with many of its ghosts dating to its colonial past.

One of the phantoms is a caballero, which, in the Southwest, simply meant a gentleman on horseback. The spectre is most often seen waving a sword as he rides down Alto Street, which is now just a short, paved road along the Santa Fe River. What distinguishes this ghost is that he has no head. An old wives' tale claims that two Spanish witches removed the horseman's head after he complained that a love potion they'd concocted for him didn't work.

South Canyon Road
Alamogordo

Monte Vista Cemetery is the largest cemetery in Alamogordo, and interments date back to the 1860s. With a main entrance on East 1st Street, the burial grounds are flanked by Washington Avenue to the west, Playa Azul Street to the south, and South Canyon Road to the east. The graveyard has long been the site of numerous nighttime hauntings, including the appearance of an unknown female dressed completely in white, sudden patches of fog, and balls of light that dart above the headstones.

It seems the paranormal phenomena aren't confined within Monte Vista Cemetery's borders, however. They're known to frequently float out onto South Canyon Road, especially the Woman in White.

State Route 14
Madrid

Madrid is located about twenty-five miles southwest of Santa Fe on State Route 14. Also known as the Turquoise Trail, the highway passes through the center of Madrid and is the tiny community's principal street. Before the Spanish came looking for silver, local Native Americans collected iron and turquoise in the area. Gold was discovered around 1800, but it was soon depleted. The town, founded in 1869, turned to mining coal, which continued until the mid-twentieth century. Once the mines closed, Madrid emptied out. Artists discovered the ghost town a few decades later, as did tourists, and today there's a small but thriving artisan community in Madrid.

The apparitions haunting the town all seem to be revenants of the Old West. The restored Mine Shaft Tavern seems to be particularly active. The two phantoms encountered most often show up outdoors. They're the spectres of a Spanish woman and a cowboy, both dressed in period garb, and they stroll together down the main street of Madrid after dark.

NEW YORK

Sweet Hollow Road, Mount Misery Road
West Hills

Sweet Hollow Road, located on Long Island, New York, stretches to the southeast from the West Jericho Turnpike (New York Route 25) to Walt Whitman Road (NY 110). Along the way, it bisects West Hills County Park.

The route has several fascinating and very different hauntings. One is the phantom of a policeman who pulls over cars for seemingly no reason. He asks motorists a few trivial questions and then always lets them go without a ticket or even a warning of any kind. No one would give such an encounter much further thought, except that when the officer turns to return to his patrol car, the motorist sees that the back of the policeman's head is missing. It's as if it had been blown off by a gun. Indeed, local lore says that's exactly how the phantom policeman lost his life, and it happened not too far from where his spirit reappears.

Then there's the ghost of Mary, a Woman in White, who either jumped or was pushed out of a moving vehicle on Sweet Hollow Road during a heated argument with her boyfriend. She might have survived had she not been run over and killed by another vehicle. Her apparition has returned to reenact her death by hurling itself in front of passing cars.

Some nights, a small group of children is seen walking along Sweet Hollow Road, all of them dressed in clothing from the early twentieth century. It's said that there used to be a day camp for kids in the area in the 1930s—until all the children were slaughtered in a horrific mass murder.

Of course, the youngsters could be the revenants of an entirely different bunch of kids. People still talk about the snowy winter day that a school bus skidded out of control on a Northern State Parkway overpass and plummeted onto Sweet Hollow Road below, killing all of the students onboard. Rumor has it that if you put your engine into neutral in the underpass, the children's spirits will push your car out of the tunnel to prevent another accident from happening there. (In a variation of this particular legend, there were no children and no bus. Instead, the ghostly Samaritan is a woman who died after crashing her car at the underpass.)

Oh, and that's not all for the Northern State Parkway. It's purported that, at some uncertain time in the past, three teens committed suicide by hanging themselves from the bridge above Sweet Hollow Road. Every so often, motorists driving that way at night see the spectres of all three bodies swinging from the overpass.

Mount Misery Road, less than a mile to the west, parallels Sweet Hollow Road. It starts at the junction of Chichester Road and Hartman Hill Road and runs to the south toward the Northern State Parkway. The paved portion of Mount Misery Road runs alongside West Hill County Park for about 0.75 miles before ending abruptly. The route continues as a walking trail through the recreational area, and the path continues southward until it merges into the Walt Whitman Trail, which is part of the Long Island Greenbelt Trail system.

An urban legend says that a mental asylum was located on or near Mount Misery Road back in the 1700s. The sanatorium was allegedly burned to the ground by one of its female patients, who also threw herself into the flames. Her ghost, garbed in a white hospital gown, roams Mount Misery Road at night.

Unfortunately, none of the incidents that supposedly led to the hauntings on Sweet Hollow Road and Mount Misery Road has ever been verified as having occurred.

NORTH CAROLINA

Mt. Misery Road
Brunswick

Among the options for those who want to drive the sixty miles from Brunswick to Fayetteville, North Carolina, is Mt. Misery Road, a section of SR 1426, a two-lane, rural blacktop that runs between highways US 74/US 76 and the city of Northwest.

The road takes its name from Mount Misery, a 25-foot-high knoll, now leveled, that was located about seven miles north of Wilmington. The landmark only appeared on maps dating from 1770 into the early 1800s.

According to historian Claude V. Jackson III, Mount Misery received its unflattering moniker because the sandy soil made it and surrounding fields difficult to cultivate. The name Mt. Misery Road was apt because, in pre–Civil War days, it was the preferred route for slave traders to march their human chattel inland from the coast. Many of the captives died along the way, and others were left for dead.

Today, many motorists on Mt. Misery Road find themselves inexplicably overcome with feelings of sadness, anxiety, or dread—even those who know nothing of the street's notorious past. Other folks swear they've heard the sounds of clanking chains and disembodied groans while on the roadway.

Edwards Road, formerly Payne Road
Rural Hall

There are probably more creepy tales about Payne Road than any other street in North Carolina, and they've been circulating since the 1960s and 1970s. The events actually occur on a street formerly known as Payne Road that is now called Edwards Road (SR 1903/SR 1961). The new name comes from an Edwards family that lived on the route back when the lane was still narrow and gravel.

Today, Edwards Road is paved and has two lanes, but navigating it is still tricky because of its many twists and bends. Traveling it at night can be down-right spooky. The road runs northward from State Highway 66 in Rural Hall, close to the intersection of NC 56 and NC 66, until the junction with the street that now bears the name Payne Road.

That's right. There's another Payne Road in Rural Hall: State Road 1961/1962. Once again, however, all of the events in the ghost legends took place on a section of the old Payne Road that's now known as Edwards Road. According to local lore, the lane was named for an Edward Payne, who was a plantation owner somewhere in the immediate area, even though there's no mention of Payne or his estate in the historical records.

According to legend, in the 1800s a farmer (who was possibly named Edwards) went on a rampage and murdered his entire family, one by one. His wife escaped with the baby, but he caught up with them on Edwards Road at the bridge over a small stream called Paynes Branch. The man decapitated his wife, drowned their baby (either in the brook or back in the well at the farmhouse), and then hanged himself from the bridge or a nearby tree.

This gruesome story may have grown out of an actual event that took place about five miles away in Germanton, North Carolina. On Christmas Day 1929, farmer Charles Lawson murdered his wife and six of his seven children and then committed suicide. His son Arthur, sixteen, only survived because he was away on an errand at the time of the killing spree.

Regardless, a rumor spread that if you stopped your car on the bridge on Edwards Road, turned off the ignition, and waited a few minutes, supposedly you'd be unable to restart the engine. In some versions of the old wives' tale, you had to whistle "Dixie" or walk around your vehicle before it would turn over. Otherwise, you had to push your car until it was off the bridge before it would run again. The original bridge is now gone, having been replaced by a culvert under Edwards Road.

There's another entirely different haunting that also allegedly takes place on the rural byway today. It's claimed that sometime around the start of World War II a young man was killed on Edwards Road after losing control of his car on a sharp curve. The vehicle slid across the gravel, crashed, and caught fire. Still alive but trapped inside the wreckage, the man suffered a slow, agonizing death. (In some tellings of the tale, the man managed to get free from the car but was engulfed in flames. Onlookers stood by helplessly as he burned to death.) Many modern-day motorists have reported seeing the headlights of a phantom car suddenly appear on the road, approaching them from behind. After a few tense moments, the lights simply disappeared. On rare occasions, the ghostly headlights would pop up in the opposite lane, approaching a vehicle instead. Drivers have identified the spectral car as a late 1930s Ford sedan.

East Main Street, Vickrey Chapel Road at US 70
Jamestown

Jamestown is home to North Carolina's most famous phantom hitchhiker: a spectral "damsel in distress" named Lydia who appears on East Main Street. Supposedly Lydia died in a car wreck in the early 1920s that occurred about half of a mile outside of town on a secondary road as it entered a railroad underpass. Her ghost was first reported in 1923 or 1924 (sources vary) by a motorist who had given the spirit a lift. The crash site became known as Lydia's Bridge, but the road leading to it no longer exists. It was replaced by today's East Main Street, which passes under the same railway a few hundred feet to the north. It's thought that Lydia's apparition, which still manifests itself occasionally, simply drifted over to the new street and underpass.

A variation of the tale locates the story about 1.5 miles to the southeast. The spectre, also named Lydia and dressed in white, flags down cars at the Vickrey Chapel Road underpass of US Highway 70. She tells those who stop that she's returning from a dance in Raleigh, which is 90 miles away, and needs a ride for the last 10 miles to her home in High Point.

The rest of this version follows the classic rendition of the ghost hitchhiker legend. (See chapter 1.) A driver agrees to take Lydia to her house, but as his car nears the address, she vanishes from the vehicle. Lydia's parents come to door to tell the puzzled stranger that, several years back, their daughter died in a car accident on that very night at the Highway 70 underpass where the motorist picked her up.

Getting between the two haunted sites is rather straightforward. If you're traveling east on East Main Street, Vickrey Chapel Road turns off to the right (south) about one thousand feet after you pass under the railroad tracks. Travel down Vickrey Chapel Road for about a mile until it intersects US Highway 70.

NORTH DAKOTA

137th Avenue Northeast
Backoo

137th Avenue Northeast (also known as County Road 12) runs in a straight north-to-south line for more than fifty miles. Its upper terminus reaches to within a few hundred yards of the Canadian border. Although there's a farmhouse and outbuildings every few miles, the road passes through vast, seemingly endless fields that stretch out flat in all directions to the horizon.

The haunted section of 137th Avenue Northeast is about ten miles long and runs from 94th Street Northeast (State Route 5) near Akra northward to 104th Street Northeast, close to Leroy. About halfway along the route is the small community of Backoo.

The apparition that's seen most frequently is a Woman in White wearing a noose around her neck. She only materializes after dark. Motorists' first sight of her usually occurs when she steps in front of the headlights of their cars as she crosses the road. Sometimes drivers reencounter the same, unmistakable spirit several miles farther down the road. Her identity remains unknown, but it's believed she hanged herself during World War II after she received news that her husband had been killed in action.

OHIO

US Highway 40
Cambridge

In the music world, the phrase "deep cut" can mean many things. It might refer to an obscure song that's relatively unknown to the public, a track that receives little radio play, a piece that's seldom performed in concert, or one that wound up not being included on a released album. But when it comes to the construction industry, the words "deep cut" should be taken literally: It's a physical slice dug deep into the ground, often through a hillside, to create a passageway for, say, a road, a canal, or even a pedestrian walkway.

The ghost of an unknown laborer haunts the Deep Cut in southeastern Ohio on US 40 between the towns of Cambridge and Old Washington. The man was killed by a fellow employee in a robbery gone bad, and to get rid of the body, the murderer buried the victim's decapitated body beneath the Deep Cut section of US 40. Now, drivers often see the victim's headless spectre walking along that stretch of highway.

A headless female apparition has returned to another part of the same highway. In the 1800s, she lived with her husband in a rustic cabin close to the trail that eventually became US 40. During a horrific argument, he chopped off her head. To his alarm, the woman's spirit began popping up soon after the incident, riding sidesaddle on a phantom white horse. Now she usually materializes at a switchback near the top of a grade on the highway, so locals gave her the sobriquet Lady Bend and nicknamed the slope Lady Bend Hill.

Intersection of State Routes 125 and 222
Amelia and Bethel

Several different kinds of hauntings take place at the intersection of Ohio State Routes 125 and 222, a spot that's been known as Dead Man's Curve for generations. The place got the nickname back in the 1800s when SR 125 was the old Ohio Turnpike. The section of road approaching today's OH 222 had a very steep grade. Getting to the top was difficult enough in the horse-and-buggy era, but at the summit there was also a sharp bend in the road. Over the years, many horses lost their footing and stumbled, leading to the carriage behind them toppling over, sometimes with tragic results. Hence the name Dead Man's Curve.

Accidents continued at the bend even after the stretch was incorporated into SR 125 and improved for motor vehicles. In fact, a larger percentage of the crashes were fatal because of the greater speeds involved. Finally, beginning in 1968, the State of Ohio did an "extreme makeover" of the highway, getting rid of the hill, flattening the road, softening the curve, and, for added measure, widening that part of SR 125 from two to four lanes.

No sooner had officials celebrated the reopening of the highway than it claimed another set of victims at the junction of SR 125 and SR 222, more or less where "Dead Man's Curve" used to be located. On October 19, 1969, a 1968 Chevy Impala carrying eight teenagers was struck by a 1969 Plymouth Roadrunner traveling more than one hundred miles per hour through the intersection. Only one person survived the collision.

Ever since, a shadowy male figure has been seen on the shoulder of the road near the site, usually around 1:30 a.m. The man often appears to be struggling to walk, as if he might be injured. As a car approaches, the spectre often sticks out an arm to hitchhike. Motorists who slow down enough to get a good look at the man will discover the phantom has no face. If the driver looks back after passing the guy, the spirit is gone. The apparition has also been known to throw itself in front of moving vehicles, and if drivers stop to see whether they've actually hit someone, the ghoul will suddenly pull himself out from under the front of the car, wrap his hands around the bumper or hood and try to drag himself onboard. And even if the spook can't get within arm's reach, it may chase the car or shower it with stones as it races away.

People have spotted ghost cars matching the descriptions of the Impala and Roadrunner from the accident, seemingly fully restored, tearing down the highway with no drivers or passengers inside. Occasionally one of the vehicles is seen parked on the side of the road, and a few brave individuals have gone up to touch it to find out if it was real. The car always seems solid enough, but later, if the person turns to take a last glance at the ghost car before leaving, it's gone, vanished without a trace.

Now that SR 125 has been reconfigured, there's some question as to exactly where Dead Man's Curve was located when it first received that moniker. There's almost no dispute, however, that the current intersection of SR 125 and SR 222 is haunted.

OKLAHOMA

East Easton Place
Tulsa

Highway 20
Tulsa and Pryor

North 289th East Avenue
Catoosa

It's always tragic when a child dies. The young ghosts of three otherwise unrelated hauntings on Oklahoma highways are all boys. There are few details about who they were, but one thing is certain: Their time on earth was cut short. Perhaps that's why they've returned from the Next World.

One of the spirits is seen on East Easton Place in Tulsa, very close to where the Admiral Twin Drive-In is located. The boy only appears between 2:00 a.m. and 4:00 a.m., and he's always barefoot. Although usually quiet, he's been known to suddenly burst out screaming. No one knows when or how he died.

The phantom of an eleven- or twelve-year-old hitchhiker has been seen several places along the forty miles of Highway 20 between Tulsa and Pryor. If he's given a lift, the phantom lad disappears from the vehicle long before it gets anywhere near whatever destination he gives the driver.

North 289th East Avenue is a north–south road in Catoosa that runs from the Verdigris River down to just beyond US Highway 412. According to local lore, a young boy was riding his bicycle on the road when he was struck and killed. His revenant now returns to finish his ride. He most often appears in the half mile of North 289th East Avenue north of US 412. Over the years, a few of the people who seemingly hit the ghost reported that they thought they had run over a living child, but when they stopped and checked, the boy and his bike were gone.

Quapaw

One of the most reliable ghost lights in the United States appears almost nightly down a straight, 3.5-mile, packed dirt-and-gravel road located about 6 miles east of Quapaw, Oklahoma. The east–west lane is technically East 50 Road, but everyone in the area calls it Spook Light Road or the Devil's Promenade. The country path ends at the Oklahoma–Missouri border.

The bright orange orb seems to be the size of a basketball, and it's always in motion. Some folks have claimed it gives off heat. It's acquired many names over the years, such as the Neosho Spook Light, the Devil's Jack-O'-Lantern, and the Hornet Ghost Light, but it's probably best known as the Joplin Light. Another moniker gaining popularity is the Tri-State Spook Light, because it manifests close to the shared borders of Kansas, Missouri, and Oklahoma.

According to Native American folklore, Indians first saw the spooky orb as they were forced to march westward on the notorious Trail of Tears in 1836. The light was probably seen by pioneer settlers by the time of the Civil War, and its name appeared in print no later than 1881 when it was mentioned in a publication as the Ozark Spook Light.

Scientists have no definitive explanation for the Spook Light, and even paranormal enthusiasts can't agree on what it is. One legend says it's the spectral lantern of a ghostly miner. He's searching for his wife and children, who were kidnapped by Native Americans warriors. Another tale suggests it's a spirit lamp or torch being carried by a decapitated Osage chief looking for his missing head. Yet a third story claims the radiant orb is the combined spirits of a young Quapaw couple. The girl's father, the tribe's chief, forbade their marriage, so the lovers eloped. Before they could be captured and separated, they took their own lives by jumping off a cliff into the Spring River.

If you're in Oklahoma, the best place to view the orb is about halfway down Spook Light Road between I-44 and the state line. If you're in Missouri, travel to the small hamlet of Hornet, about nine miles southwest of Joplin. The perfect time to see it is between 10:00 p.m. and midnight, preferably on a clear, moonless night. Obviously you should turn out all other illumination or lower it to an absolute minimum. And keep your distance: The orb tends to stay far away from crowds and loud noises.

OREGON

Oregon Coastal Highway
Cannon Beach

Starting in the 1960s, motorists on the Oregon Coastal Highway (US Route 101) about three miles northeast of Cannon Beach began to see what appeared to be a man, his face wrapped with bloody strips of cloth, standing on the side of the road close to the overpass above Sunset Highway (US Route 26). The man—actually a ghost—vanishes, only to instantly materialize in the back seat of a passing car. Almost before the driver can react, the unwelcome guest disappears. The awful scent of decaying flesh sometimes lingers in the car for days, and occasionally the motorist finds tangible proof of the haunting: a piece of the wound's dressing that was inadvertently left behind.

The apparition is known as the Bandage Man.

The phantom also loves to hop into the beds of passing pickup trucks. The driver is usually unaware of the ghostly visitor being there, however, until it starts to bang on the back of the cab. The spirit always vanishes before the truck has time to pull over.

While usually docile, the apparition has been known to smash vehicles' windows. Also, some versions of the story have most of his body wrapped, not just his face, making him look more like a mummy than a mere accident victim.

No one knows who the spectre might have been. Because the logging industry has such a big presence in Oregon, some believe he may have been a lumberjack who died in a sawmill mishap or while felling a tree.

Croisan Creek Road
Salem

Croisan Creek Road is a two-mile, two-lane paved street on the west side of Salem. It runs through a forested ridge from River Route South down to just past Kuebler Boulevard. (The road should not be confused with Croisan Creek Trail, also known as the Croisan Scenic Way, which is an abandoned road slightly to the east that's been turned into a nature walk.)

Although the trail can feel spooky at times, it's Croisan Creek Road that's home to a haunting. The scenario always unfolds in the same way. In the distance, the motorist sees a young girl and boy playing with a ball on the shoulder of the road. The ball gets away, rolls into the street, and the girl chases after it. As the car slows to avoid hitting them, the girl (and presumably the ball) suddenly vanishes. The boy wags his finger at the stunned driver, and then he too disappears.

The ghosts usually materialize close to the intersection of Croisan Creek Road and Kuebler Boulevard, where a car supposedly struck and killed a little girl sometime in the past. Most of the sightings take place on a Friday night, which is when the fatal accident allegedly occurred. As happens with so many ghost stories, though, the mishap that precipitated the haunting is impossible to verify.

PENNSYLVANIA

Bordentown Road
Tullytown

At first glance, it's easy to see why fans of the paranormal mistake the female spectre seen on Bordentown Road for a phantom hitchhiker. After all, she ticks off all the boxes: She's young, alone, wears a soaking-wet gown, and appears in the middle of the night. Also, now and then she actually does hitchhike! But usually the spirit isn't looking for a ride. Instead, she floats down to the edge of Van Sciver Lake or one of the nearby ponds and walks across on the water until she fades out of sight. At that point, ghost aficionados know they're not dealing with your ordinary, everyday hitchhiking spook.

Bordentown Road is a two-lane blacktop built on a narrow land bridge crossing Van Sciver Lake about twenty miles northeast of Philadelphia. Tullytown is located at the western end of the two-mile stretch. The street nominally ends on the other side of the lake just past New Ford Mill Road, but it continues as Old Bordentown Road for about another mile until it reaches the Delaware River.

Because of the late hours she manifests, the spectre acquired the nickname Midnight Mary. It's believed that she and her boyfriend were coming home from the prom when, tragically, their car ran off the road and sank in the lake. Both drowned. The boy's body was found, but Mary's remains were never recovered. She now spends eternity trying to get home from the dance, but her spirit is always drawn back to her watery grave.

Constitution Drive
Allentown

Although Constitution Drive is located on the south shore of the Lehigh River directly across from Allentown, Pennsylvania, it's hard to believe that it's located anywhere close to a city of 121,000 people. The 1.5-mile, bumpy stretch is only partially paved as it passes through a wooded stretch with no streetlamps. Even when one travels it in midday, there's an eerie sense of isolation and foreboding. The road begins at Cardinal Street to the east and parallels the Lehigh until the river bends northward. At that point, Constitution Drive curves south and continues until it ends at East Susquehanna Street. There's also a set of railroad tracks between the trees lining Constitution Drive and the river, and they're a central part of our story.

There have been rumors for years that motorists driving down Constitution Drive after dark sometimes hear the disembodied screams of a phantom little girl. It's also possible to pick up the sound of a high-pitched whistle wafting through the trees, day or night. But the ghost everyone in the area has heard of—and some have actually encountered—is a man who lost his life trying to cross that now-hidden set of tracks.

Little is known about the victim, including his age. He could have been a railway worker or was simply taking a shortcut across the tracks. In the most popular rendition of the legend, he was out walking his two dogs. No matter why he was there, he was fatally struck by a passing train. But he didn't die instantly. Instead, the grisly accident tore off one of his legs, and in such a desolate area there was no one there to get him to a hospital.

Most versions of the story say that the man's dogs stayed by his side as he clawed his way down the deserted asphalt street trying to get help. Eventually, the man bled out and died. Some variations of the folklore say it took him two days to finally give up the ghost. A few accounts add that, even after their master's remains were taken away, the trusty canines wouldn't leave the spot until, eventually, they too died. Of course, in some takes on the tale, the train killed them all instantly.

Regardless, the man's ghost and those of his faithful friends have apparently returned to haunt Constitution Drive. The stricken stranger's apparition has been seen struggling down the pavement, with blood streaming out onto the road behind him, usually with the spectral dogs at his side. Even when the man's spectre isn't around, folks have reported seeing the animals' fiery red eyes glowing in the darkness. In the winter months, those walking down Constitution Drive have often observed a double line of paw prints in the snow, always accompanied by a single line of human footprints.

Kelly Road
Industry

Kelly Road (State Route 4043) is a paved 1.6-mile rural lane in Industry, a small borough on the Ohio River about 25 miles northwest of Pittsburgh. The route runs north to south from Engle Road to Wolf Run Road. Its southern end wends its way through dense forest. People in the area have nicknamed this last stretch the Mystery Mile because of all the weird things that happen there.

In addition to playing host to several white apparitions that stay their distance, the road has a hitchhiking ghost. If you pick up the phantom, it will dutifully disappear before you get too far down the road. Wild animals that normally remain out of sight are unnaturally aggressive and sometimes run out to attack passing vehicles. Even pets act strangely if they're in the car with you on the Mystery Mile. Humans are not immune to the dark aura either, and some people become angry, anxious, or afraid until they emerge from the woods.

One of the most fascinating stories to come out of the forest tells of a man whose truck engine died on Kelly Road. As the driver was considering what he could do to fix it, a curious haze inexplicably appeared up ahead. Then, a group of young boys, dressed in clothing from the late 1800s or early twentieth century, strolled out of the mist and silently passed in front of the vehicle. As soon as they disappeared between the trees on the other side of the road, the truck instantly started up.

There's never been a good explanation for the paranormal activity on the Mystery Mile.

RHODE ISLAND

State Route 37
Cranston

Running for just 3.4 miles, State Route 37 is an east–west highway located about halfway between the cities of Cranston and Warwick. Also known as the Lincoln Avenue Freeway, its primary purpose is to connect I-295 to I-95 and US 1. The road was constructed between 1963 and 1969.

After a series of heavy rainstorms in June 2006, human remains were discovered along the westbound lanes of RI 37. A subsequent investigation discovered that the highway had inadvertently been built over an old, forgotten burial ground, the State Farm Cemetery. About three thousand people had been interred there between 1873 and 1918, but all of their wooden markers had worn away, leaving no trace of what lay beneath the surface.

As a result of the grim discovery, seventy-one bodies were exhumed, identified, and relocated, but the rest of the graves weren't disturbed and remain extant. The unearthed remains were reinterred in the State Institution Cemetery in Warwick, where a memorial service was held on July 14, 2009.

Spirits don't like to be disturbed, and one of the easiest ways to do that is to damage, disregard, or disrespect their final resting places. No wonder that, for more than fifty years, there have been reports of ghostly activity occurring on State Route 37 between what are now Exits 1C through 1E. In addition to the many apparitions that have been spotted, including sightings of glowing orbs, people frequently report having car trouble on that stretch of highway.

Tower Hill Road
Cumberland

Tower Hill Road links State Route 114 (Diamond Hill Road) to West Wrentham Road northwest of Cumberland. The narrow asphalt lane twists and turns its way for roughly 2.5 miles, much of it through a heavy forest scattered with small farms and private homes. Some of the houses are historic, dating back to the 1700s. There are many blind curves and few streetlamps for illumination.

Many of the ghosts seen along the route are children, such as a little girl, standing on the side of the road or sitting in front of one of the houses. There's the spectre of a young boy running with his dog and a phantom toddler who was struck and killed while riding his tricycle on the street. Youngsters' disembodied laughter rings out from behind the trees.

Native American apparitions are sometimes spotted along Tower Hill Road as well, and the sound of phantom war drums can be heard coming from the woods. Both of these hauntings may be revenants from King Philip's War of 1675–1676, in which many local warriors were killed. There have also been accounts of mysterious lights and inexplicable, radiant orbs along the road. A few people claim to have encountered zombies! Many motorists felt they were being watched, even if they didn't see or hear anything to cause that sensation.

The strangest sightings, however, aren't of ghosts or even the living dead. They're of a weird creature that's been nicknamed the Man Monkey. The elusive Bigfoot-like cryptid has stalked Tower Hill Road and the surrounding woods since the 1970s. Some say he's actually an extraterrestrial and can travel through dimensions and space at will.

SOUTH CAROLINA

Old Buncombe Road, Maybinton Road, Ebenezer Road, Brazzleman's Bridge Road
Newberry

Newberry lies just off I-26 about forty miles northwest of Columbia, South Carolina's capital. European colonists began to settle there in large numbers in the 1750s. Most of them were planters of English, Scots-Irish, or German descent. The village became the county seat in 1789 and, centuries later, still retains its small town charm.

The urban legend told most often around Newberry is probably that of the Hound of Goshen. The story has its roots in an incident that allegedly occurred somewhere outside Newberry on a highway named Old Buncombe Road, so-called because, at the time it was constructed, it linked Charleston with Buncombe County in the mountains of North Carolina. It's said that at some time in the long-gone past, an itinerant peddler came to Newberry with his trusty dog at his side. The huge canine was unmistakable, because it was the size of a mastiff or Great Dane but had white hair.

A rumor began that the itinerant salesman, the only stranger in town, was responsible for a series of small thefts that had recently beset the community. Mob justice reared its ugly head, and the vendor was unceremoniously dragged to a large tree and hanged. No sooner was the deed done than folks began to take notice of the traveling merchant's dog standing at the base of the tree. The forlorn canine stayed there, howling, for about a week, until one of the locals took it upon himself to "quiet" the dog for good.

You might think that would be the end of the story. Instead, it was just the beginning. Almost immediately after the execution, the true thief was discovered. Instead of the innocent trader's ghost returning to seek revenge, however, it was the spectre of his canine companion. Reports of it in the area have continued into the present.

Much of Old Buncombe Road was torn up and rerouted long ago, but sightings of the white spirit dog, now known as the Hound of Ghosen, still continue on the few extant sections of the original roadway. The majority of the segments are now within Sumter National Forest, and visitors may be driving on part of the highway without even knowing it. The ghost hound has also been encountered on other streets in the Newberry area, including Ebenezer Road and Brazzleman's Bridge Road.

Interestingly, the phantom dog's name refers to a place he began haunting in the nineteenth century: the community of Goshen Hill in neighboring Union County. The hound repeatedly materialized on Maybinton Road (SR S-44-45), which connects Goshen with Maybinton in Newberry County. This eight-mile stretch of highway passes through thick and largely uninhabited woods. The area is also prone to dense fog, which alone makes the route spooky.

The ghostly canine has an unnaturally toothy grin, which led to the spectre's other nickname, Happy Dog. But is the phantom friendly? Above the lopsided mouth, there's a set of flaming-red eyes! Most folks encounter the Hound of Goshen from afar, but there have been reports of the dog chasing after people, animals, and motor vehicles. The ghostly canine has also been known to pass through walls and closed gates! Seeing the demon dog is always frightening, but reviews are mixed on just how ferocious it is.

Carson Drive
Draytonville

Starting around 2014, residents of Carson Drive in the Draytonville community outside Gaffney began noticing an enormous white canine that loped down their lane from time to time. None of the neighbors had a dog matching its description, but no one was concerned—that is, until they realized what they were seeing was not flesh and blood but a ghost! The giveaway was when the hound raised itself up, stood on its hind legs, and began to chase them. There doesn't seem to be a link between the Ghost Hounds of Goshen and Gaffney—after all, they're sixty miles apart—but there's also no explanation as to why the otherworldly dog suddenly showed up on Carson Drive.

South Dakota

Spook Road
Brandon

Spook Road, technically 264th Street, is alleged to be the most haunted highway in South Dakota. Not that it's a highway in any sense of the word. The wide, east–west lane has a dirt-and-gravel surface and is closely lined by trees for most of its three-mile length. The haunted section is located about two miles south of Brandon and stretches from 481st Avenue (State Route 11) to 484th Avenue (County Highway 109).

There are several weird legends about this country road that has earned it the nickname Spook Road. The one heard most often is that you'll cross five bridges on 264th Street if you count them as you travel west to east, but you'll only cross four going east to west. There may be a supernatural explanation, but more likely people simply miscount because four of the concrete bridges are nondescript and look very similar. The other is a steel truss bridge.

But the road is haunted too, and all of the paranormal activity takes place at night. There have been claims that ghosts walk along the stretch after dark or peek out from behind the trees. Motorists and passengers all along the route have declared that they felt as if they were being watched. Sometimes phantoms suddenly pop into view from nowhere or vanish while you're looking at them. Several shadowy figures have been seen hanging from branches overhead, and a white phantom reportedly lingers outside South Beaver Valley Cemetery. One of the apparitions may be the spectre of a deceased person who was found on the side of the road in the late 1990s.

Spook Road is quite tranquil during the day, but it can be quite unnerving if you're caught on it after the sun goes down, especially during the dark fall and winter nights.

Spook Light Road
Fedora

A spectral glowing orb appears in Fedora on 224th Street, known locally as Spook Light Road (not to be confused with the similar-sounding Spook Road seventy miles away in Brandon).

Spook Light Road is a gravel path that heads north off State Route 34 about three miles outside of town. As the road's nickname suggests, the entity is an ethereal, illuminated sphere, and it's been seen all along the route for as long as anyone can remember.

The shining anomaly seems to have a mind of its own. It will suddenly materialize in front of your car and then vanish just before there would be a collision. Sometimes the ghost light creeps up to your car from behind. It chases your vehicle for a bit, but then picks up speed, passes up and over your car, and speeds on ahead. Occasionally, the ball takes a shortcut and passes straight through a vehicle, from bumper to bumper. People outside the cars have seen this eerie penetration happen, but the folks inside the vehicle were often blithely unaware that it had occurred.

Is it swamp gas? The reflection of distant headlights? Such explanations satisfy those who have never experienced the glowing orb on Spook Light Road, but believers in paranormal phenomena know better. Ghost experts are stumped as to the origin of the flickering light in Fedora, however. The legend heard most often is that the mysterious luminescence is the spectre of a lamp that once hung from a pioneer family's wagon. The westward-bound settlers were told that a snowstorm was fast approaching. Foolishly, they continued on, got caught in the blizzard, and died.

TENNESSEE

Netherland Inn Road
Kingsport

Netherland Inn Road, once known as the Old Stage Road, runs between a set of railroad tracks and South Fork Holston River in Kingsport. The stretch is named for the eponymous three-story Federal-style hotel, which was built on the north bank of the river between 1802 and 1808 and is located at the furthest navigable point to which goods could be shipped from the East.

Today, the west end of the two-lane blacktop road feeds into State Route 11W, and its other end merges into a roundabout with West Center Street and West Industry Drive. Even though it's only about two miles long, the street has at least three ghosts.

The apparition seen most often is that of Albert "Hugh" Hamblen. Back in 1922, he was visiting his son Charles, who was a patient at a hospital just down the road from the Netherland Inn. Hamblen sat at his unconscious son's bedside for hours, but as the evening wore on with no change in the young man's condition, the staff suggested Hamblen go back to the hotel to get some sleep.

As often happens along that waterfront, the night was foggy, and as Hamblen walked down the road toward the inn he could barely see his own hands in front of his face. Suddenly a vehicle emerged from the dense mist coming straight toward him. Hamblen frantically waved his arms to warn them he was there, but it was too late. The car stuck Hamblen, killing him instantly. Today Hugh Hamblen's ghost, dressed in period hat and trench coat, appears on Netherland Inn Road on foggy nights, his arms in the air trying to tell drivers to slow down. Some nights the car that hit him, an old Ford, also appears in the middle of the road, lying tipped over on its side.

Ironically, Hamblen's son, Charles, was in the hospital because he had been a passenger in a fatal car crash on the nearby Rotherwood Bridge, which is also located on Netherland Inn Road. Charles had been the only survivor.

Appearing less often on Netherland Inn Road is the revenant of an old carriage, and usually by the time onlookers figure out what they're seeing, the coach has vanished. Supposedly the phantom carriage disappears when it reaches the spot where it was struck by a train while trying to cross a set of tracks back in the nineteenth century.

Sensabaugh Hollow Road
Kingsport

Sensabaugh Hollow Road, located northwest of Kingsport, is a paved street that follows the Sensabaugh Branch of the North Fork Holston River between Big Elm Road and Ripley Lane. The two-mile route takes its name from the family whose land it crossed.

So, too, does the infamous single-lane Sensabaugh Tunnel, which was dug as a railway underpass for Sensabaugh Hollow Road in the early 1900s. Almost from the day it opened to traffic, the tunnel has had a reputation for being haunted.

Several legends claim to explain the reason for the paranormal activity, even though some of them have absolutely no basis in fact. The most popular story is that a man in the neighborhood killed his family, including his baby, dragged their bodies into the tunnel, and then committed suicide. A variation has a stranger breaking into the Sensabaugh house and stealing their baby. The father, Ed, chased the intruder into the underpass but, by the time he got to him, the kidnapper had drowned the infant in a nearby stream.

Another old wives' tale claims that Ed Sensabaugh was the murderer! He went mad, killed his wife and child, and hid their bodies in the tunnel. (Some say he tossed their remains into the creek instead.)

Yet another piece of lore says that a young woman was chased into the tunnel and almost immediately gave birth. The baby's cries have reverberated down through the ages to haunt the path.

And what exactly do people experience at the tunnel? Sounds of a bawling baby, a woman screaming, footsteps, and unrecognizable eerie noises regularly drift from its dark interior. If you brave driving through, don't shut off your car's engine in the middle of the passageway for any reason. It may not restart, and you'll have to push the car all the way out before the engine turns over. Whatever you do, don't leave your car in the tunnel. Supposedly, a woman who left her stranded vehicle in the tunnel to go look for help was never seen again.

Finally, there's also word that a spirit sometimes materializes in the back seat of your car before you enter the tunnel to warn you not to drive through. Sometimes the phantom waits and appears midway through the tunnel instead. Depending upon who's telling the tale, the ghost is either Ed Sensabaugh, the vagrant, or the woman who vanished after leaving her car behind.

Urban myths aside, there are practical reasons to be cautious if you decide to drive through the underpass. It's very narrow and not overly high, so some cars and trucks simply don't fit. Check the width and height of your vehicle carefully before starting in. Speaking of which, also make sure the tunnel is empty and that no one is about to enter from the other side. If you don't, one of you will have to back your vehicle all the way out to let the other one pass. Finally, check to see whether a stream of water is coming out of the passage before you go inside. For some reason, the tunnel is prone to flooding. There are no reports of any vehicles being washed away but, as they say, it's always better to be safe than sorry.

Stones River National Battlefield
Murfreesboro

Theaters of war are notorious for being haunted by the spirits of those who died there, and the Stones River National Battlefield in Murfreesboro is no exception. The skirmish took place at the height of the Civil War.

At the time, Murfreesboro was the largest town between Nashville and Chattanooga, and it was a major rail hub linking the state with Atlanta. Union General William Rosecrans had his men march on General Braxton Bragg, who was headquartered in Murfreesboro and whose Army of the Tennessee was the largest militia in the Confederacy. Bragg decided to stand his ground. Fighting began around 6 a.m. on December 31, 1862. Battle lines shifted constantly throughout the engagement, but by the night of January 2, 1863, Bragg realized his forces couldn't win. His army's retreat began the next evening, but rather than pursue them, Rosecrans stayed and occupied Murfreesboro.

Though not as well remembered as the larger mêlées at Antietam, Shiloh, Bull Run, and Gettysburg, the Battle of Stones River was one of the war's deadliest clashes, with a full 30 percent of the combatants dead, wounded, or missing.

Apparitions of soldiers are spotted throughout the park. Some are hazy, shadowy, or indistinct, but many can be seen quite clearly. Occasionally a visitor to the park will see a spectre fall to the ground, a residual haunting of the moment the soldier was shot and killed more than 150 years earlier.

In addition to numerous walking trails, Stones River National Battlefield also has two connecting, one-way paved roads that allow guests to explore the park by car. There are six signposted places of particular historical importance on the self-guided tour. By far, the most paranormal sightings along the 1.5-mile route occur near the former Nashville Pike (Stop 4) and at the McFadden Farm (Stop 6).

Be wary, though. Not all of the spooky-looking figures you'll see are ghosts. There are often costumed reenactments of the battle as well as occasional special ceremonies in which participants wear period uniforms. Also, the Park Service has placed several life-size cutouts of soldiers on the grounds to give visitors a sense of how the terrain affected the battle.

TEXAS

Bragg Road
Sarasota

Bragg Road, also known as the Ghost Road Scenic Drive, is located north of Sarasota between Farm to Market Road 787 (FM 787) and FM 1293. The 7.8-mile, dusty, unpaved path lies in a perfectly straight line because it was once a bed for Santa Fe Railway tracks. The road is named for the small community of Bragg, which was established at the terminus of a rail link to Sarasota in 1902. The entire town was razed, however, when the Santa Fe changed its route and removed the tracks in 1934.

Ghost hunters drive down the two-lane dirt road at night hoping to get a glimpse of the famous Bragg Road Light, which is also called the Sarasota Light, the Ghost Light, and the Big Thicket Light. (Sarasota lies within a biodiverse region of southeast Texas called the Big Thicket.) The bright, glowing spot has been seen for more than fifty years, and it doesn't seem to be going away. It usually appears as a twinkling yellow light far off in the distance, swaying gently as if it were being carried inside a lantern. As it comes closer, the light intensifies and changes to white, then red, and then instantly goes out.

There are many reasons given for the anomaly, including the old standbys: car lights and swamp gas. Most of the explanations are paranormal, however. One legend says that it's the spirit of Jake Murphy, a brakeman for the Santa Fe who was decapitated when he fell under a moving train. A variation suggests that the light comes from the lantern he uses to search for his missing head.

Another tale suggests that the light is indeed that of a ghost lantern, but it belongs to a phantom hunter who's trying to find his way home. He got lost in the Big Thicket and died before he could find a way out.

A third old wives' tale says that sometime during the construction and opening of the Bragg to Sarasota line, a railroad foreman killed four of his workmen so he could keep their salaries. He buried the men alongside the tracks, but their spirits wouldn't stay in the ground. The Ghost Light comes from the lantern they're carrying to track down their murderer—and their money. A variation suggests that it was actually the four laborers who killed their boss because he refused to pay them. The supervisor's avenging ghost, lantern in hand, has returned to look for the men.

Some people believe the eerie light is the headlight of an approaching ghost train traveling on the long-gone tracks.

Finally, there's one more story worth mentioning, and it's a bit more contemporary. Sometime after the rail tracks were torn up, a young bride was murdered on Bragg Road. The groom, who was not guilty of the crime, died not long afterward of an unrelated cause. His revenant has supposedly come back from the Other Side to be reunited with his beloved wife. There are no more details available about the spirit, but presumably instead of a lamp, he's carrying a flashlight.

UTAH

Provo Canyon Road
Provo

Ogden River Scenic Byway
Ogden

There are certain ghost stories that have such a strong grip on the imagination that they turn up time and again across the country. There's the legend of the haunted hitchhiker, for example, that gets into a motorist's car only to disappear before reaching the destination. There are the invisible ghosts of children that push cars up hills, across bridges, and off railroad tracks. And then there are the sightings of cryptids, such as Bigfoot, the Goatman, and other strange creatures.

Two legends in Utah are fascinating because they show how easy it is for folklore to spread and then become established as having happened in an entirely different location. The myth was first associated with Provo and dates to pioneer days. To escape an unhappy marriage, a newlywed threw herself into the Provo River near the base of Bridal Veil Falls and drowned. Today, her ghost appears to motorists on Provo Canyon Road (State Route 189) as they drive through Provo Canyon.

An almost identical haunting is said to occur seventy miles north at the Ogden Canyon Waterfall in, well, Ogden. Its phantom appears on the Ogden River Scenic Byway (State Route 39, also known as Canyon Road) as the road passes through a ravine.

The cascade in Ogden was originally called Bridal Veil Falls as well, but unlike the waterfall in Provo, Ogden's is manmade. It was created in the late 1880s to help manage the overflow from irrigation pipes on the land above the canyon. The name appeared everywhere, including on early tourist postcards. As late as June 28, 1912, the *Standard* newspaper was still referring to the cascade as the "Bridal Veil Falls of Ogden." At some point, however, the name of Ogden's Bridal Veil Falls was changed to its current, more prosaic one, perhaps so Utah visitors don't confuse it with the natural cascade in Provo.

Of course, it's always possible that a ghost appears at both waterfalls, and the stories' similarities are merely coincidental.

Big Cottonwood Canyon Scenic Drive
Salt Lake City

Big Cottonwood Canyon is located about twenty-two miles outside of Salt Lake City. The main road through the chasm is Big Cottonwood Canyon Scenic Drive (State Route190). It stretches for fifteen miles from I-215 to the bypass loop around Salt Lake City and up through the canyon to two ski resort towns, Brighton and Solitude.

The highway follows the course of Big Cotton Creek, which swells and becomes quite treacherous during the spring thaw. Over the years, many people have lost their lives in the rushing waters due to suicide, accidents, or misadventure. A female phantom walking along Big Cottonwood Canyon Road is always dripping wet when seen, so it's assumed she was a drowning victim.

Her ghost is only one of several spirits that regularly materialize in the ravine. An adult male is often sighted walking alone near the entrance to the canyon. Like his female counterpart, he disappears if you pull over to offer him a lift. Even after he's vanished, motorists hear the jangling of the metal coupling-link carabiners that were hanging from his belt. He's believed to be the revenant of one of several rock climbers who have fallen to their deaths while trying to scale the steep canyon walls.

Another male spectre is seen walking with his dog down Big Cottonwood Canyon Scenic Drive. If you offer to give him a ride, he'll hop into the backseat with his canine companion, but before you reach the mouth of the canyon they'll both disappear.

Sightseers may want to visit at least one of what the state calls its "Mighty Five" national parks when they're in Utah. But ghost hunters are often looking for something else entirely. Provo Canyon, Ogden Canyon, and Big Cottonwood Canyon are just three supernatural wonders they might consider exploring.

VERMONT

Washbowl Road
Northfield

Washbowl Road is a rural lane located about five miles south of Montpelier, the capital of Vermont. It cuts south off of Morehead Mountain Road/Cox Brook Road and runs for about two miles before its name changes to Bean Road. Almost the entire route is thickly forested, and only about a dozen houses and small family farms lie along the way. For such a short distance, it has many twists and turns and even a couple of near-hairpin turns. Most of the road is unpaved.

You don't have to worry about running into ghosts on Washbowl Road. Instead, you have to be on the lookout for a peculiar creature that's been dubbed the Pig-man. It's unclear whether the beast is human or a cryptid, like the half-man half-animal anomalies in Kentucky and Maryland known as the Goatman.

Stories about the Pigman only began to circulate in 1951 after a local seventeen-year-old boy went out one night to take part in some Halloween mis-chief but never returned. Despite a massive search, neither the boy nor any remains were ever found. It was as if he had disappeared off the face of the earth.

But had he? It was only a few months later that sightings of a hulky, human-oid figure walking along or crossing Washbowl Road began. Most folks that saw it agreed that the creature had the body of a man but the head of a pig or boar. It was bipedal and walked upright, but reports differed on whether the Pigman had human feet or hooves. Some people had heard squealing noises coming from the woods as they passed through, even though the beast itself never appeared. Sightings are rare, some more believable than others, but they definitely continue.

The Pigman's origin story remains a mystery. At first it was all dismissed as a prank: The monster was just someone wearing a realistic pig mask to scare people. But other folks believed that some sort of bizarre, swine-like fiend had killed and eaten the missing teenager and that somehow the two had merged to become the elusive Pigman.

VIRGINIA

Coast Artillery Road
Virginia Beach

Cape Henry, situated at the southern entrance to the Chesapeake Bay, juts into the Atlantic Ocean just north of Virginia Beach. Named for the son of King James I, the promontory has played an important role in early US history. The first English colonists to permanently settle in America landed at Cape Henry in 1607 before moving on to Jamestown. At the end of the Revolutionary War, a French fleet blocked the entrance to the bay at Cape Henry, which prevented British rein-forcements from reaching Yorktown. As a result, Lord Cornwallis was forced to surrender to George Washington's forces, ending the War of Independence. One of the new country's first lighthouses was built on Cape Henry in 1791. Fort Story, a military installation, occupies much of the cape today.

Dozens, if not hundreds, of lighthouses in the United States are purportedly haunted, and there are entire books chronicling their stories. The paranormal activity at today's Cape Henry Lighthouse doesn't take place inside the tower, however. Instead, it occurs on Coast Artillery Road leading up to the beacon.

The lighthouse is on the grounds of Fort Story, but it can be visited after passing through a checkpoint. There are guards on duty twenty-four hours a day, and there have been whispers among those who serve at night that an apparition regularly materializes on Coast Artillery Road. Whenever they approach the figure demanding to see ID, the ghost instantly disappears. Rumor has it that the spectre was a soldier, perhaps one who committed suicide on the base many years back.

Elbow Road
Virginia Beach

Elbow Road is a two-lane paved highway that stretches between the City of Chesapeake and the Virginia Beach city line. Numerous bends make the route extremely dangerous. Also, there are no street lines or shoulders on the side of the road, and several sections of it pass through dense woods, limiting visibility, especially at night.

Elbow Road may be haunted or perhaps cursed. There are frequent vehicular accidents, some of them fatal, with more than three dozen people having lost their lives since 2010. It's rumored that many of the crashes on Elbow Road are caused by the sudden appearance of a ghost, an elderly, blood-soaked woman standing on the highway at one of its many curves. The manifestation causes drivers to either freeze up or swerve off the highway.

Allegedly, the spectre, when alive, was a Mrs. Woble—elbow spelled backward—who lived in a ramshackle house on Elbow Road. Police investigating the property one night found broken glass by the door and a cold, uneaten meal in the kitchen, but no Mrs. Woble. There were indications that a murder had occurred, but no body was ever found. Eventually, the house was demolished. Nevertheless, several motorists have seen inexplicable lights on the side of the road, and many claim that they must be a revenant of the long-gone cabin.

The ghost of a little girl who drowned in Stumpy Lake haunts a shore-side section of Elbow Road. An urban legend claims that if you park on the shoulder there at night and climb onto the hood of your car, muddy footprints will soon appear on the ground as the invisible entity walks toward you.

Witchduck Road
Virginia Beach

Witchduck Road, sometimes seen as Witch Duck Road, takes its name from an event that occurred there in July 1706. Belief in witchcraft came to the Americas with settlers from Europe, as did the practice of executing those convicted of practicing it. Although colonial Virginia never fell victim to the witchcraft hysteria that shook New England, it had its fair share of witchcraft trials.

Grace White Sherwood, a farmer, herbal healer, and midwife who lived in the village of Pungo (today part of Virginia Beach) was charged with witchcraft several times throughout her life. In 1706, she was accused of causing a neighbor, Elizabeth Hill, to miscarry. Virginia courts demanded proof that the defendant was, indeed, a witch in order to render a guilty verdict. In Sherwood's case, they ordered a "trial by ordeal" known as "ducking."

Basically, the accused woman—it was almost always a woman— was bound and tossed into a river or cast into a lake. This led to a classic Catch 22, no-win situation for the defendant. If she floated, it meant the water, which was considered pure, had rejected her. She was therefore deemed unclean and guilty of witchcraft, usually resulting in her execution. If the water accepted her and she sank, she was deemed innocent but was, unfortunately, drowned. (In some instances, instead of being thrown into a lake or river, the accused was strapped to a chair and repeatedly dipped into water until a final judgment was rendered. The seat was variously known as a ducking stool, cucking stool, scolding stool, or stool of repentance.)

Sherwood's test was carried out at the end of a dirt path that led to the mouth of the Lynnhaven River. She was bound, weighed, and placed in a sack before being tossed from a boat into what is now Witch Duck Bay. Luckily, she bobbed to the surface, and her conviction resulted in several years in prison rather than being hanged. She was released from jail no later than 1714, managed to regain her farm, and died in 1740 at the age of 79 or 80. The Witch of Pungo, as

Sherwood came to be known, was the last person to be convicted of witchcraft in Virginia.

After a campaign by biographer Belinda Nash to "restore the good name of Grace Sherwood," Virginia Governor Tim Kaine informally pardoned her on July 10, 2006, the three-hundredth anniversary of Sherwood's conviction.

Nowadays the old lane to the river is known as Witchduck Road. It's said that if you travel down the path at night and stand where it meets the Lynnhaven River, a spot now called Witch Duck Point, Grace Sherwood's ghost may join you. Local legend also claims that a bizarre, otherworldly light, thought to be Sherwood's spirit, appears every July, flitting over the bay at the precise location the Witch of Pungo was thrown into the water.

WASHINGTON

Holland Road Northwest
Bremerton

Bremerton, the largest city on the Kitsap Peninsula, lies directly across Puget Sound from Seattle and can be reached by one of several ferry routes or by land and bridge via Tacoma. The city has more than forty thousand residents and is home to Puget Sound Naval Shipyard and the Bremerton Annex of Naval Base Kitsap.

Holland Road Northwest is a two-lane blacktop on the peninsula about five miles north of downtown Bremerton. It's about a mile long with a northern terminus at Central Valley Road Northeast, and it merges into Tracyton Boulevard Northwest at its southern end. The route is completely straight except for two easy curves and one ninety-degree bend. Although it passes through or by numerous clumps of trees, there are also several houses and open fields along the way.

Holland Road is unremarkable, and if it weren't for its lingering ghost stories, it wouldn't draw much attention or capture anyone's imagination. But, oh, what stories they are!

According to urban legend, sometime around 1937, a young girl was riding her black horse on Holland Road around midnight when a drunk driver smashed into them, killing them both. He called a couple of friends who quickly came to take the girl's body away and bury it. (Sources don't mention what they did with the horse.) The motorist never admitted he had anything to do with the girl's disappearance.

And then one day, with no warning or symptoms, he keeled over and died. No cause of death was ever found. Had the victim's spirit exacted revenge?

The girl's parents continued to reside in the same house after their daughter's death, and when they, too, eventually passed away, the house was sold to an elderly woman. The new occupant began to keep a journal of her time living there. Police found it when locals asked them to do a welfare check on their neighbor and discovered the lady's corpse. There was no sign of a struggle, but, other than age, no cause of death could be determined. According to the woman's diary, almost immediately after she moved in, the apparition of a girl—and sometimes also a horse—began to visit her every night. The youngster demanded the stranger get out of her house, but despite the continued haunting, the woman refused to leave. Had that been a mistake?

The house was torn down along with a barn in the back, where the remains of several horses were recovered, their original owners unknown. Before long, people started hearing the disembodied clip-clopping of horse hooves on the macadam road in front of the property. Motorists on the narrow lane have seen the spectre of a little girl with long black hair, and sometimes she's on horseback. She materializes most often when there's a thick fog, and she always stands out from the mist as if haloed in light.

There's a second legend that also involves someone being struck and killed by an inebriated driver on Holland Road Northwest. In this tale, the victim was an upper-middle-aged man who had just gotten back from vacation. Even though it was late at night, he went out to check his mailbox. Tragically, just as the man reached the end of his driveway, a car filled with drunken teenagers appeared, racing down Holland Road with the vehicle's headlights out. Before anyone could react, the man was struck and killed. They say that, today, if you slowly drive down Holland Road at night with your car lights off, the man's ghost, or at least a dark, human-shaped form, will manifest in front of your vehicle.

There's yet another old wives' tale that if you drive Holland Road at night with your headlights off, the spectre of a huge black horse will materialize in front of your car.

It's possible these stories may be variations of the same legend, because they share several details. Could they all be throwbacks to the story of the little girl?

WEST VIRGINIA

22 Mine Road
Logan

Mine Road snakes its way southward from State Route 119 to a three-way junction with Holly Ridge Road and Pine Creek Road. The area is mountainous, heavily forested, and mostly uninhabited. The secluded, two-lane, asphalt path is named for the Island Creek Coal Company's No. 22 Mine, which was located on the route. Tragically, on March 8, 1960, the mine suffered a fire and subsequent rock fall that trapped eighteen miners, leading to their deaths, most likely from smoke and carbon monoxide.

Although heartbreaking, that wasn't the event that led to the haunting of 22 Mine Road. That honor, such as it is, comes from a vicious murder that occurred decades earlier on June 22, 1932. The victim was thirty-one-year-old Mamie Thurman, who had moved to nearby Logan eight years earlier with her husband, Jack, a police officer. Garland Davis, a thirty-two-year old deaf-mute, discovered Mamie's lifeless body along 22 Mine Road, which at that time was called Trace Mountain Road. She had been shot twice in the head, and the murderer had also slashed her throat for good measure.

Evidence of the killing was found in the home of her landlord, Harry Robertson, and both he and an African American handyman, twenty-nine-year old Clarence Stephenson, were arrested. Although Robertson admitted having an affair with Thurman, he was never indicted. Instead, the handyman was arrested, and the jury found him guilty.

Now, almost a century later, no one can locate Mamie Thurman's grave. Perhaps that's why her ghost is restless and walks 22 Mine Road at night. Occasionally, truck drivers have seen her hitchhiking along the road, dressed in clothing from the Jazz Age. If they pick her up, she'll sit silently in the cab for a few miles, then suddenly disappear.

She's not the only apparition on 22 Mile Road. There's a tall, thin male phantom dressed in clothing from the 1920s or 1930s whose ghost, like Mamie Thurman's, will vanish in the blink of an eye. Also, some of the anonymous workers who died during the road's construction have come back to haunt the highway. Little wonder: Rumor has it they were unceremoniously buried beneath the road in unmarked graves. If that weren't enough, there have even been reports of a Bigfoot sighting or two.

Lick Fork Road
Mossy

Lick Fork Road (County Route 15/3) branches to the northeast off of Okey L. Patteson Drive (State Route 612) about 1.5 miles east of the small community of Mossy. It follows Lick Fork, which is a tributary of Mossy Creek, and runs for about two miles before coming to a dead end in the heavily forested hills. As for the stream, it flows between two mountain ridges, and the narrow gulch has become known as Witchy Hollow.

Despite the gully's name, it's the road that's haunted, and almost all of the paranormal activity takes the form of ghost vehicles. The phantom car that most people encounter is blue. It's not a current model, but it's no older than the late twentieth century. No one is ever behind the wheel.

You don't have to worry about being chased or rear-ended. When the ghost car appears, it's always approaching your vehicle, with both of its headlights uncommonly bright and beaming directly into your eyes. The downside is that Lick Fork Road isn't too wide, and the spectral vehicle hogs the middle of the road. It seems certain there's no way to avoid a head-on collision, and there wouldn't be if the ghost car didn't invariably vanish just before impact.

WISCONSIN

Bray Road
Elkhorn

There have been reports of a strange, enormous creature appearing on the back roads near Elkhorn since 1936. It's most often seen on the 4.3-mile, two-lane, macadam Bray Road, which is located east of Elkhorn, Wisconsin. The route passes through the farmland between Highway 11 and County Road NN.

When rumors spread of multiple sightings on Bray Road in the late 1980s and early 1990s, a local newspaper named the *Walworth County Week* sent out a reporter, Linda Godfrey, to have a look. After interviewing a number of people who claimed to have encountered the weird animal, she was convinced they had seen something extraordinary. She wrote a book based on her investigation and news articles entitled *The Beast of Bray Road: Tailing Wisconsin's Werewolf.*

It's still uncertain what people saw. Witnesses described the cryptid as being covered in coarse brown hair, weighing four hundred to seven hundred pounds, and being two to four feet tall when on all fours or seven feet tall when standing on two legs. Some described the animal as having a dog-like face or resembling a bear. Others compared it to a Sasquatch or were sure the beast was a werewolf. There are no accounts of its ever attacking anyone.

Although sightings are rare these days, they still pop up from time to time. In February 2018, for example, *Southern Lake Newspapers* reported that a Danny Morgan had spotted the enigmatic animal on State Route 20 outside the town of Spring Prairie the previous month. According to MyRacine.com, a site managed by *Southern Lakes Newspapers*, Lake Geneva resident Ron Rice saw it from a distance of just 150 feet in May 2000. He was a few miles west of Lyons, parked in a driveway on Highway 36, when he spotted the beast ducking into a forest. Rice saw the mysterious creature again two weeks later. Both times it was broad daylight!

Dyreson Road, East Dyreson Road
McFarland

Dyreson Road, a rural, north–south, two-lane blacktop, is located close to the western shore of Lake Kegonsa southeast of Madison. The street runs for about five miles between East Dyreson Road (to the north) and Schneider Drive (to the south) and is more or less bisected by US 51. A phantom, older-model black car has been chasing other vehicles on Dyreson Road for years. No matter how fast the front motorist drives, the ghost car manages to keep up. It races up to the first car's bumper but always disappears just before impact.

East Dyreson Road is also haunted. It, too, is about five miles long, and it connects Dyreson Road to County Highway AB. Most of the spooky phenomena on East Dyreson Road take place on or close to a bridge over the Yahara River that was built by the Milwaukee Bridge and Iron Company in 1897. Many drivers have reported seeing a seemingly solid car teetering over the side of the bridge, plummeting, and then vanishing just before hitting the river. Disembodied screams have also been heard in the immediate vicinity.

Jay Road
Boltonville

Jay Road runs fifteen to twenty miles from Wisconsin State Highway 28/144 in the Boltonville community of Farmington all the way to the shore of Lake Michigan. Two female phantoms haunt the stretch of road.

One of the spectres was an elderly woman who lived with her cats in a house on Jay Road. For some reason, a few local teenagers started taunting her. Over the weeks, their pranks escalated until one night, perhaps hoping only to scare the old lady, they set her house on fire. Neither the woman nor her beloved pets got out; they all died in the flames. Now her spirit—usually accompanied by the ghosts of some of the cats—walks Jay Road at night. (A variation of the story says that some of the cats managed to escape, and they fled into the nearby forest. Their offspring, or perhaps their revenants, are sometimes spotted in the woods or wandering on the roadway without the ghost of their former mistress.)

Another old wives' tale claims that at some time in the past a drunk driver struck an unidentified woman jogging on the side of the road. The vehicle hit her with such force that she was tossed into the air and thrown into a bordering swamp. Her body was never recovered, but her spirit has returned to the proverbial "scene of the crime." Today, motorists will be driving at night on Jay Road just east of Boltonville when they see an unusual mist hovering over the street up ahead. As they approach the fog, it coalesces into the apparition of the deceased jogger. Often she'll disappear while the driver is watching. Some motorists claim to have accidentally hit the spectre, but when they stop and step outside to check, no one is there. Even folks who had no interaction with the phantom jogger have reported having car trouble as they passed through the area.

WYOMING

State Route 70
Slaughterhouse Gulch to Encampment

The fifty-eight-mile long Wyoming Highway 70 (WYO 70) is located in the southern part of the state very close to the Colorado border. The road stretches eastward from the town of Baggs (on WYO 789) to Riverside (on WYO 230). Much of the highway is within Medicine Bow National Forest and is closed during the winter due to snow. The road cuts through the Sierra Madre Mountains and crosses the Continental Divide at Battle Pass. The gap was the site of an 1841 skirmish between fur trappers and Native Americans. In 2012, WYO 70 was officially designated the Battle Pass Scenic Highway.

Its hauntings take place on the section of road between Slaughterhouse Gulch and the small town of Encampment, which is located about eight miles to the northeast.

It's claimed that sometime in the late 1880s, a prospector was rigging dynamite at a mine in Slaughterhouse Gulch when it unexpectedly went off. The man's body was blown to pieces. Just after the turn of the century, the driver of a coach for the Charles M. Scribner Stage Line was traveling on what is now WYO 70 and saw the miner's ghost up ahead standing on the side of the road. As the carriage passed the phantom, the spirit turned toward the team of six white horses and walked right through them. The apparition then instantly vanished. (Some sources say the spectre passed between the cantering horses rather than through them before disappearing.)

There was another recorded sighting by a group of park rangers in 1917. As they sat around a campfire, the silent revenant strolled past them and then simply evaporated. At least one source says the visitation took place in 1918 instead and that the party consisted of two men, who were there to mark trees for the Forest Service, and their wives. In this telling, only one of the women, Dorothy Peryam, and her brother John saw the spirit. They were standing close to WYO 70 when they heard a cough and turned toward the road. The pair then watched in a mix of curiosity and wonder as the ghost of what appeared to be a miner or prospector passed them by. The night shade stared straight ahead, not acknowledging the couple and making no further sound, not even the quiet shuffle of footsteps.

Although sightings are rare, they've continued into modern times. The spectre is always dressed in period workmen's clothes as he walks along the Battle Pass Scenic Highway late at night. It's believed the apparition is earthbound and is searching for his grave—which, of course, he'll never find. After the explosion, there was nothing left of him to bury.

One of the most enduring fables of the Old West is that of a prospector who discovers a vein of gold, travels to town to tell others and stake a claim, but then is unable to find his way back to the deposit. Many of these secret mines also have ghost legends attached to them.

Take the story of Lost Cabin Mine, which is purportedly located somewhere in Slaughterhouse Gulch. In the bare-bones version of the account, three men were guarding the entrance to the secret mine when they were attacked by a band of Native Americans. Two of the men were killed; the other one survived and escaped into the dense forest. He had become so disoriented as he fled, however, that he was never able to get back to the mine. Presumably he perished during his long search. It's said that the spectres of the two men who were slaughtered are still there at the mine, guarding its entrance. The ghost of the prospector who lived through the attack supposedly walks WYO 70 at night looking for the mine.

US Route 287
Jeffrey City
In Wyoming, much of what used to be the Oregon Trail is now part of US Route 26. (See chapter 12.) Many other wagon trails funneled into the main route, however, including today's US 287. It joins up with US 26 in the center of the state in the Wind River Reservation, just east of Grand Teton National Park.

Jeffrey City sits on US 287 about ninety miles southeast of that junction. The community was founded in the 1930s when three World War I veterans and their families settled there as homesteaders. Uranium was discovered in the nearby hills in 1954, and Jeffrey City became a boomtown—that is, until 1979, when the accident at Three Mile Island curtailed the construction of new nuclear power plants. Demand for uranium ore waned, jobs disappeared, and people moved out. By 2017, the population of Jeffrey City had fallen from a high of about four thousand to just fifty people.

The decline in the number of residents hasn't stopped Jeffrey City's hometown ghost from materializing. There's been a legend since the stagecoach era about a mysterious male figure dressed in a green parka seen wandering over the area's empty plains. The phantom's modern incarnation seems to stick close to US 287, but he always appears miles outside of town. Drivers on the road late at night will suddenly spot the dark, enigmatic man, hunched over and wearing an oversize coat, methodically making his way through the brush toward the highway. Less than a mile down the road, the driver is startled to see the same man again, but this time much closer to the highway. Sometimes, after another mile or so, the spectre will show up a third time, standing on the shoulder of the road about to step in front of the vehicle. Fortunately, no traffic accidents have ever occurred—or been reported—as a result of these terrifying encounters.

WASHINGTON, DC

M Street Bridge, M Street NW, K Street Bridge, K Street NW

The Georgetown neighborhood in Washington, DC, was founded in 1751 at the uppermost point that ocean vessels could navigate the Potomac River. It also happened to be the spot that Rock Creek flowed into the Potomac.

Several bridges have spanned Rock Creek over the centuries, the first being a simple wooden structure in 1788. The current bridge at that site was constructed in 1930, and the road that crosses it is now called M Street NW. The bridge spans not only the creek but also a major roadway alongside the stream known as the Rock Creek and Potomac Parkway (or simply Rock Creek Parkway).

Sometime between the end of the Revolutionary War and the War of 1812, a drummer boy, name unknown, drowned in Rock Creek after being blown off the bridge by a strong blast of wind. For many years, people regularly reported hearing disembodied drumbeats approach and then start onto the bridge. The sounds grew louder and louder until halfway across the span they suddenly stopped. Presumably it was the spot the young man was swept from the bridge.

It's said that, later, the original bridge collapsed during a severe storm, plunging a stagecoach, its driver, and horses into the swollen waters below. Ever since, their soundless ghosts have been seen on moonless nights in Georgetown, galloping down M Street toward the existing bridge. Halfway across M Street Bridge, the phantoms simply vanish, often accompanied by a clap of thunder and a bolt of lightning, even on otherwise clear nights.

Although there are fewer reports of the hauntings these days, both still take place.

Another spectre, that of a headless horseman, is seen on the streets of Georgetown as well as on K Street Bridge, which also spans Rock Creek. It's possible he's the same headless ghost that was seen south of the K Street Bridge, riding a towpath between the Potomac River and the Chesapeake and Ohio Canal. There has been speculation about the man's identity and the cause of his decapitation since the early nineteenth century. The spirit is almost never spotted these days, but the haunting is still considered active.

Former Site of the Van Ness Mansion
17th Street and Constitution Avenue NW

The Van Ness Mausoleum, Oak Hill Cemetery
3001 R Street NW

Rock Creek Parkway

John Peter Van Ness led a full life, including stints as a US Representative from New York, a major general in the DC militia, an alderman and then mayor of the City of Washington, and, for the last thirty-two years of his life, president of the National Metropolitan Bank. He married into a wealthy, well-connected family, and in 1816 he and his wife moved into a Greek Revival mansion built on an estate bordered by today's 17th Street, 18th Street, C Street, and Constitution Avenue.

Van Ness's wife, Marcia, passed away in 1832, and soon after her death her ghost, usually wearing a bonnet, began to materialize in the mansion's upstairs hallway. Even when the spectre didn't appear, servants often heard her disembodied footsteps. Soon the hauntings included alternating laughs and screams, but they were thought to be coming from the spirit of Van Ness's daughter, Ann, who had died in childbirth in 1822. When Van Ness died in 1846, a cortege led by six gleaming white horses carried his coffin to rest next to his wife and daughter in the family's spectacular circular columned mausoleum on the grounds of the Washington City Orphan Asylum on H Street. (Marcia Van Ness had founded the orphanage in memory of her daughter.)

Before long, rumors began that the apparitions of six snow-white horses were parading around the block of the Van Ness estate. Some folks claimed the equines were headless! The sightings continued, even though the house was demolished in 1907 after a series of owners and tenants. Today, if the steeds appear at the site of the old mansion, it's usually at or near the corner of 17th Street and Constitution Avenue.

In 1872, the Van Ness mausoleum was moved to a commanding hilltop location in the tranquil Oak Hill Cemetery overlooking Rock Creek. And yes, the team of stallions now silently circles the Van Ness tomb on moonlit nights, and motorists sometimes encounter them on the Rock Creek Parkway as the horses head toward the mausoleum.

"BOO"K REPORTS

There have been hundreds, if not thousands, of books written about ghosts, hauntings, and spirit phenomena. For this bibliography, I'm providing a short, representative list of the books I used in collecting the tales for *Haunted Highways*.

Some of these books focus on a particular city or state. Several deal with a specific road (such as US Route 666 or Archer Avenue in Illinois) or even a short stretch of the highway. The titles of some of the books make their contents self-evident.

Books

Asfar, Dan. *Haunted Highways*. Edmonton, Alberta, Canada: Ghost House Books, 2003. A lively collection of hauntings including ghost lights, cursed roadways, and haunted bridges in the United States, Canada, and the United Kingdom.

Bielski, Ursula. *Chicago Haunts: Ghostlore of the Windy City*. Chicago: Lake Claremont Press, 1998. A good source for information about the apparition of Resurrection Mary and the streets that border various cemeteries in the Windy City.

Brunvand, Jan Harold. *The Vanishing Hitchhiker: American Urban Legends & Their Meanings*. New York: W. W. Norton & Company, 1981. Brunvand, a folklorist and college professor, surveys dozens of old wives' tales, particularly automobile legends, while attempting to explain their sociological and cultural impacts on American tradition.

Carroll, Rick, ed. *Hawai'i's Best Spooky Tales: The Original*. Honolulu: Bess Press, 1996. This collection of new and traditional tales of hauntings on the Hawaiian Islands include those that occur along the Pali Highway on Oahu.

Clyne, Patricia Edwards. *Ghostly Animals of America*. New York: Dodd, Mead, 1977. Nineteen spooky stories of phantom animals that haunt the United States.

Dudding, George. *Haunted Highways USA*. Independently published, 2018. A wide-ranging selection of American ghost-ridden streets.

Godfrey, Linda S. *The Beast of Bray Road. Tailing Wisconsin's Werewolf*. New York: Dystel, Goderich & Bourrett LLC, 2015. Godfrey tells the story of her initial

1992 investigations of the titular creature and gives insight into similar enigmatic, folkloric features.

Granato, Sherri. *Haunted America: The Highway to Hell*. Independently published,
2018. Paranormal legends of the highway formerly named US Route 666—
not to be confused with the historic Route 66.

Hauck, Dennis William. *Haunted Places: The National Directory*. New York: Pen-
guin, 1996. This must-have book lists more than two thousand haunted sites
as well as tales about alien spacecraft, Bigfoot, and other strange anomalies,
all sorted by states and cities. There's a short description of each location,
along with contact information and general travel instructions on how to get
to it. The volume includes an extensive bibliography of books on ghosts and
the paranormal.

Kaczmarek, Dale David. *Field Guide to Haunted Highways and Bridges*. Oak Lawn,
IL: Ghost Research Society, 2012.

Kelemen, Ed. *Route 30: Pennsylvania's Haunted Highway*. Altoona, PA: Piney
Creek Press, 2013.

Knowles, Zachery. *True Ghost Stories: Real Haunted Roads and Highways*. Independently published, 2018.

McNeill, W. K., ed. *Ghost Stories from the American South*. Atlanta, GA: August
House Publishers, 2005. Part of the American Storytelling Series.

Nord, Joy. *Haunted Texas Highways: Legends & Lore of the Lone Star State*. Dallas,
TX: Atriad Press, 2012.

Oberling, Janice. *Ghosts and Legends of Nevada's Highway 50*. Charleston, SC:
The History Press, 2018. Part of the Haunted America series.

Robson, Ellen, and Dianne Freeman. *Haunted Highway: The Spirits of Route 66*.
Phoenix, AZ: Golden West Publishers, 2003. You'll find ghost stories about
several sections of the road itself, but the book centers on creepy buildings
and eerie sites located along the highway.

Southall, Richard. *Haunted Route 66: Ghosts of America's Legendary Highway*. St.
Paul, MN: Llewellyn Publications, 2013.

Taylor, Troy. *Weird Highway: Illinois Route 66. History, Hauntings, Legends & Lore*.
Alton, IL: Whitechapel Productions, 2015. This is the first volume of a three-
book, state-specific series covering haunted venues and parts of old US
Route 66. Two subsequent similarly titled books are dedicated to the portions

of Route 66 in Missouri (Alton, IL: Whitechapel Productions, 2016) and Oklahoma (Alton, IL: Whitechapel Productions, 2017).

Tremeear, Janice. *Missouri's Haunted Route 66: Ghosts along the Mother Road*. Charleston, SC: The History Press, 2012. Part of the Haunted America series.

White, Thomas, and Tony Lavorgne. *Haunted Roads of Western Pennsylvania*. Charleston, SC: The History Press, 2015. Part of the Haunted America series.

Wilder, Annie. *Trucker Ghost Stories: And Other True Tales of Haunted Highways, Weird Encounters, and Legends of the Road*. New York: Tor Books, 2012. A collection of around forty tales about roadway wraiths, told from the point of view of the drivers who encountered them.

Witzell, Michael Karl. *Strange 66: Myth, Mystery, Mayhem, and Other Weirdness on Route 66*. Beverly, MA: Voyageur Press, 2018. This book is well illustrated. In addition to several ghost legends associated with America's "Mother Road," Witzell catalogues many of Route 66's unusual roadside attractions and monuments, crime venues and hideouts, odd buildings, and unique restaurants. The book also details deadly stretches of highway and touches on the road's connection to Native American paths, including the so-called Trail of Tears.

Wolf, Christopher E. *Haunted Highways and Ghostly Travelers*. Atglen, PA: Schiffer Publishing, 2011. A representative assortment of paranormal sightings on roads, bridges, railways, airplanes, and ships at sea.

DVDs, Downloads, and Audio

Grant, Glen. *Ghostly Tales for Over the Pali*. Audiotape. Honolulu: TimeWalks. Undated. Glen Grant (1947–2003), a Hawaiian historian, radio host, folklorist, and storyteller, popularized the many "chicken skin" (that is to say, goose bump–producing) ghost stories of the island chain. Among his best-loved tales (which he shared in books, on audiotape, and on Oahu Island tours) were those of Madame Pele. For years he owned and operated The Haunt Cafe, a bookstore and coffee shop in Honolulu. His ashes were scattered at Kaena Point, which, according to ancient Hawaiian myths, is a "jumping off" point for spirits, a bridge between this world and the next.

Haunted Highway. HD downloads. Syfy Network, 2012 and 2013. Each season consists of six episodes. Available online by full season or individual episode. Ghost investigators Jack Osbourne, Dana Workman, Jael de Pardo, and Devin Marble examine famous paranormal legends at the sites where they occur.

Only about half of the stories concern roads or streets. Most of them involve the world of mythic cryptids, such as hellhounds, the Vergas Hairy Man, Skinwalkers, and the Louisiana Swamp Woman.

Websites

There are several aggregation websites that collect and distribute tales of the paranormal. They receive the stories from users, write short descriptions about the haunted sites, and list them alphabetically by country, state, and/or city in directory format. These sites change constantly as users update the posts or add new ones. Some paranormal directory sites contain thousands of listings.

theshadowlands.net

Founded by Dave Juliano in 1994, The Shadowlands contains perhaps the largest internet collection of hauntings from around the world. The individual listings are broken down by country (and for the United States, by state and city), which makes it easy for amateur ghost hunters to find haunted sites in their own backyards.

haunted-places.com

In addition to its list of hauntings by state, haunted-places.com also has the URLs of other ghost-related websites and ghost hunter groups, as well as Amazon.com links to recommended books.

youtube.com/TheSpeakeasyGlobal

For those who are more visually oriented, this YouTube channel may be for you. The site features more than two hundred ghost-related videos consisting of narration under a series of still images. Each video highlights the hauntings of a specific state, city, type of venue, site, or type of haunting. There are also videos about other paranormal topics and urban legends, such as cryptids, curses, and more.

In addition, paranormal investigation societies and individual ghost hunters have posted videos of their investigations on a variety of social media sites. To find them, type the word "ghost" or "haunted" into any major search engine along with words or phrases that would narrow the topic to your particular interests. If you want to further explore the subject of this book, for example, include the word "road," "street," or "highway" in your search.

ABOUT THE AUTHOR

Tom Ogden is one of America's leading experts on the paranormal and, as a professional magician for the past fifty years, he has a special insight into ghost phenomena, hauntings, and all things that go bump in the night.

Ogden's first book, *200 Years of the American Circus*, was released in 1994. The American Library Association and the New York Public Library named it a "Best Reference Work," and Tom was subsequently profiled in *Writer's Market*. Ogden's other early books include *Wizards and Sorcerers* and two magic instructional books for the Complete Idiot's Guide series. In 1998, Tom Ogden released *The Complete Idiot's Guide to Ghosts and Haunting*. This expanded second edition of *Haunted Highways* is his twelfth book of ghost stories for Globe Pequot.

Nicknamed "The Ghost Guy," Ogden has been interviewed by numerous radio programs, podcasts, and periodicals, and he's in demand as a speaker on the Spirit World. His original ghost videos can be found on his "Hauntings Channel" on YouTube, and he is a member of the Paranormal Investigation Committee of the Society of American Magicians.

Tom Ogden resides in haunted Hollywood, California.